"You might be J
Annie said

"I'm not Mata Hari. trying to seduce me?"

"No." Simon lifted her chin with his finger, forcing her to look at him. "If Ky does have someone out in the garden watching this room, he's going to see just enough to convince him you're not alone. And won't be for the rest of the night."

"Oh." He felt her relax just a fraction. "I see. You want to give them enough of a show to ruin my reputation and probably save my life."

Simon traced the outline of her lips with the tip of his finger. "They aren't going to think our little act is for real unless you kiss me." He lowered his mouth to hers....

ABOUT THE AUTHOR

Marisa Carroll is a pseudonym for a successful two-sister writing team. The sisters are close in more ways than one: they live only about two miles from each other in the town of Deshler, Ohio, where they are both raising their families. The authors have published four Harlequin American Romances, and *Rescue from Yesterday* is their third Superromance.

Books by Marisa Carroll

HARLEQUIN SUPERROMANCE

268–REMEMBERED MAGIC
318–GATHERING PLACE

HARLEQUIN AMERICAN ROMANCE

127–NATURAL ATTRACTION
160–JENNA'S CHOICE
190–TOMORROW'S VINTAGE
256–COME HOME TO ME

Rescue from Yesterday

MARISA CARROLL

Harlequin Books

TORONTO • NEW YORK • LONDON
AMSTERDAM • PARIS • SYDNEY • HAMBURG
STOCKHOLM • ATHENS • TOKYO • MILAN

Published September 1990

ISBN 0-373-70418-6

Printed in U.S.A.

...for those who wait

PROLOGUE

"I DON'T CARE WHAT THE HELL your State Department sources tell you, Simon, I know Rachel's alive and I intend to get her out of that damn jungle if it's the last thing I do."

Simon McKendrick remained silent, regarding his elder brother through narrowed hazel eyes. They were the same height, a couple of inches over six feet, but Micah outweighed him by thirty pounds and always had. "Are your sources any more reliable?" Simon asked quietly, turning his back on the other man to look out the window of his Maryland apartment at the Washington skyline in the distance.

"They can't be any less reliable," Micah growled.

Simon didn't acknowledge the taunt but he felt its sting, nonetheless. "We haven't had a hint of a lead, even a rumor of her whereabouts, in over two and a half years. Now, all of a sudden, you show up on my doorstep convinced our sister is alive and that you know where in Laos she's being held."

Micah shoved his big, scarred hand into the pocket of his jeans. He ran the other one through the shaggy salt-and-pepper beard on his chin. His hair, thick and night-black like Simon's, was just as shaggy as his beard. "She's been seen, Simon," he responded in a less belligerent tone. "It's a positive ID. Tiger Jackson cabled me three days ago. He's been in Thailand since '68. He's got contacts all over Southeast Asia. Hell, even the CIA uses him to get information in and out of Laos. You three-piece-suit types over at State have probably seen his reports, too.'' Simon began an automatic denial but Micah forestalled him with a wave of his hand. ''Spare me the 'I don't know what you're talking about' routine, little brother. You can swear on every Bible in this town that you're nothing but a middle-echelon flunky for the Census Bureau, but we both know different. Hell, by now you're probably reporting directly to the secretary of state, himself.''

Micah was closer to the truth than he knew but Simon sidestepped an answer. Instead, he said in a carefully neutral tone, ''I do know Tiger Jackson's selling guns to the Laotian resistance.''

''That's no secret,'' Micah said, propping one hip on the back of Simon's couch. ''He's been doing that ever since the war ended.''

''He's branched out.'' Simon looked straight into his brother's eyes. ''He also deals in opium as a sideline.''

Micah let out his breath in a low, disgusted whistle. ''I didn't know that,'' he admitted. ''But it doesn't change what he told me. I flew with him in the Ravens. We saved each other's butts a half dozen times apiece. I don't approve of how he's living his life now, but that doesn't have anything to do with Rachel. He has the contacts, the people I need to get me in and out of Laos, and to bring Rachel back with me. If I didn't believe what he told me about her being alive, I wouldn't be here today.''

Simon didn't have to hear Micah's last statement spoken aloud to know his brother was already committed to tracking down this tenuous lead to their sister's whereabouts. Micah would never have left his raptor research in Michigan's Upper Peninsula at this time of year, during the critical spring nesting season, for any other reason.

"Give me a few weeks to follow up on the information," Simon suggested. He might as well have saved his breath. Micah's answer was more growl than speech.

"I'm tired of waiting, of not knowing what happened to her." He banged his fist on the couch but it only sank into the soft, overstuffed upholstery with a hollow thud. "I'm going to Thailand and then on into Laos. I'm going to find out for myself this time."

"I don't think that's wise." Simon had always been the sober, steady one of Harold and Frances McKendrick's three children. He was always the one who counseled prudence when his elder brother and sister had been hell-bent to rush into new love affairs, new causes, new adventures. He was forty-one years old now and the pattern still held. But, Lord, it was hard to stand here playing the voice of reason when his heart was beating fast and heavy with excitement and renewed hope. *Rachel, alive.* It had been more than fourteen years since their sister had disappeared in the chaos that was Saigon in those last days of April, 1975. And in all those long days and months and years, Simon had never once forgotten that her loss was at least partially his fault.

"I'm tired of waiting," Micah said again, looking past Simon, staring at something only he could see. "It's been too damned long. I can't sleep at night thinking of what she's gone through, is still probably going through. Not knowing for certain if she's dead or alive." He broke off abruptly.

Micah had his own nightmares to contend with, Simon knew. Anxiety about their sister's whereabouts was added stress he didn't really need. Silence rushed in to fill the void. Each man was busy with his own thoughts, his own fears, and long-suppressed hopes now clamoring for new life, new release yet again. Hope died hard, and each time it was resurrected it hurt more to deny it at the end.

Outside the window the sounds of traffic filtered up from the street six stories below. Micah shook his head and focused intense blue-gray eyes on Simon's face.

"I'm going whether you think it's a good idea or not."

"I knew I was wasting my breath trying to talk you into letting me handle this, but I had to try." Simon smiled ruefully, resting one long-fingered hand on the window frame just above his head.

"It's not a false lead this time, Simon, I'm sure of it." Micah smiled too, stiffly, reluctantly, as though he didn't attempt the expression very often. But when he did, the engaging, roguish grin made him look far younger than his forty-three years, despite the wildly curling gray-streaked hair and beard. "I've already made most of the arrangements. I'm leaving for Bangkok the day after tomorrow. Tiger will meet me in Chiang Mai and take me across the border into Laos. I'll be back with Rachel by the Fourth of July. Wait and see."

"WHAT DAY IS IT, MICAH?" His sister's voice was weak but stronger than it had been for many days. Micah took the time to finish tying up his bedroll before he answered.

"It's Tuesday."

"Tuesday? It was Sunday evening when I asked you last." She pressed her hand to her temple as if to push away the pain. "Oh, Micah, I've slept away another day, haven't I? I'm so sorry. We'll never get home if I keep holding you up like this." A hint of despair seeped into her words, but her enormous, scared eyes were dry. She stared off into the gloom beyond the small jungle clearing where they were camped.

Micah hadn't seen her cry. Not once. Not even when he walked into the tiny, remote village high in the mountains to find her grinding rice among a group of black-clad women of the tribe. That was three weeks ago. It was almost as if she didn't dare allow her emotions that much freedom. That perhaps once she did let herself go, let the tears come, they might never stop.

"We're making good time," he assured her. If Rachel hadn't been so ill with the bout of malaria she would have heard the lie in his words as he spoke. They'd missed their rendezvous with Tiger Jackson by many days. Thank God he'd had enough sense not to let Rachel know that they were supposed to have an escort by now, an expert jungle tracker, an expert fighter. Now it was up to him to get them out of these mountains and into Thailand on his own.

"I can walk today, really. The fever's gone. I'm feeling much stronger." Rachel sat up from the makeshift bed of broad palm leaves he'd made for her three days earlier, pulling at the shapeless black skirt and baggy blouse she wore, the standard garb of Hlông women. Except that a true Hlông woman would have covered her garments with ornaments of silver and gold, complements to the towering wrought-silver headdress she wore, not only as adornment but as a symbol of her standing in the village. Rachel had no silver baubles, no headdress, because she had no family, no man to provide them for her. Even though the Hlông had welcomed her and the Dutch priest, Father Pieter, who had escaped from a Vietnamese work camp with her, the superstitious and clanny tribesmen had never fully accepted them. For ten years Rachel had lived and worked among the Hlông, but still always apart, always alone.

Micah knew all this without being told because it was the way he lived his own life, solitary, separated from his fellow men by an invisible wall of his own making, alone even in a crowd.

"I shouldn't have left the village when we did. I could feel the malaria attack coming on." Rachel sighed listlessly and plucked at a strand of hair that had straggled out of the bun at the back of her head. Her hair had far more gray in it than his. And she was so thin, so small and childlike that Micah feared she couldn't make the long, hard trip even in good health. But she kept going, kept moving even when the fever had been at its worst.

"We're making good time, Sis. Don't worry." Micah felt his anger at the way fate had treated his sister grow and throb within him as though it were some living thing. It pushed against his restraint, battering away at the barricades he'd erected so long ago. The ferocity of his feelings surprised and dismayed him.

"I just wanted to go home so badly..." Her voice broke. Rachel stopped talking and he could see her pull the tattered edges of her composure together once again. "...to leave with you before I woke up from my dream to find you'd never really been here at all." She gave a small, strained laugh and the sound was full of sadness and bewilderment. "I'm not even sure I've been using the right words. It's been so long, Micah. My English..." She made a helpless little gesture with her hands.

"Your English is great. Come on. Breakfast's ready and if you feel strong enough to walk on your own for a while I think we'd better get started. It's going to rain."

What made this woman different from Elaine, Micah wondered as he handed Rachel a rice cake and some dried fruit. Why had Rachel found the strength within herself to survive every hardship when Elaine had felt her life was so hopeless she couldn't stand the pain? He knew the answer to that question even before he'd asked it of himself. Because Elaine had been betrayed, terrorized, assaulted, physically and mentally, by the one person in the world she should have been able to trust above all others. Her husband. Him.

"It always rains here," Rachel commented, choking down the food with some of the same determination and will to survive that must have sustained her through trials and privations she hadn't even begun to allude to yet. "And when it stops raining they take the opium to market." She looked up with a start, her blue gray eyes locked with his. "Micah. We've been moving down out of the mountains for almost a week, haven't we?"

"Yes." He could see her making connections, coming to conclusions. "We're getting close to the border," she said. "The patrols will be out looking for opium smugglers."

"To confiscate their cargo. Certainly not to destroy it. Too many Vietnamese officials and their Laotian counterparts are on the take up here. We'll have to be careful." He knew, as weak as she was, that Rachel wouldn't appreciate being patronized. They were in a bad situation. Avoiding the truth wasn't going to make it any easier to get out of it.

"We'll have to be more than just careful. But maybe we'll be lucky." She attempted another small smile.

"Why do you say that?" Micah didn't smile in return but began breaking their Spartan camp in preparation for the day's travel.

"You said it was Tuesday." Days and dates had been of great importance to Rachel ever since he'd arrived at the village. It seemed to make it easier for her somehow to accept the march of months and years that had passed if he put a specific date and time on everything he could.

He looked at his watch. "Yeah, Tuesday. The fourth."

"The Fourth of July," Rachel said, pleased to have caught him unaware. "Tell me how can anything bad happen to two loyal Yankee-Doodle Dandies like us on the Fourth of July?"

Plenty, Micah thought to himself, *when those two Yankee-Doodle Dandies happen to be damned near lost in a jungle in Laos.*

I'LL BE BACK WITH RACHEL BY the Fourth of July. Simon McKendrick remembered his brother's promise as he hunched his shoulders against another pelting shower of hard, cold raindrops that seemed determined to find their way inside the upturned collar of his trench coat. The Fourth of July had come and gone without any sign of Micah or Rachel. Now it was September, at least for a few more hours, Simon corrected himself, glancing at his watch in the dim glow of a street lamp halfway down the block, and the latest information he'd received on his missing brother and sister was as grim as the Chicago weather.

It was only seven o'clock in the evening but with the steady rain that had been falling ever since he'd landed at O'Hare, it seemed much later than that. He wondered how much longer he'd have to stand here, in the shadow of a big wet pine at the edge of the small park directly across the street from Anne Simpson's home, waiting for her to return.

He couldn't remember if they'd ever met. He didn't think so, although he did recall Rachel mentioning an air force nurse named Anne something who had volunteered to help with the evacuation of the orphanage where Rachel worked during those last chaotic days before Saigon fell. Lieutenant Anne Norton. Simpson, of course, was her married name. He'd been gleaning bits and pieces of information about Anne Norton Simpson, R.N., over the past few weeks. She was in all probability the same woman who'd known his sister briefly that long-ago spring.

She was also the perfect cover he needed to deliver the ransom a Vietnamese official was now demanding for the safe release of his brother and sister. *Damn Micah's impatience.* It had landed him in danger, as well as jeopardizing their chances of getting Rachel safely out of Southeast Asia. Yet, at the same time, Simon envied Micah his freedom to act as he chose. There was no way Simon could have gone to Laos as Micah had without cutting through enough red tape to strangle an elephant. And if he'd been caught—as Micah had—the consequences would have been decidedly grim.

A car pulled into the driveway of the thirties-era, two-story frame house that was Anne Simpson's home. Simon watched as two bareheaded blond boys jumped out of the back seat of the middle-aged Chevy station wagon, followed more sedately by a slim teenage girl with long, straight black hair that shone with steel-blue highlights in the reflection of the porch light. Simon knew without consulting his notes that the boys were Anne Simpson's twin sons and the girl was Leah, her only daughter, one of the three Amerasian orphans Lieutenant Anne Norton had brought with her out of Saigon, April 29, 1975.

He heard laughter and voices calling as two tall, broad-shouldered young men appeared on the porch of the house. Anne Simpson's two eldest adopted sons. They sprinted out into the rainy evening, each accepting a loaded brown paper grocery bag from their sister. The two youngest boys carried cartons of soft drinks, Leah, a pile of schoolbooks. Simon found himself waiting impatiently for his first sight of the woman herself.

Anne Simpson got out of her car. Simon had a quick glimpse of long legs and her attractive backside as she reached across the seat for her purse. Then she straightened and turned toward him.

He didn't know what he'd been expecting, maybe Wonder Woman or Supergirl, he wasn't sure. But he was disappointed. Anne Simpson was decidedly ordinary. Not too short or too tall, five-five or -six, he'd guess. Her figure was slight but rounded beneath her white nurse's uniform. Her features were blurred with rain and distance but she didn't look anywhere near thirty-nine, which was the age given on the dossier he'd compiled. And her hair was red, not copper or auburn, or strawberry blond. It was just plain red. He could see that even in the pale light shining off the porch.

She was laughing and joking with her children, issuing orders right and left as Simon melted farther into the shadows, realizing he'd have to postpone his initial encounter with the woman to a more private moment. He pushed away the feeling of impatience with the ruthlessness of long years of practice. The time would come.

She laughed again and Simon decided he liked her laugh. It was light and sweet, carrying across the street on the heavy wet air like a sudden flight of butterflies dancing in the sun. He watched as she marshaled her brood and marched them into the house with the ease and aplomb of a four-star general. A large shaggy yellow dog of indeterminate breed appeared around the side of the house. Anne Simpson greeted it with affection. She stooped to pick up a stray scrap of soggy paper that had blown up next to the sidewalk and crumpled it into a ball. Seconds later she'd disappeared inside the house.

"The perfect cover," Simon muttered aloud as he retreated farther into the darkness along the main path of the little park. Anne Norton Simpson, widow, mother of five, veteran, owned her own business: quite a lot of hats for one woman to wear. She liked kids and animals and she was neat; he'd learned that much about her tonight. Not much to go on, really. And he'd bet she had freckles, too, with that red hair and creamy white skin. But best of all, from Simon's point of view, was the fact that in three days' time she'd be leaving for Vietnam as part of a delegation of veterans and concerned parents interested in speeding up the process of allowing Amerasian teenagers to come to the United States.

Three days. That was all the time he had to convince her to do what he needed her to do. It was going to take every ounce of his vaunted persuasive abilities to get the job done. He'd bet Anne Simpson was no pushover. She was honest, upstanding, a pillar of her community. Just how did you go about talking a woman like that into committing a crime?

CHAPTER ONE

"MICHAEL! JONATHON! Turn off that TV and get to bed. It's almost ten. There's school tomorrow, in case you've forgotten."

"Awww, Mom. We're watching *Star Trek: The Next Generation*. We can't go to bed until we see what happens to Mr. Data. Somebody zapped his circuits," Mike said earnestly, turning his head to gaze at his mother over his shoulder from where he was sprawled on his stomach in front of the family room TV.

"No kidding," Annie replied, moving away from the rumbling dishwasher to see for herself.

"Yeah, some dorky mad scientist or other that snuck onto the *Enterprise*." She smiled fondly at her twin sons. Although the boys were identical, Annie thought Mike looked most like his father. She couldn't explain her feelings logically, because everybody else had trouble telling the boys apart at all, but there was just something, the curve of his smile, the twinkle in his dark brown eyes, that reminded her so strongly of her dead husband. Annie waited for the choked, teary feeling that usually burned her throat and misted her eyes whenever she thought about Michael Jonathon Simpson, but, surprisingly, the familiar stab of sorrow didn't come. Was she finally coming to terms with her grief? She hoped so. The last thing Mike would have wanted her to do was spend her life mourning for what could never be again.

But he'd died so suddenly...and she'd loved him so very much....

"The guy who plays Mr. Data does a pretty good job of looking like a dead robot," Jon piped up, adding his two cents' worth to the conversation.

"Android," Mike corrected with a snort. He was the elder by fifteen minutes and never let his brother forget the fact. "Don't you know anything, dummy?" he added provokingly.

"Android, robot. What's the dif?" Jon rolled back onto his stomach and continued to watch the show, ignoring his brother's attempt to start a bedtime free-for-all. Jonathon, like Annie, was even-tempered and easygoing. Again, it was Mike whose temperament more closely resembled his volatile and high-spirited father. Annie turned back into the kitchen with a final word of warning that the two were to be on their way upstairs to bed before the credits were finished rolling.

"It's your fault they're Trekkies, Mom," her eldest son, Chad, said from the depths of the refrigerator, where he'd been studying the contents for the past five minutes. "You got them hooked on the old reruns when they were babies. Then the movies, now this new TV show. It was inevitable." He straightened to his full six feet, towering over Annie as she gently but firmly shut the refrigerator door in his face.

"Nothing in there has mutated into anything else since you first poked your nose inside. What are you looking for, anyway?"

"Something to take back to the dorm for snacks. How about this pound of Colby cheese and that box of crackers over on the cupboard? Think you can spare them?"

"Be my guest," Annie motioned with an expansive wave of her hand. "It's got to be cheaper than having you feed quarters into a vending machine faster than the human eye can follow."

"That's exactly the way I see it," Chad agreed with a devastating grin that showed two rows of perfectly straight white teeth. Annie never ceased to marvel at that brilliant smile. Considering the deprivations of the first six years of his life, Chad was a remarkably happy and healthy young man. He draped his arm around her shoulders. "Besides, just consider how much better for me this wholesome, all-natural dairy snack will be than that prepackaged, preservative-ridden junk food."

"Not to mention, this stuff is free."

Chad laughed. "That's what I like about you, Mom. We think alike. We've got real business sense."

"No, just common sense." Annie laughed, too. "You'd better get started back to campus or you won't make it in before curfew." Chad was attending a small private Catholic college in another Chicago suburb about twenty miles away. He'd won a partial basketball scholarship and was planning to major in accounting. Annie was looking forward to the time he could take over some of the endless bookkeeping chores at the clinics.

"On my way. You two squirts behave," he ordered his brothers as he grabbed his jacket off the hook near the kitchen door. He bent over to peer through the shuttered pass-through that he'd helped Mike build over the Christmas holidays three years ago—just a few months before his perfectly healthy, forty-two-year-old father had died of a massive stroke. This time Annie did have to blink away tears. Mike would have been so proud of the young man their adopted son had become. Of their three eldest children, all Amerasian orphans, Chad's Vietnamese ancestry was least apparent. His hair was light brown and curly, his eyes a deep, sexy blue, with only the slightest tilt to the corners. Annie knew nothing abo biological parents except that his mother had been prostitute in a Saigon brothel and that his father was an American GI.

"Doug working late at Burger King again tonight?" Chad asked, altering the course of her thoughts as he halted on his way out the back door to add a bag of taco chips and a jar of salsa to his goody bag.

Annie nodded, her memories, if not her emotions, under control once again as she felt her usual faint anxiety for her second child's welfare escalate into a tight knot in her chest. "Someone on the late shift called in sick. Doug volunteered to close up."

"Won't be home till after midnight, huh?" Apparently Chad had no trouble picking up on the concern in her voice. He grabbed a handful of chocolate-chip cookies from a container on the kitchen counter. His hand was on the doorknob but he stopped to look back at her.

"I don't like him working this late on a school night," Annie admitted, but that wasn't the real reason for her anxiety.

"He's seventeen and a junior. You can't regulate every minute of his day. His grades are okay," Chad remarked, touching on the real problem. He was well aware of how much his brother's lack of enthusiasm for continuing his education beyond high school bothered their mother. "Let him get his fill of flipping burgers and mopping floors. So what if it takes him a year or two to make up his mind what he wants to do with his life? Just be thankful he's not into drugs, or getting blitzed on beer every night, or trying to run with one of those street gangs from the south side, like two or three of the kids in his class are doing."

"Thanks for cheering me up," Annie said with a wry twist of her lips. "It's just that your father wanted all of you to make something special of yourselves."

"Dad was a damn good electrician. He owned his own business and he never went to college, either. Maybe you ought to let Doug be what he wants to be."

"It's not that easy. I'd be happy if Doug wanted to learn to work with his hands. It's that he doesn't seem to want to do anything at all with his future that worries me."

"Lighten up, Mom. He's still a kid. You worry about us too much. You'll get old before your time."

"I am old." At least sometimes she felt that way. Especially if she let herself think of all the people who depended on her. She couldn't help but worry about her children. She was a mother, after all, and worry is what mothers do best. There were also her patients, her employees, the pressures of owning her own business. Maybe it had been a mistake to borrow the money to open the third clinic? But so many women and children, both low and middle income and the elderly on fixed incomes, all needed the medical care provided by family nurse practitioners like herself.

"Hey, Mom, don't talk like that. You've still got a while to go before you hit the big four-oh."

"Five months and eleven days, but who's counting?" Annie said, putting a lid on the container of cookies before Chad could decimate their numbers even farther. She gave his hand a playful slap. "Save some for your brothers and sister. It's hard feeling young when you have a house full of teenagers and almost teenagers eating you into the poorhouse."

"Hey!" Chad clapped his hand to his chest in the general region of his heart. "Is it my fault you and Dad got a head start on parenting by adopting the three of us?"

"No, it's not." Annie's slim, carefully darkened eyebrows came together in a quick frown. She searched Chad's face for any shadow of old fears, of remembered terror and suffering, but saw nothing but a teasing glint in his eyes. She made her own voice deliberately light and playful.

"It was just a moment of weakness on our part. We couldn't pass up the opportunity to start out with two of the three of you already potty trained."

"You sure know how to let the air out of a guy's ego." Chad tried to look properly chastised but the wicked glint remained in the depths of his blue eyes. "I thought it was because we were all so darn lovable you just couldn't turn us back over to the orphanage people when we got to the States. And just remember, you'd never have met Dad if you hadn't shown up at the embassy gates dragging me and Doug by the hand, carrying Leah in your arms...."

"Enough." Her emotions were too close to the surface this rainy night to be able to match his playful mood. "Get going. It's late and the streets are slippery, so drive carefully." She smiled to erase any sting in her words.

"Not to worry, Mom. That old crate of a VW won't go over thirty-five without a tail wind."

Annie reached up on tiptoe and planted a quick, light kiss on his cheek. "Will you be home before I leave Thursday?" The trip to Vietnam was important to her but she'd never left her children alone for more than a day or two since Mike had died. This time she'd be away for two weeks, in a part of the world where travel was difficult at best and Americans were still regarded as enemies of the people.

"I'll be here Wednesday evening to get all your last-minute instructions. Don't worry, Mom. I've arranged my classes to be home every night by eight. I won't leave in the morning until the brats are on the school bus. Leah gets home first to referee and Doug will be around to haul them back and forth to anything that's going on after school. Just get their schedule down on paper and don't forget to leave the checkbook so I can keep all of us fed. It'll be a piece of cake. I bet we'll hardly even notice you're gone."

"Thanks," Annie said, making a sour face.

"Just kidding, Mom. Can't you take a joke anymore? See you Wednesday." He was out the door before Annie could muster a suitable retort. Instead, she herded the twins, protesting loudly every step of the way, upstairs to bed and knocked on the door of Leah's room to wish her good-night.

"Hi, Mom," Leah answered from her desk in front of the window. She looked up, smiling absently in Annie's general direction.

"What are you working on, honey?" Moving across the room to get a better look at the sketch pad under Leah's hand, Annie saw a quickly executed line drawing of her twin sons roughhousing in the backyard with the dog.

"The perspective's a little off," Leah said with a frown and a quick shake of her head. "I'll have to work on it some more."

"I think it's very good."

Leah giggled. "You think everything I do is great. You have since you bought me my first box of crayons."

"You were good then, too," Annie said with a proud smile. Leah was already moving beyond what her latest private instructor could teach her. She needed first-class professional guidance, and, unfortunately, right now Annie couldn't afford to get it for her.

Her daughter giggled again, rippling crystal laughter like the ringing of tiny temple bells. "I drew stick people and houses with crooked chimneys and no windows just like every other little kid."

"Not quite like every other little kid," Annie replied softly as she watched her daughter add a quick stroke here, a suggestion of movement there to make it seem as if the clean-lined images of her sons might come alive before her very eyes.

What would Leah's life have been like if Annie had not entered that dark, twisting little street in her frantic haste to reach the American Embassy that long ago April day? Would Leah's childlike and terrified young mother have kept the newborn baby girl, raised her as best she could? Or would she have abandoned her in her own terror at being deserted in the beleaguered city, to survive or not, like thousands of other half-American children? If she closed her eyes she could still see the young mother's beseeching look as she thrust the baby into her arms and disappeared into the milling crowd outside the walls of the embattled embassy.

"It's still not right." Leah's impatient exclamation snapped the line of Annie's thoughts. The past was very close tonight, too close. Annie welcomed the interruption.

"Why don't you sleep on it." She bent and placed a quick kiss on the top of Leah's head. Her hair was the color and texture of ebony satin, her skin a rich, creamy olive. Only her eyes, pale gray like a cloudy spring day, betrayed her American heritage. "It's late, honey, better get to bed. School tomorrow." Somehow she'd find the money for Leah's lessons. She'd contact someone at the Art Institute as soon as she returned from Vietnam.

"In a minute." Leah was once again engrossed in her sketch.

"Now." Annie made her voice firm. "The drawing will still be here tomorrow."

"And so will a million other things that have to be done."

Annie laughed as she turned to walk out of the room. "You sound just like Grandma Norton when you talk like that."

Leah frowned, making a face. She wasn't altogether certain she liked being compared to her autocratic and strong-willed grandmother. "I guess I did. Well," she said with a fourteen-year-old's devastating candor, "it's better than not having anything you want to do, like Doug. Night, Mom."

"Pleasant dreams, sweetie," Annie reminded, not letting the dart of pain Leah's careless remark inflicted on her heart seep into her words. "I meant what I said—turn out the light."

"I will."

Annie closed Leah's door, and paused a moment outside the twins' room to see if they were really asleep. It seemed they were. Annie continued on down the stairs. It had been a long day. She was tired. She had a thousand things to do before she left for Saigon in three days' time. *Saigon.* Annie had trouble thinking of the capital as Ho Chi Minh City. Would anything be as she remembered it?

"I doubt it," Annie said aloud as she picked up a pair of sneakers belonging to one of the twins and deposited them on the wide overhang of the steps that projected beyond the banister edge. "The war's been over for almost fifteen years." Saigon had been a city on the verge of collapse when she'd arrived, beleaguered, almost paralyzed by imminent defeat and the Americans' withdrawal. She never wanted to live through times like that again.

She might as well wait up for Doug to get home, Annie decided, flipping through the TV channels, finding nothing she wanted to watch. Sleep was very far away and would be a long time coming. She turned off the set and picked up a magazine from the coffee table in front of the couch. She really didn't want to go upstairs yet. Without Mike's strong, loving arms to hold her safe in the dark, lonely hours before dawn, the nightmares sometimes came back to haunt her, still. She'd thought she'd put the war and the months she'd spent as an air force nurse in Southeast Asia behind her. And for the most part, she had. But not always...and not tonight....

"MRS. ANNE SIMPSON?"

"Yes." Annie didn't release the chain lock on the door. The man on her porch was tall, with midnight-black hair, harsh angular features and eyes that might be either hazel or brown. It was difficult to tell in the dim overhead light on the front porch.

"I'd like to talk to you." The words were spoken politely enough, but the ring of command in his speech couldn't be entirely suppressed.

Annie stiffened. She hadn't heard anyone use that particular tone of voice since she'd mustered out of the air force. Yet, the man didn't look like officer material. There was a hint of danger about him, of lean, coiled strength, of too much drive and energy held in check to fit the mold of some one-star general's trained flunky. "Who are you?"

"My name's Simon McKendrick." He reached into the pocket of his wet trench coat. The collar turned up. His thick, dark hair just brushed the edge. Water dripped from the brim of his soft gray fedora. The hat was very wet also, as if he'd been standing in the rain for a long time. *Watching the house?* A small shiver of alarm coursed down Annie's spine. He was dressed like a spy. He looked like a spy, too. The man flipped open a small leather folder and held it in front of her nose. "I work for the Bureau of the Census."

He smiled then, for the first time, and Annie felt her breath catch in her throat. "The Bureau of the Census?" Had she heard him correctly?

"Yes." Maybe he wasn't a spy after all, Annie decided, oddly disappointed by the conclusion. His smile grew a little broader as though he'd read her mind and knew what she was thinking about him.

"Why are you here, Mr. McKendrick?" She released the safety chain but didn't invite him inside.

"To discuss your trip to Vietnam." The smile disappeared. He was all business once more. Annie wondered if she'd only imagined the warmth of that fleeting grin.

"I, and my group, have all the necessary government clearances for our trip. I can't see where the Census Bureau would have any interest in Amerasian children until they are actually in this country."

"That's correct." Again she sensed, for an instant, great impatience held in check by the force of his will. "My business is of a more personal nature." It was possible that he had fathered a child during the Vietnam War himself and wanted some information on how to go about finding the teenager. He was the right age, Annie guessed, early forties, moderately successful, settled in life. *No, not settled in his life.* He might be trying to pass for some sort of middle-management civil servant, but she sensed the truth was far more complex than that. Annie trusted her woman's intuition and it told her this man was dangerous.

"It's late, Mr. McKendrick. Please state your business." Annie let her own impatience seep into the words. She didn't like being made to feel intimidated in her own home. A gust of wind howled down the street, blowing rain onto the porch and across their legs. Annie shivered as the cold, wet drops peppered her bare feet.

"May I come in?" Simon looked pointedly at her wet feet. Her toes were coral-tipped, curled up, away from the chill blast of wet autumn wind. Funny, he hadn't thought of Annie Simpson, businesswoman, mother of five, as the kind of woman who wore coral polish on her toenails. For some reason he liked knowing she wasn't as straightlaced and by-the-book as she might appear at first glance. He looked back into her face. "I promise I won't keep you from your bed very long." A faint wash of color stole across her cheeks. She did have freckles, a small gold smattering of them across the bridge of her nose. "What I have to say is very important."

He watched her hesitate once more, then step reluctantly away from the door. A very careful lady, Annie Simpson. She didn't entirely trust him. That was good. A little healthy skepticism never hurt. In his line of work it was damned near a necessity if you wanted to stay alive and healthy. Annie Simpson wouldn't be easily intimidated by anyone, including conniving, corrupted Vietnamese officials.

Simon didn't know when he'd started calling her Annie in his mind. Up close she just didn't look like Anne.

Maybe it was the freckles, or the coral-tinted toenails, or the way she'd pulled her red hair back off her face to try to keep it from curling wildly about her cheeks. The comfortable, old-fashioned form of her name suited her best, and Annie she would be from this moment on. At least in the privacy of his thoughts.

"Would you mind if we talked in the kitchen? I have lunches to pack for tomorrow. It's just too much of a madhouse around here to get it done in the morning."

"With four kids to get off to school every day before you leave for the clinics, I can imagine that it is."

Annie stopped in the middle of the entry hall and turned to confront him. "You seem to know quite a bit about me already, Mr. McKendrick."

"Yes, I do." He didn't seem perturbed by her sudden attack. Annie looked him over carefully. He returned her scrutiny from gold-flecked hazel eyes. She was a little afraid of him; it showed in her eyes, in the tense set of her shoulders. Good. She had sense, this woman. She wouldn't panic or blow his cover at the first sign of trouble. He didn't stop to analyze his decision. It came from somewhere deep inside, below the level of conscious thought. Annie continued to watch him, her brown eyes narrowed in concentration. Simon was aware of the exact moment she decided to trust him.

"Would you like a cup of coffee?"

"Thanks." He was dripping rainwater on the carpet.

"You can hang your coat here." She gestured to a plain oak hall tree at the foot of the stairs. "We might as well be comfortable while you say whatever it is you have to say."

He seated himself at the round kitchen table when she invited him to do so, accepted the cup of strong, black coffee she poured and watched her set out ingredients for sandwiches, fruit, pudding cups and homemade cookies. She handed him a plate with three of the oatmeal cookies on it. He thanked her gravely and ate in silence for a minute or two more. Annie made ham-and-cheese sandwiches with the assembly-line finesse and skill of long practice. She started sealing them inside plastic bags.

"I can talk and work at the same time, Mr. McKendrick." She glanced pointedly at the clock above the sink. "What exactly is it you want from me? If it's information about the various groups of Vietnam veterans who are trying to find and bring to America the children they fathered during the war..."

"I know about your work with the Amerasian Children's League, Mrs. Simpson. That's not why I'm here, however." Simon decided not to beat around the bush. He wasn't going to lie to Annie Simpson—any more than he absolutely had to. "I need your help."

"In what way?" Five identical brown-bag lunches were lined up on the counter. Annie began putting initials on them with a black felt-tip marker. She carried her lunch, too, just like the kids.

"I have a small package that I want you to deliver for me."

Annie poured herself a cup of coffee and leaned back against the counter. "Try UPS, Mr. McKendrick. They're fast and reliable."

"I want the package delivered to a gentleman in Ho Chi Minh City."

"You want me to smuggle something into Vietnam?"

"Yes." She was quick on the uptake. Simon didn't let any of what he was thinking show in his expression. He met her wide-eyed gaze head-on. Her eyes were the deep, rich brown of a chocolate bar. So were her delicately arched brows and lashes. He wondered, for a moment, if the color was natural and decided it wasn't.

"You're crazy." She shook her head in astonishment. "Why in the world would I do something like that? It's taken eighteen months to get this trip organized, to cut through the red tape and overcome all the State Department foot-dragging. I won't jeopardize this project for you or anyone else. There are lives at stake here, Mr. McKendrick." He saw her glance quickly at the telephone on the wall at the end of the counter. She had probably decided he was a lunatic and was calculating how long it would take the police to get here after her call to 911.

"Sit down." Her brown eyes widened in alarm. He lowered his voice. "I'm sorry. Please, join me." He pointed to the seat across from his. "Let me explain."

"There's nothing to explain," Annie stated, but she sat down anyway. He saw righteous anger begin to replace the spurt of fear that had darkened her eyes, quickened her breath and sent her pulse racing in the creamy hollow where her throat and collarbone met just above the neck of her plain gray sweatshirt. Her voice was steady. "Explain yourself, Mr. McKendrick, or I'll call the police."

"Why don't you call me Simon?" She ignored the offer to use his first name. "It's imperative that this package is safely delivered to a contact, a member of the Vietnamese delegation, most likely."

"You don't know the man's name?" She looked skeptical.

"No. Most kidnappers prefer it that way." Her expression was filled with anxiety and just a hint of excitement. It was the excitement that made him decide to trust her. Annie Simpson was brave and intelligent, and somewhere beneath the washed-out sweatshirt and faded denims there beat the heart of an adventurer. He reached into his back pocket and produced a slim, black jeweler's box.

He held it out to her. She took it reluctantly, and opened the lid. Annie sucked in her breath, her mouth a round O of wonder and surprise. "It's beautiful. It must be priceless."

Annie didn't know anything about jewelry, not really, but even a child would have been able to tell the exquisite necklace of perfectly matched pearls she held in her hand was worth a fortune. She shut the lid with a snap and set the box on the table in front of him. She squared her shoulders and folded her hands. "I can't be responsible for something so valuable." She didn't look at him again. Somehow, seeing the necklace made it all seem very real. Simon McKendrick was some kind of crook and he was asking her to become one also.

"Believe me, the next time you see this necklace it will look just like a piece of costume jewelry. No one will take a second look at it." His voice was harsh and cold. The quick, delightful flashes of humor she'd detected now and then in his speech had disappeared.

"I'm not making myself clear," Annie fumbled for words. "I don't intend to commit a..." She just couldn't say the word *crime* for some reason. "I don't intend to risk my freedom and the safety of my companions by carrying this necklace into a foreign country."

"You used to take risks for a good cause, Annie." It was the first time she'd heard him say her name. Annie suppressed a shiver as the warm, dark sound of the word washed over her skin like smoke in the night. "Once you even volunteered to leave a cushy assignment in Manila to fly into Saigon and help evacuate an orphanage full of babies and small children."

She raised her eyes to meet his. "Who told you that?" Was it the combination of excitement, fatigue and anxiety that made her think she heard the thunder of mortar shells and the sharp staccato bursts of automatic-weapons fire in the distance? She shook her head to clear the echoes of the past from her mind.

"It's all in your record, Annie. I know you stayed in Saigon until April twenty-seventh, trying to get kids out in buses that broke down time and again, through streets clogged with mobs of frightened refugees and deserting ARVN soldiers. I know the kind of courage it must have taken to go out in those streets alone with two small children clinging to your hand, to accept a babe in arms from its terrified mother and carry all three of them through the chaos outside the embassy walls. That's the kind of courage I need from you now, Annie Simpson."

"It doesn't take courage to smuggle a necklace into a country so poor its people can't feed themselves. Are those pearls destined for the neck of some corrupt bureaucrat's mistress, or to keep his wife from complaining too loudly about her?" Annie tried to hold back the memories of the past his words evoked by the sheer strength and weight of her indignation. "You don't need someone with my kind of courage, Mr. McKendrick. You need someone who's stupid and greedy and who doesn't give a damn about anyone but himself."

"The necklace is the ransom required to free two Americans held captive in Vietnam." His hand closed over hers when she tried to push the jewelry box back across the table. His fingers bit into the flesh of her wrist. Annie looked down at the strong, tanned fingers holding her. She felt them tremble ever so slightly before he released her.

"There's no proof that any MIA/POWs are still alive over there, Simon," she said very gently. She was active in the MIA/POW program also. She knew the grief and frustration their families and friends still felt, the agony of not knowing what had happened to their loved ones. But she had no proof there were any living captives still in Vietnam. She covered his hand with her own. Beneath their intertwined fingers, the jeweler's box rested on the tabletop.

"Not MIAs," Simon said, his hazel eyes holding hers by the sheer force of his will. "My brother...and my sister were being held in Laos. Now I have reason to believe they're in Vietnam."

"How long?" Annie's words were hardly more than a breathy whisper. A woman, a woman held captive in the jungle?

"My brother, Micah, since the spring. My sister, Rachel..." Simon closed his eyes and took a deep breath "...since April thirtieth, 1975."

"Rachel." A memory stirred to life in Annie's mind. Her heart began to beat so hard and fast she was afraid she wouldn't be able to hear him when he started talking again. A small, childlike woman with a will of iron and a smile that charmed birds from the trees. A smile very like Simon McKendrick's. Rachel Phillips was an ex-army nurse, several years older than Annie, who'd been working for the orphanage that Annie was assigned to during the evacuation. The last time she had seen Rachel Phillips was when their bus broke down in the middle of a clogged Saigon street and they had been separated by the relentless milling of the panicked crowds, unable to return to the orphanage. Annie remembered being dragged along like helpless flotsam, two small boys in tow, toward the beleaguered compound of the American Embassy. "I knew a nurse in Saigon named Rachel Phillips."

"I know." Simon's voice was raw with emotion. "My sister, Rachel McKendrick Phillips. She's still alive. And still in Vietnam."

CHAPTER TWO

IT WAS FOUR O'CLOCK THURSDAY afternoon and O'Hare was a madhouse, as usual. Annie fingered the strand of disguised pearls at her throat as she waited for the rest of the group to check in for the flight to Bangkok. Simon McKendrick had made her task sound so simple. Wear the necklace through each customs checkpoint. Hand the pearls over to the kidnapper and accept the documents that would allow Micah and Rachel to legally leave the country. So simple. So terrifyingly simple.

Perhaps it had been the sound of Simon's dark, rough voice, calm and matter-of-fact as he explained his plan. The perfect, large, white South Sea pearls would be slightly altered to hide their luster and value from the casual observer. Perhaps it was his strength of purpose, the unmistakable tenor of knowledge and authority in his words as he explained why he believed pearls, revered since ancient times in Asia and China, as well as being easily converted into gold or currency, had been chosen as the medium of exchange. He talked of the danger, the possibility they might not succeed and the reasons why he was determined they should. There had been a dream-like quality to the entire visit. In the clear light of day she knew it would only be the work of a moment to undo the clasp, hand the necklace to Chad or Doug and instruct them to return it to the messenger service that had delivered it the night before.

That quickly, that easily, she could rid herself of the whole affair. She wasn't a spy or a smuggler, or even very brave, really. She didn't want to be responsible for the necklace or the lives of the people connected with it. Simon McKendrick had told her it was impossible for him to get into Vietnam with the necklace without encountering major difficulties that could further endanger the lives of his brother and sister. She believed him. Almost. Somehow—her intuition again?—he struck her as a man who would find few obstacles insurmountable. She had her own safety to consider after all—for the sake of her children.

And of course it was because of the children, of all the children she helped, and those she could not; because of Mike's memory, because of the memories of Rachel and the others who had cared, of the times and places, the fear and terror of her escape from Saigon . . . an escape that would have been impossible if Rachel Phillips hadn't stayed behind. That's why she knew there was no question but that she would have to do whatever lay in her power to help bring Simon McKendrick's brother and sister home.

"Mom, you're going to break that necklace if you keep twisting it like that." Doug was watching her with a frown on his face. His dark brown, curly hair was long and pulled back into a short ponytail at the nape of his neck. Brown eyes, slightly tilted, regarded her closely.

"Nervous, I guess." She gave him a lopsided smile. Simon McKendrick had been as good as his word. When the necklace was delivered it looked like nothing more than a fairly good piece of costume jewelry. Something she could feel comfortable wearing with the pale peach cotton shirtwaist dress she had on. No customs agent would give it a second look. But it wasn't comfortable.

It was heavy and constricting and seemed to burn with cool fire against the skin of her neck.

"Don't forget to bring us something," the twins chorused, dancing back and forth in front of her like mechanical toys that had been wound too tight.

"I'll bring you both something great," Annie promised. "Sit down," she added automatically. For once the twins did as they were told, sprawling in two of the contoured plastic chairs the airline provided for passengers waiting to board its international flights. She started listing last-minute instructions for Chad. The twins began fidgeting again almost immediately.

"Go watch the planes take off, brats," Chad ordered. He pointed to the big plate-glass window with its view of busy runways. "We've been all through this, Mom," he said serenely.

"Are you sure you have everything you'll need in that one bag?" Leah frowned disapprovingly at Annie's single oversized canvas carryall. It was only slightly larger than the bag she carried to school each day.

"I'm sure." Annie smiled at the memory of Leah's scandalized expression when she'd informed her daughter she wasn't taking a blow-dryer or curling iron with her to Vietnam. Doug's brusque explanation that neither appliance would work because of different electrical systems hadn't impressed Leah very much.

"Mom, with all that heat and humidity, your hair's going to look like a rag doll."

"It won't be the first time," Annie had said, and laughed. But that was before the necklace had arrived; before she'd had to admit to herself that her late-evening visit from the mysterious dark-haired stranger hadn't been a disturbing dream after all.

"There's the boarding call for your flight," Chad said, signaling the fractious twins to come and kiss their mother goodbye.

Annie bent to scoop the boys up in her arms. They felt small, but strong and sturdy as she held them close for the space of several heartbeats. *God, was she doing the right thing, leaving her babies behind like this?* "Be good," she said, and her throat burned with tears.

"We will," Mike said, uncharacteristically subdued.

"Don't forget our presents," Jon reminded her with another quick, hard hug.

"Bye, Mama." Leah hugged her, too. She was crying a little.

"Bye." Doug let her kiss his cheek but he didn't offer a kiss in return. Annie's tears came closer to the surface. He was so angry that life seemed to be moving too slowly. How could she tell him that all too soon it would go speeding by, instead, and he would wish he could reach out and slow time in its relentless march toward the future?

"Have a safe trip." Chad hugged her so hard, she gasped. "Don't worry about us, okay?"

"Okay," Annie said in a shaky voice. "Drive carefully."

"We'll go straight home." Chad winked as the twins burst into indignant speech.

"McDonald's."

"You promised."

"Don't forget to study for your American history test, Doug," Annie called as she watched them move away into the steady flow of people along the concourse.

"Mom." Doug's voice cracked in annoyance. "Lay off it."

"Promise," Annie called once more.

He held up his hands in surrender, but smiled, striding backward, away from her. "Promise." They walked around a corner and were gone.

"Nice kids."

Annie had knelt to retrieve her carryall. The rough, dark voice was familiar. She looked up. "You." She stood all in a rush. The tall, broad-shouldered figure of Simon McKendrick seemed to fill her field of vision. She stepped back, away from him, away from the slight, ever-present hint of danger that seemed always to surround him. "What are you doing here?" His eyes flickered over the necklace. The heat of his gaze warmed the skin of her throat. Annie almost raised her hand to touch the affected area.

"I'm going to Bangkok," he told her in a quiet, forceful tone that brooked no argument. "As Peter Leyton, the free-lance reporter the Amerasian Children's League hired to cover the trip. Pleased to meet you, Mrs. Simpson." He held out his hand.

Annie looked around, hoping to spot someone from airport security. When she looked back, his hand was still extended. She took it reluctantly, unwilling to cause a scene. "No one is going to believe you're Peter Leyton." She let him grasp her cold fingers for a moment, then pulled away. His grip was warm and solid, just like the rest of him. "He's five feet tall and bald."

"Everyone will believe what you tell them. You're the only one who's seen Peter Leyton." He was right. Their group was small: three fathers of Amerasian teenagers, their lawyers, two members of the league, including herself, and two representatives of Vietnam veteran groups who would be meeting with Vietnamese officials regarding the questions of Agent Orange and MIA/POWs. A State Department official was to meet them in Bangkok for last-minute instructions before the trip to Vietnam. Simon McKendrick's identity was safe. As long as she kept her mouth shut. "Why are you here? Why are you impersonating a man you've never met?" The dreamlike quality of their first meeting wasn't with her now. This man was cold, hard reality and she wondered what she'd gotten herself into.

Simon shifted his carry-on bag to his shoulder and put his arm under her elbow. "I'll explain on the plane." He showed his ticket to the steward at the gate. His grip on her arm was strong enough to be uncomfortable.

"You'll never get away with this," she said through clenched teeth. "Someone will recognize you."

"Who?" Simon asked, nodding pleasantly to the flight crew standing in the cockpit doorway as they boarded the big DC-10. "You're the only one who knows my real name."

"Where's Leyton?" Annie smiled, too, but it felt as false as the disguised pearls at her throat were supposed to be.

"Your Mr. Leyton has a problem with alcohol abuse," Simon said, his eyes the hard, reflecting gray-green of lake ice in winter. "He's checked himself into a clinic to dry out. I'm afraid he'll be incommunicado for quite some time." He pushed Annie's carryall into the overhead bin above her seat.

"Why are you here? I agreed to—" this time she did raise her hand to touch the pearls "—to do what you asked of me. You said it was impossible for you to leave the country. I don't understand."

"It is impossible for Simon McKendrick to leave the country." He shut the lid of the storage compartment with a snap. "I'm here because you are," he said quietly. "Because, as of right now, we're both in this together." He turned on his heel and walked down the aisle to his seat.

It was almost morning before he got a chance to talk to Annie again, alone and undisturbed by group members wanting to get acquainted, stewardesses trundling drinks and food up and down the aisle, movies playing across the screen. They had changed planes in London. Annie had told him the Chicago–London–Bangkok route, although longer and less convenient than a direct flight across the Pacific, was also cheaper, and that was a major consideration for the financially strapped Amerasian Children's League.

Annie had breezed through customs like a pro. No one gave her necklace a second glance. Bartman, the ex-jewel thief turned government informer he'd hired to temporarily mask the gems' perfection, had done his work well. The pearls had a street value of one hundred and fifty thousand dollars, every cent he could scrape together. The price of freedom for Micah and Rachel, all hanging, literally, on a thread, fastened around the throat of a very brave woman.

"We have to talk," he said, leaning over the seat where she sat staring out the window. His tone was brusque. He meant it to be. This woman stirred his emotions too strongly to allow any softness, any hint of sensuality to slip into their conversation. She was dangerous. Already he'd put himself into a precarious position with his superiors by even being on the plane. By going to Vietnam with Annie Simpson he was probably putting his life in jeopardy as well.

She looked at him for a long moment. "You're right. We have to talk."

The steward had distributed pillows and blankets. Annie's were piled on the empty seat beside her. Simon moved them and sat down. He glanced at his watch. Six hours before they landed in Bangkok. "Are you tired?"

She nodded. "It's been a long day. I haven't any idea what time it is in Bangkok."

"About 3:00 a.m." He kept his voice low. Almost everyone in their section of the plane was asleep.

"I'm glad we have two days to spend in Thailand. I'm sure it will take me that long to get used to the time change."

"Have you ever been to Bangkok?"

She shook her head. "I flew directly into Tan Son Nhut from Manila. Mike always planned for us to come here someday. He said Thailand was one of the most beautiful countries in the world."

"It is." He made a steeple of his fingers, then dropped his hands between his knees. "I was stationed there for two years during the war."

"Are you really with the Census Bureau?"

"Yes," he said, smiling a little. "The Census Bureau pays my salary."

"That's not an answer." Annie looked down at her hands folded in her lap.

"It's the truth."

"Or part of the truth. Are you a spy?" She turned a little in her seat. The remark caught him off guard for a moment. He hesitated. Her gaze held his. Her eyes were clear and guileless, and she studied him with an intensity that made his heart jump in his chest. There was so much passion hidden inside this woman.

He recovered quickly. "Let's just say I'm not a census taker and leave it at that for now, okay?"

"No." Annie shook her head. "It isn't okay." She pulled her lower lip between her teeth. She wore very little makeup; still, her lips were moist and pink and very, very kissable just as they were. "But it will have to do. Did you lie to me about the rest?" She touched the altered pearls at her throat.

Simon laid his head against the back of the seat and closed his eyes. He supposed he had that one coming. The fatigue he'd been holding at bay rushed over him in a black, suffocating wave. He opened his eyes and turned his head to look at her once more. "I wish I had been lying, but it's the truth. The Vietnamese have both my sister and brother hostage somewhere near the Thai border."

"How do you know that?" She should have asked these questions that night at her kitchen table, but then the whole thing had seemed so unreal, so dreamlike that she hadn't thought to do so. He had told her then she would be in no danger, and like a fool she'd believed him. Now, thirty-five thousand feet in the air, speeding toward a time and place that was still so much a part of her nightmares, she wasn't so sure.

"We've been trying to get information on Rachel's whereabouts almost from the beginning. She was a civilian nurse so the military was no help. My parents have spent nearly all their life's savings tracking down leads. Most of them turned out to be dead ends. But there was always just enough detail, just enough of a possibility to keep us hoping. Off and on we've gotten bits and pieces of information from my brother, Micah's, expatriate air force buddies in Bangkok and . . . other places. But God, it was frustrating. Always just a rumor here, or a garbled third- or fourth-hand refugee account of seeing an American woman in some godforsaken jungle village in the mountains. Nothing concrete, nothing we could work with, build on. Until this spring." Simon stopped talking, thinking back to that warm day in Washington. What if he'd insisted Micah go back to his eagles and falcons until he could verify Tiger Jackson's report? What if...

"Your brother took off to find Rachel and was detained, himself." Annie spoke softly. He looked tired, as tired as she felt. James Bond never got tired. If Simon McKendrick was some kind of spy, and Annie suspected he was, then the life of a spy was very different from what she'd seen portrayed in movies and written about in books. It must be a lonely, cold kind of existence, shutting yourself away from all the comforting things in life, relying always on your own strength and judgment and never allowing yourself to completely trust another living soul.

"How did you guess?" Simon turned his head and smiled at her, the corners of his mouth barely curving upward, his eyes still grim and devoid of light.

"I knew Rachel, remember? She used to tell stories about the three of you to the children at bedtime. It helped to soothe them. Most of them were too young, or didn't understand English, so it was only her inflection, the tone of her voice that mattered to them. It was the words that mattered to me. I was scared and homesick. I missed my parents and sisters. So family stories were especially appealing. Funny, I haven't thought about those nights in years. Blocked them out of my mind deliberately, I suppose." Annie smiled. "Rachel was such a small thing, so fragile-looking, yet she was strong and hardworking. She had a will of iron. And she was so impulsive." She leaned back in her seat, lost in memories of the past, quicksilver images of working with Rachel, of the children, of the sweet-faced nuns and the old, white-haired Dutch priest. "She bossed everyone at the orphanage, the nuns, the children, even Father Pieter. Did he get out of the city...or was he left behind, like Rachel?"

"Two Dutch nuns were reported airlifted out the day after you and the kids. Rachel and Father Pieter were to have followed them as soon as possible, but they never arrived at the embassy."

"Mike and I could never find out about the others. We tried for a while after we were married but just kept coming up against a brick wall. I've often wondered about them...." They always figured in her dreams, the bad ones and the good one, where everyone made it safely inside the embassy and Mike was there, smiling at her, and she felt loved and secure.

"We got the same runaround for years. Then, later, after I got clearance...after I started working for the Census Bureau I...uh...met some guys who had access to that kind of information."

"I see," Annie said, wondering if she really did. "You never gave up hope." There was just enough inflection in her voice to make the statement a question if he wished.

"My parents never gave up hope," he corrected her. "We decided not to tell them this time, Micah and I. They don't know he's missing yet. They're on a six-week Mexican cruise now, and during the summer he's always out of touch, climbing dead trees, banding eagles and raising peregrine falcon chicks from eggs they send him from all over the country, so they aren't worried about not hearing from him, yet."

"So it's Simon, the youngest, the levelheaded one, who's going to make everything right again." She wondered just what risks he was running by being on this plane. What strings had he pulled, what threats had he made to get the alcoholic journalist he was impersonating signed into a detox program where she had no doubt he was as much a prisoner as Rachel and Micah? What would he do to her if she revealed his true identity?

"How did you know I'm the youngest?"

His eyes were still shuttered, as though he was used to keeping all emotion from his expression, but they were no longer as cold and hard as ice. He didn't smile at her but she felt as if he had. Was her first instinctive assessment of his character correct? Was he a gentle man capable of violence when provoked, as Mike had been? She watched him closely for a long moment. She had to be right about him; she'd put her own life—as well as the welfare of her children and the others—into his hands with little more than a second thought.

"It just popped into my head," she said, trying to concentrate on their conversation and not the doubts and questions squirreling around in her brain. "From one of the bedtime stories, probably. We were so busy with the children we didn't have much opportunity to talk about ourselves any other time." She yawned, suddenly so tired she could barely go on speaking.

She still wore her wedding band, Simon noticed. "Your husband was a marine guard at the embassy." Again, it was a statement of fact.

Annie answered it as such. "He helped me get inside the walls. He held back the crowd and let me slip inside the gate with the children." She shivered and wrapped her hands around herself as though she were chilled, although the cabin was almost uncomfortably warm. Then she smiled, and for Simon it was as if the sun had left the sky and found its way inside the plane. "He watched over us all that day and night, even found powdered milk and a bottle for Leah. She was only a few days old."

"I know." Annie's courage was amazing. Fourteen years ago she had to have been very young and probably scared to death, but she hadn't given in to panic or terror. He needed that kind of grit and determination from her now.

She looked at him from the corner of her eye and smiled again, impishly this time. "Do you know the rest of the story or shall I go on?"

He grinned, too, and felt heat rise above the collar of his khaki shirt. "Go on, I want to hear you tell it."

"Mike watched over us all that day and night. He went to his CO and swore on a Bible that the children were his, even though he'd only been in Vietnam a few months."

He knew his cue. "What happened next?"

"The colonel fined him five dollars per child and told him to get me inside the embassy and get the paperwork taken care of. He asked me to marry him then and there. I told him he was crazy but even then I was falling in love with him. I know that sounds ridiculous." She laughed self-consciously.

"No, it doesn't sound ridiculous at all. I think Lance Corporal Simpson was probably one of the smartest men in the world."

"I loved him very much." Annie stared out the window for a moment, then took a deep breath and went on talking. Her eyes were misty but serene. "He stayed with us as much as possible, got us on a helicopter, promised to find me when he got back to the States, even though I was so panicked I forgot to give him my parents' address. I couldn't give the children up after all we'd been through, so I got a hardship discharge from the air force and went home." Simon knew it hadn't been that easily accomplished, but he didn't interrupt again. He just let her go on telling the story in her own words. "Six months after I got back to the States, Mike showed up on the doorstep. We were married two weeks later." Her voice trailed off, blurred with fatigue.

"Why don't you try to get some sleep." Simon surprised himself by reaching over to pull her head down onto his shoulder. She didn't resist him. Her hair smelled sweet, like lemons and soap. It was soft to the touch; the curls brushing against his cheek felt like the touch of butterfly wings against his skin.

"Little Simon," she said with a chuckle that ended in another yawn. She snuggled against him, already more than half asleep. "Always the sober, stable one—always there to rescue Micah from his flamboyant, daredevil stunts, and to smooth over Rachel's broken love affairs and not always successful attempts to right the wrongs of the world."

"That sounds like Rachel's description of me, all right."

"I still think you're a spy," she said, as stubborn as ever.

"I am." Annie didn't hear him. She was already asleep and he knew it.

Annie slept on as the plane sped toward its destination. She dreamed of the past but the dream playing itself out against the velvet backdrop of her mind's eye was the good one; the one where everyone was safe and happy. It was the dream that, always before, she'd had only when sleeping in the safety and security of Mike's loving embrace.

CHAPTER THREE

BANGKOK: THE NAME ALONE conjured up visions of temples and canals, crowded marketplaces and saffron-robed monks, but the trip in from the airport passed Annie by in a blur of barely perceived sights and sounds, colors and smells. She was exhausted by the flight and the time change and the emotional uncertainty of her involvement with Simon McKendrick. Consequently, she slept away most of her first day in Thailand. The next morning she woke feeling only slightly out of sync with the world and eager to savor at least a small portion of the beauty and culture of the ancient capital in the few hours of free time available to her.

Annie stretched and yawned, pushing herself up against the pillows and looked at her watch. She calculated the time and day in Chicago once more, and then decided it was a useless exercise unless she was going to call the children, which she did not intend to do until just before she left for Vietnam. Regardless of the day and date in Illinois, it was Sunday morning in Bangkok and she was eager to be out and about. She showered and dressed and ate a hurried breakfast in the coffee shop in the hotel. It was a restaurant like any she might wander into back home, all chrome and vinyl and hanging plants. If it weren't for the fact that the menu was printed in four languages, that the maître d' greeted her in Thai, and that her waitress had the grace and beauty of a rare and delicate tropical flower, she might have been lunching in the mall two blocks from her clinic.

Outside the air-conditioned lobby of the hotel, the heat and humidity assailed her senses. It was the first week in October and still very hot, but the rainy season was nearing an end and the sky, though overcast, showed no signs of an imminent downpour. Annie hesitated a moment, undecided where to go or what to do. A number of the three-wheeled motorized rickshaws that are one of the most popular means of transportation in the city, were lined up in front of the hotel. She was just about to ask the doorman to start bargaining with one of the drivers to set her fare when she was hailed by several members of the delegation. To her surprise and discomfort, the group included Simon McKendrick—no, she decided resolutely—not Simon McKendrick but Peter Leyton.

"Morning, Annie," Jacob Paderwiski greeted her with unquenchable good humor. An ex-combat engineer, his seventeen-year-old son and the boy's mother were still in Vietnam. This was Jake's second trip to Southeast Asia to try to gain custody of the boy and return him and his mother to the States. He was more or less the official leader of the group.

"Good morning, Jake." She greeted him with a smile.

"I think you've met the others. You know my lawyer, Billiup, here." He gestured to the small, nondescript man, in a loud red and blue plaid sport shirt and wrinkled white pants, standing beside him. He might look like a balding insurance salesman just off the golf course but Annie knew he was a first-rate immigration attorney. She smiled at him, too.

"We've met." The lawyer grinned and gestured to the busy street scene surrounding them. His voice was surprisingly low and resonant. "I don't think we're in Kansas anymore, do you?"

Annie recognized the misquoted line from *The Wizard of Oz* at once. "Bangkok could easily qualify as the Emerald City in my book."

"Then you can't miss seeing the Emerald Buddha in the royal chapel of the Grand Palace," Annie heard Simon say. He was standing a bit apart from the others. She turned to him politely. There was something different about him this morning, something she found hard to describe. It was as though he'd banked the inner fire that she sensed burned so brightly within him, lowered the energy level that seemed to spark and crackle around him like heat lightning on a summer night. He had become, she realized suddenly, Peter Leyton, second rate free-lance reporter and photographer, and he would remain Peter Leyton for as long as it suited him to do so.

"I'm not sure there's enough time—" Two could play this game. She couldn't resist a wicked little pause before speaking his name "—Mr. Leyton. Is it worth a visit?"

His mouth wasn't smiling but his eyes were. Annie felt their touch on her skin as though his fingers had brushed across the pearls she'd fastened around her throat. The pearls. Suddenly she remembered why she was wearing them. Teasing Simon McKendrick didn't seem quite as appealing as it had a moment before.

"Well worth a visit. Legend has it that as long as the Emerald Buddha remains in his temple, Thailand will never fall under the domination of a foreign government."

"Only country in Southeast Asia never to have been colonized by another country." Billiup sounded impressed.

"I do know that much Thai history," Annie said. "I was just about to ask the doorman for help in getting a trishaw."

"Have to bargain for the trip," Jacob advised her. "Insult the driver if you just ask, 'How much?' "

"I'm aware of the custom." She wondered if they were going to keep her standing on the sidewalk all day.

"Waste of time, this bargaining," Billiup complained. Annie couldn't recall if she'd ever heard his first name spoken aloud. Jacob Paderwiski always referred to him merely as Billiup. "Set the fee, fair and honest, and pay it. Get on with business, that's what I say."

"Well, my business is getting some breakfast. We've been out to watch the sunrise over the river with Leyton, here. Pretty impressive. Join us for breakfast?" Jacob added as an afterthought. He was already moving his considerable bulk toward the hotel entrance, pulling Billiup along in his wake like a leaf in a whirlwind.

"No thanks." Simon's dismissal was curt, out of character for the laid-back Leyton. "I had coffee earlier in my room. If Mrs. Simpson has no objection, I'll join her on her tour of the city." His lapse was momentary. Annie was the only one who noticed at all. "I can get some background shots for my articles at the same time." He patted the camera case hanging from a strap over his shoulder. The movement pulled the khaki fabric of his shirt tight across the width of his shoulders. The material was clean and well pressed but looked as if it had seen a lot of wear. He didn't appear out of place at all in these exotic surroundings, Annie realized with a small, sharp dart of envy. He probably looked good in whatever he was wearing, wherever he might be wearing it.

"I don't know." The words came out sharp and defensive. Annie blushed and tried again. "I mean, I'm sure a busy man like you, Mr. Leyton, has more important things to do than act as a tour guide for a mother of five on a souvenir shopping trip." She had the satisfaction of seeing him momentarily taken aback.

Annie Simpson was getting a kick out of making him squirm, Simon decided, watching the dimple at the side of her mouth come and go when she smiled. She was a worthy adversary in a duel of words. She would be a worthy adversary in a duel of hearts and minds and bodies, also. He wanted to spend time with her, learn to know her mind and body, discover and unleash the passion he sensed just below the surface. That realization was staggering enough without the added tantalizing distraction of trading quips with this beautiful woman in one of the most romantic and exotic cities in the world.

Beautiful woman? When had he started considering Annie Simpson in those terms? When they first met he'd found her pleasant-looking enough. "Ordinary" was the way he recalled describing her, but not this morning. This morning she looked fresh and vibrant in a turquoise sundress of gauzy cotton. The skirt was full and swirled around her knees. The bodice was fitted like an old-fashioned camisole and her breasts pressed full and firm against the fabric. He felt his body stir and harden at the thought of those breasts pressed tight against his chest.

Simon looked away, down at the pavement beneath his feet. Annie was wearing rope-soled sandals, as if she intended to do a great deal of walking. She was also speaking to him. He raised his eyes to her face. The blue of her dress brought out golden sparkles in her brown eyes, complemented the creamy perfection of her skin and the fiery glow of her hair. She was beautiful and he wanted to tell her so, but instead he made himself concentrate on what she was saying.

"... really, I can find my own way."

Peter Leyton waved off her dismissal. "No, you won't. We'll start our tour with the Grand Palace, then make our way to the weekend market." It was Simon McKendrick, however, who took her arm and began leading her away from the hotel. "You'll find everything in the world for sale there. Even with five children to find souvenirs for." She started to protest. "Don't worry." He was back in character again. "We'll still have plenty of time to check out of the hotel and catch the plane to Sai... Ho Chi Minh City."

"For me, it will always be Saigon."

"For me, too." They were of the same generation. They shared a time and place in the universe. Annie looked at him for another long moment, seemed to come to a decision and fingered the disguised pearls at her throat. She was wearing pearl studs in her ears, too. They peeked out from the riot of curls held back from her face by a pair of amber combs. The pearls were small but genuine. A gift from her dead husband?

"Thank you for wearing the pearls." *Peter Leyton be damned.* This cloak-and-dagger playacting confused and distressed her; he sensed it. When they were alone together he would be himself—whoever that was. Simon held out his hand. She hesitated, her troubled brown eyes searching his, as if for reassurance of some kind. Simon smiled down at her. He folded his hand around the thin, delicate bones of her fingers, warming them with his touch.

"I feel safer when I have them with me," she said quietly. "So valuable." He felt her hand tremble slightly within his grasp. "So many lives depending on their safe delivery." She shook her head. "I'm not sure..."

"It will all go like clockwork." Simon did nothing to soften the harshness of his words. *If anything happened to her because of what he was asking her to do, he'd never forgive himself.* But nothing would go wrong. He'd been in this business for twenty years. He wasn't about to start making mistakes now. "I promise you." Their eyes locked and held for a long moment. "Trust me."

"I do." Annie's tone was full of wonder; so were her eyes. She smiled. Simon's heart jerked out of rhythm and began to hammer against the wall of his chest. He wanted to take her in his arms there and then, hold her, kiss her, take her somewhere dark and quiet and make love to her. Instead he started walking, remembering after a few yards to slow his pace to match his long stride to hers.

"If we get away from the hotel a block or two, we can strike a much better deal with a *samlor* driver. That's Thai for three-wheeler. I warn you, though, it takes nerves of steel to ride in one of these things. Are you sure you wouldn't rather take a taxi? It's safer."

"I feel like tempting fate." Annie realized her voice sounded breathless even to her own ears. Why in heaven had she chosen to say something so needlessly provocative?

Simon looked at her for a long moment through narrowed hazel eyes, then unexpectedly held out his hand. "I'm willing if you are." He started walking again without another word, still holding her hand. At the same moment the gilded spires of the Grand Palace came into view. Surely it was that combined with Simon's headlong pace that caused her pulse and heartbeat to quicken alarmingly. It had nothing to do with the close proximity of Simon's lean, hard body to her own.

ANNIE HAD FORGOTTEN HOW early the day started in Vietnam. Or perhaps she'd never really known, having spent only two weeks in Saigon when it had been under siege. But by her third morning she was used to being awakened long before 6:00 a.m. by motorcycle and moped traffic in the street outside her hotel. Crowds of people were everywhere. There were fewer cars and trucks now, it seemed, but that might be because she remembered only an endless stream of vehicles of all shapes and sizes, filled with frightened people trying desperately to escape the advancing North Vietnamese army. When Annie thought back to that time at all, she could remember only days and nights of hard work and incipient panic mixed together in anxious tumult. She hadn't remembered Saigon as a beautiful city, but in many ways, it was. So many things were still the same. And yet so many were different.

Tan Son Nhut airport was familiar, the terminal building, the camouflaged hangars, big fleecy white clouds in a blue-washed sky, chain-link fences, guard towers. A few Vietnamese army soldiers were scattered around the terminal. Her first sight of the familiar gold star on red background on their collars and hats made Annie's heart skitter with old fear. Then Simon came up behind her, loaded down with cameras and light meters, snapping shots here and there, being Peter Leyton for the benefit of one and all. She found herself oddly comforted by his presence. The moment of almost paralyzing terror passed, and Annie moved forward again over the blistering-hot concrete runway. She was even able to watch without flinching the official welcoming flight of Soviet MiG jets that passed overhead. She recalled the sights and sounds of other aircraft, in another time, with only a lump of tears pressing against the back of her throat for so many lives lost, so many futures wasted.

Customs, the final barrier, was housed in a small, hot building adjacent to the now almost deserted main terminal. She passed through the formalities with a smile and surprisingly friendly greeting from the officials behind the desk. The paperwork was quickly taken care of. She didn't touch the pearls at her throat once. Perhaps it was because her thoughts were elsewhere. Even the paper here was strange, made of thin slices of pulpwood. Annie remembered that, too, from her days in Manila. It only served to underline the continuing poverty of this war-ravaged country.

With another smile and a bow, the customs agent waved her out the door to a big black Russian-made limousine that waited to take the group into the city. That quickly and easily the last hurdle was crossed. Now she had only to wait to be contacted by those men who held Simon's brother and sister hostage somewhere far to the north.

The next two days passed in an endless succession of meetings with government officials. Annie talked with various groups about the continuing problem of documenting Amerasian children. Bureaucrats were the same the world over, she decided, sitting across the table from four smiling, well-dressed men as they explained the difficulties of finding relatives to corroborate the Amerasian teenagers' claims. They talked of families who had actually sold their half-blood children to other Vietnamese who would then pose as relatives in order to be allowed to leave for the United States along with the child. This could not be tolerated. She must understand their position as well.

Annie smiled politely and said that she did, all the time in the back of her mind wondering which one of these intelligent, sophisticated men might be a kidnapper and extortionist. She doubted if it was any one of the committee members. Not one had given the pearls a second glance, and too often she'd met their counterparts in the States, foot-dragging State Department officials who used the same arguments to justify their procrastination in repatriating the thousands of half-American children still living in Vietnam.

It was exhausting, heartbreaking work. Her nerves were stretched to the breaking point. In the evenings, after being driven back to the hotel in the limousine, she wanted nothing more than to collapse in her bed and forget her frustrations in sleep. But sleep wouldn't come. Or if it did, it was full of dreams of running and hiding, trying to get the children and others to safety, moving through air as thick as molasses. Instead of courting old nightmares she usually found herself out in the garden that surrounded the hotel, sitting on a stone bench in the darkness, listening to the sound of the city at rest, wondering how she could move the smiling, inscrutable Vietnamese to do her will.

This evening had been no different. Tomorrow was her last full day in Saigon. One more round of meetings capped off by a formal dinner and reception with some of the country's most influential leaders, including a deputy minister of Foreign Affairs, Hoang Van Chi, whose cooperation could be most helpful in the future. It was her last chance to make someone listen, understand, work with her instead of putting obstacles in her path.

The sound of a match being struck alerted Annie that she wasn't alone. The bench she was sitting on was in the shadow of the high stone wall that surrounded the hotel, the former home of an ousted general. She watched as the match was applied to the tip of a cigarette, illuminating for a moment the stark angles of Simon's face. Annie relaxed as he moved forward, the cigarette still in his mouth, the match flame dying with a sizzle as it was flicked into the lush green border of small, white flowers that edged the pathway.

"I didn't know you smoked," she said as he sat down on the stone bench beside her.

"Leyton does." Simon rested his forearms on his knees and watched the glowing tip of the cigarette in his hand.

"I see." There were so many things she wanted to ask him but did not. He spoke easily enough of his family and of Micah and Rachel when they were all children. But of himself, of the here and now, of the future, he said little.

"I'll need the pearls tonight." He dropped the cigarette onto the gravel path and ground it under the toe of his boot.

"No one has approached me." Annie's hand went protectively to the pearls.

"It will be tomorrow night. At the reception."

"Oh." She probably should have expected that. After all, it would be too much of a coincidence that one of the four bureaucrats she'd been dealing with should be the man they were looking for.

"I'll clean and polish them tonight. It's my guess, whoever engineered this whole setup will make the contact himself. The fewer people that know about a deal like this the better."

"Won't the others notice the difference in the pearls?"

"I doubt it. They'll be more likely to notice when they don't see you wearing them again after the reception."

"I suppose you're right." Annie fumbled with the clasp of the pearls, suddenly reluctant to be parted from them.

"Here, let me help." Simon shifted on the bench. His hands grazed the back of her neck. He brushed her hair aside and Annie felt a tingle of electricity all the way to the tips of her fingers. Once again her heartbeat slipped into a faster cadence. She didn't have the excuse of physical exercise or a panoramic view of Bangkok to blame for the anomaly this time. They were alone in the darkened garden. There was only the sound of Simon's breathing, and the touch of his strong fingers against the skin of her neck, as he unclasped the necklace.

"Thanks." She turned away as quickly as possible, flustered by her reaction to his touch. "Is there anything else I should know? Anything special I should be on the lookout for?" She'd asked the same questions several times before and they both knew it, but Simon didn't say anything about it. The moon slipped out from behind a cloud. She saw his face for the first time. He smiled but his eyes were grim.

"Don't worry," he said just as he always did. He didn't touch her again, just looked down at the pearls in his hand before dropping them in the pocket of his shirt. "Trust me, Annie. I won't let anything happen to you. It will all go like clockwork." He balled his hand into a fist, but then reached out and tucked a wisp of her hair behind her ear, reluctantly, as if he didn't want to touch her but couldn't help himself. "I promise everything will come out right in the end."

IT WAS THE BEST MEAL HE'D eaten since leaving Bangkok, spicy crab and fish dishes, crisp vegetables, clear soup, the ever-present boiled rice and fresh fruit for dessert. It was too bad the tightly coiled nerves in his stomach hadn't allowed him to do justice to the food. Simon rested his shoulders against the high, carved back of his chair and surveyed the other diners at the long teak table. Paderwiski, massive in a seersucker jacket and white shirt, was engaged in earnest discussion with the under secretary of Cultural Affairs, Ha Thuck Ky. Billiup leaned across the table, interjecting his own comments into the one-sided conversation. Ky smiled and nodded, benign and inscrutable, the perfect diplomat. Simon watched the trio from the corner of his eye. Unless he missed his guess, Ky was his man. It was a gut hunch, nothing more, but Simon had long ago learned to trust his instincts.

Only once had he seen the man's sharp, impenetrable, black eyes stray to the pearls at Annie's throat. His inspection had been brief but thorough. The avarice of a connoisseur flashed in his eyes, to be quickly masked by studied composure and a polite interest in what Annie had to say. The moment lasted no longer than a heartbeat, but it was long enough to alert Simon.

His quarry was ruthless, possibly dangerous, an ex-army colonel still in close contact with the military. Simon didn't intend to be far from Annie's side for the rest of the night. Even now she was sitting diagonally across the table, almost within reach of his hand. Close enough if the need arose to put himself between her and whatever danger threatened. Reaching for a piece of fruit from the heavy silver bowl presented by the white-jacketed waiter, she lifted her gaze, caught his eye and smiled. Simon felt the earth tilt under his feet.

Annie was wearing a traditional Vietnamese dress, an *ao dai* of flame-colored silk that brought out golden highlights in her red hair. The pearls, their original luster restored, were a circle of cool fire around her throat and in her ears. Her hair was pulled up in a soft knot on top of her head, wispy tendrils escaping to curl around her temples and the back of her neck. He knew she was disappointed that her last protracted session with the Vietnamese had ended in a stalemate, but nothing of the disappointment at not getting permission for the children's families to be allowed to leave with them showed on her face.

It was what she'd expected all along, she'd told him back at the hotel. The authorities would allow the seven Amerasian teenagers they'd already cleared for emigration to accompany the group home tomorrow. Their parents and guardians would follow later, when all the paperwork had been completed. She said she understood, but inside Simon knew she was hurting. Annie was one of those people who took everyone else's troubles to heart. Like his mother, she never gave up hope. Frances McKendrick believed her daughter was alive, had always believed so, and because of that faith he and Micah had kept up the search. His own belief in miracles, in happily-ever-after, had been tried and found wanting long ago.

The chiming sound of silver against crystal broke into his thoughts, drawing his attention to the man at the head of the table. Tall for a Vietnamese, Hoang Van Chi stood just under six feet. His hair was black and thick but his face showed the effects of years of fighting and living off the land. Simon settled back to listen to his speech. He spoke of putting the past behind them, of the difficulties of finding the bodies of MIA soldiers and airmen in the triple canopy jungle that covered much of his country. He spoke also of the reluctance of many of his countrymen to search for the bodies of missing GIs when tens of thousands more of their own friends and relatives were still missing in those same jungles.

For a man who had risen through the ranks of the Vietcong, Chi was an able and urbane speaker. His English was precise, his manner sincere. Simon listened closely, trying to pick up on the subtle nuances of speech and body language that gave the liar, the prevaricator away. Nothing. Chi was the only other official present, aside from Ky, whose rank and privilege would lend itself to the kind of extortion plot he was facing. No, Chi was not the man he was seeking. Ky was. The exchange of information would most likely take place before the end of the reception.

He looked across the table at Annie. She was listening intently to Chi's speech, her chin resting on her left hand, the dull gold of her wedding band catching the light from overhead chandeliers. Simon wondered how she was going to react to his announcement that he was spending the night in her room. She probably wouldn't give in easily, but there was no way he was going to leave her, or the pearls, unguarded for a single minute until the transfer was made.

Simon found himself wishing, not for the first time, that he could be spending this night with Annie Simpson as men and women were meant to spend the long, quiet hours of darkness together. He knew already how she would feel, the texture of her skin, the heaviness of her breasts in his hands, the silkiness of her lips against his mouth. Wrapped in each other's arms, cocooned within a canopy of white netting, a ceiling fan stirring lazy swirls of hot flower-scented night air, he would make love to her until dawn. He could almost feel himself sheathed within her and he knew she would be as hot and sweet as the night around them.

Minister Chi brought his remarks to a close. Secretary Ky rose to make a toast. Simon brought his thoughts back to the here and now with a mental jerk that was almost painful. His lower body was tight with the strength of his vision. He tugged at the knot of his dark gray tie. It was suddenly too tight, almost choking him. Hell, what had he been thinking of? He never let his attention wander from matters at hand that way. You couldn't in his business and survive. *Annie, why did I get you involved in this affair?* He had to keep her safe, no matter what happened to him. She trusted him and for her sake he had to bring this whole thing off without a hitch.

Annie turned her head as though sensing his regard. She smiled in sympathy at what she interpreted as his own impatience to see this very dull occasion brought to a close. Ky was still talking. Simon watched as Annie turned her brown eyes in his direction, saw her brows pull together in a slight frown. Was she picking up on the same subtle undertones in his polished words that he was? Annie lifted her glass to join in the toast Ky proposed. Her gaze shifted to Simon once more. Their eyes met and held over the rims of the champagne flutes, Annie's asking the question she couldn't voice aloud.

Simon nodded, almost imperceptibly, saw her shoulders stiffen, saw the anxiety in her expression. But only for a moment. He blinked and she was smiling again, speaking to the elderly woman seated on her right, disregarding the man who would most surely try to contact her within the next few minutes. A man who was ruthless and probably dangerous. A man who was a kidnapper and a criminal, who literally held their lives in his hands. If any of those thoughts went through her mind in the next few seconds she gave no sign of her fear. Her hand trembled slightly when she set her glass back down on the damask-covered table, but that was all. Simon relaxed very slightly. His Annie would do just fine.

CHAPTER FOUR

SO THIS WAS THE MAN. Annie didn't allow herself to look at Ky again. When would he contact her? What would he say? How did one conduct oneself with a kidnapper? How had she let herself be talked into this? If something happened to her, who would take care of her family? Her business? And most important of all, where was Simon? She was alone, or so it seemed as small groups of people broke up and formed anew all around her.

The banquet was almost over. There wouldn't be another opportunity to talk to Simon in private. She didn't know what to do. She wasn't a spy or a secret agent. She was a mother and nurse and...widow. She'd almost said wife, but she was a wife no longer. Annie looked around at the faded rose-and-gilt splendor of the ballroom in the downtown hotel, a relic of French colonial days now run by the government, as was almost everything in Vietnam. The last of the toasts and speeches had passed in a blur of polite applause and lifted glasses. When the group finally rose from the table, her legs had been almost too weak to support her. What if she made some terrible blunder, some slip of the tongue, and ruined everything?

Annie made herself stop asking unanswerable questions, squared her shoulders and pasted a smile on her face. She wasn't going to fail Simon or Rachel or Micah. How difficult could it be to say a few words to Colonel—somehow she couldn't think of him as Under Secretary—Ky, listen to whatever instructions he might give her and carry them out? She could do it.

She would do it.

Moving away from the table, Annie began saying her goodbyes, cementing tenuous connections that might, in the future, grow into another delegation such as this one. Jacob Paderwiski moved into sight, shepherding Minister Chi along before him, Billiup and a slender Vietnamese woman following in his wake. The woman's *ao dai* was high-necked and long-sleeved. The slim silk pants beneath the two split panels of the long blue skirt were white. The effect was simple and understated. She wore her beautiful ebony hair in an elegant chignon at the nape of her neck.

Madame Chi was some ten or twelve years younger than her husband, in her early to mid-thirties. She was also very lovely, her features combining the best of two races. Her European ancestry was evident in the dark blue of her eyes and the creamy ivory of her skin. There was something about the woman's quiet dignity and hesitant smile that tugged at a chord of recognition in the back of Annie's thoughts, but she had too many other things on her mind to pay it any heed.

"Annie." Jacob hailed her. "I want you to meet Minister Chi. He's been meeting with us on the Agent Orange and MIA/POW issues. He's been a real help. Minister Chi, this is Mrs. Anne Simpson."

"How do you do, Mrs. Simpson?" He bowed slightly. Like all the other Vietnamese males present, he was dressed in a dark suit of lightweight linen, white shirt and subdued tie. "May I present my wife, Le Thi?"

Annie held out her hand. "I'm honored, Madam Chi."

"I am pleased, also." Le Thi's voice was soft and whispery. She didn't look directly into Annie's eyes but focused her gaze somewhere near her chin. Once more an image stirred deep in Annie's memory, but Jacob Paderwiski started talking again and the moment passed. He gestured toward someone behind her.

"Colonel Ky." Annie didn't want to face the man whose eyes she felt on the back of her neck. "Have you met Mrs. Simpson?"

Annie turned her head to meet the inscrutable expression of Colonel Ky. What she saw there—nothing, shuttered blankness—was more frightening than any hostile emotion would have been. She held out her hand and knew that he felt her trembling, sensed her anxiety.

"Colonel Ky." It was all the greeting she could manage.

"Mr. Paderwiski has been telling me of your clinics back in America, Mrs. Simpson. Of the work you do there with underprivileged women and children. Your involvement with the Amerasian Children's League must be a great deal of extra work for a woman who has five children of her own to raise alone. You are a widow, are you not?" The condescension in his voice was so slight, so well disguised, that Annie wondered if any of the others in the group even picked up on it.

"My children are a great help and comfort to me. I'm very proud of all of them."

"The three eldest are Amerasian orphans, are they not?" A shiver ran down Annie's spine, despite the warmth of the big, high-ceilinged room. She didn't know why she was suddenly so afraid. Everything he'd said about her was common knowledge, but somehow she didn't think Colonel Ky had learned about her life from just glancing through the biography the group had put together for each delegate before they left Chicago.

"Yes." Annie stifled her fear. The man was baiting her, subtly but with a purpose. If he thought he could fluster her, cause her to make a mistake by making an issue out of her children, he was sadly mistaken.

"Two boys and a girl, I was told," the bland, dispassionate voice went on.

"Two sons and a daughter," Annie replied, meeting his blank stare head-on, allowing more than a hint of steel to creep into her voice. Who was this evil little man to intimidate her, anyway?

Someone handed her a champagne flute. Belatedly, Annie realized it was Simon and was grateful for his solid warmth at her back. She took a sip to moisten her mouth. Her throat was so tight she could barely swallow.

What was Ky up to? Simon wondered, offering a second glass of wine to Madam Chi. She smiled at him, shyly, raising her eyes to his for only a second, but the sadness lurking in the dark blue depths was plain to see. Some loss, old but no less painful for the passing of time, held the spirit of this lovely, fragile woman in thrall.

"Were your children airlifted out of the country or did they come to you from a refugee camp, Mrs. Simpson?" Simon knew Ky was using these repeated references to Annie's children to test her resistance, her courage. Ky had to know she was a novice at this game. The only advantage they had at the moment was that Simon's cover hadn't been blown. He was a nonentity to Ky, just one of the noisy, boisterous Americans in the delegation. Ky had no idea that Annie had a partner, a protector. Simon watched, satisfied, as Annie made a visible effort to rein in her escalating temper.

"I was in Saigon in April of 1975, Colonel Ky."

"You were here when the city fell... when the Americans left?" Le Thi corrected herself with haste, her eyes flickering in Ky's direction. Her breath quickened, her shoulders tensed as she waited for Annie's reply. Simon noted her agitation but had no idea what caused it.

"I volunteered to help with the evacuation. I was assigned to work with Father Pieter and the sisters at St. Dominic's orphanage. I brought the children out myself."

"A most romantic story, is it not?" Colonel Ky's voice broke the small silence that stretched out after Annie finished speaking. People were beginning to make their way out of the room. "Separated from her companions, alone in the city only hours ahead of the advance of our victorious troops, she makes her way toward the American Embassy with two small boys. And from out of nowhere a woman appears, thrusts a newborn baby girl into her arms and disappears."

Simon saw the shudder that shook Annie. He knew she had realized for certain that Ky's knowledge of her was far more extensive than it should be, but he didn't think anyone else noticed, because quietly, without a sound, except for the tinkle of shattered crystal, Le Thi sagged against her husband and slipped to the floor in a faint.

Annie wasn't even aware when Simon reached out to take the champagne glass from her hand; she only knew it was gone when she knelt at Le Thi's side. Already the other woman was regaining consciousness. Her husband held her in his arms, murmuring to her in Vietnamese. Annie recognized only one or two broken phrases, but the love and anxiety in his voice was easy to understand. It was the first hint of softness she'd seen in the older man. He looked over at her as she checked his wife's pulse, and his eyes were dark with strain.

"My wife recently lost a child, Mrs. Simpson. I feared it was too soon for her to try to resume official duties."

"I am all right. Hoang. It was a dizzy spell, nothing more." Le Thi spoke in French, which Annie had taken in high school and remembered slightly better than her rudimentary Vietnamese. Le Thi looked toward Colonel Ky with fear mirrored in her cobalt eyes.

What was the story behind this troubled and unhappy woman? Was she a child of privilege with a past that put her beyond the pale in the new Communist-dominated Vietnam? Was even a man of Minister Chi's rank and stature subject to harassment by men the like of Ky? Suddenly Annie wanted very much to go home, back to the States and her children and worrying about meeting the mortgage payments and getting the dog spayed; where complaining about the government and politicians was a right and privilege enjoyed in safety and freedom.

Le Thi was on her feet, leaning against her husband's shoulder, held protectively within the circle of his arms. She apologized for her weakness in Vietnamese and in halting English and asked to be excused. Hoang added his farewells to hers with a special thanks to Annie, who urged him to take Le Thi home and if there were any more dizzy spells, to seek medical help at once. He agreed. With a snap of his fingers Colonel Ky brought one of the armed guards who'd been stationed outside the ballroom in a ceremonial capacity to his side. He spoke a few words, curt and to the point. The soldier moved ahead of Minister Chi and Le Thi as they walked out of the ballroom.

"My man will see that their car is brought around immediately. It is so sad that Madame Chi's health is so uncertain. We all hoped that this time she would produce a healthy child, but alas, it was not to be."

So there had been other miscarriages. Annie's heart ached for Le Thi. She and Mike would have liked another child but after the twins were born she had never conceived again. She resented the slight smirk she thought she detected on Ky's bland countenance.

"It's a shame." Jacob Paderwiski's words fell into the silence like stones into a pond. "Damn shame." Annie knew he was thinking of his wife and three children back home in Illinois, and of the son he had worked so hard to be reunited with. She hoped everything went well for him. She hoped what she had to do wouldn't jeopardize Jacob's hopes and plans for the future. Ky was speaking to her again.

"I have been admiring your pearls, Mrs. Simpson."

"Thank you." She hoped her voice sounded normal. Her heart had begun beating so fast and hard it felt as if it had moved up into her throat, choking off her breath. Jacob Paderwiski and Billiup said their farewells and moved away, taking Simon with them to photograph the two sober-faced members of the Missing Personnel Committee before they left the room. Annie felt suddenly small and very much alone.

"They are of excellent quality." A little of Ky's bland good humor disappeared. His words were hard-edged.

"A gift from friends, Secretary Ky." She purposefully used his civilian title, not thc military one he obviously preferred.

"I see. Then I assume they carry a great deal of sentimental value."

Annie touched the pearls with the tip of her finger. "Even objects with great sentimental value have their price." She didn't know if she was being too direct, but there was no one nearby to overhear their conversation and her nerves were stretched to the breaking point.

"What is their worth to you?"

"An addition to our party. Nine souls to leave Vietnam instead of seven." Simon had finished taking pictures of the committee members. Paderwiski and Billiup were moving in her direction. Ky's eyes flickered to his left, gauging the distance that still separated them from the jovial American and his lawyer.

He nodded once, curtly. "A fair price."

"Where? When?" Her composure was slipping. She didn't like this cloak-and-dagger routine. She was scared and she wanted Simon by her side, not halfway across the vast ballroom.

"Tomorrow when your *bui doi* board the plane to Thailand." *Bui doi.* Children of the dust. His use of the derogatory term for Amerasian children left little doubt as to his true feelings. "I will be there myself to see that there is no problem with...the exchange." Did that mean that Micah and Rachel were somewhere in the city? So close and yet still so impossibly far away.

Paderwiski and Billiup were almost close enough to overhear.

"Mrs. Simpson." She had already turned her back to him.

Annie halted, looked over her shoulder. "Yes, Colonel Ky?"

"I would take very good care of the pearls. It would be a shame if you were to lose them before you leave my country." The threat in his words was open and plain to hear. "A very great shame indeed."

"ANNIE, ARE YOU AWAKE?" He could hear her moving around inside her room, although it was after midnight and most of the other hotel guests seemed to have retired for the night. The air was heavy with the growling of distant thunder and oppressively hot, but a breeze was beginning to stir the trees in the garden beyond Annie's ground-floor room. In an hour or two, after the rain, it might just be cool enough to sleep.

"Yes, Leyton?" She hesitated before saying his name. He knew it bothered her to call him by another man's name. Maybe you had to be born to intrigue, or learn it at the risk of your life, as he had in this very part of the world twenty years ago, to be able to bring off a masquerade like this without a qualm.

"Let me in." Not "May I come in?" He didn't dare give her a chance to refuse. He could almost see her bristle with indignation on the other side of the door.

"It's late, Mr. Leyton." There was no hesitation this time. She was furious.

"Open the door." He couldn't stand out here in the corridor sparring with her. There was too much at stake. *Damn it, didn't she know her life could be in danger?* "We have to talk."

The door opened. She was wearing a big, sleeveless pink T-shirt that said Nurses Do It with TLC and a pair of gray running shorts that were so short they barely covered the rounded curve of her fanny and made her legs seem to go on forever. She wasn't wearing a bra, either, he noticed. How long would it be before he couldn't help himself any longer and took her in his arms? How would she react? She looked angry enough, now, to slap his face.

"I thought everything was settled." A slight quaver roughened her voice. She wasn't angry, she was scared. Simon wished to hell he'd been easier on her when they had discussed Ky's conversation in the garden an hour ago.

"It is settled." He made his tone as level and ordinary as he could. "All we do now is wait." He let a hint of command seep into his voice. "And we're going to wait together."

"Why?" She walked into the room and pulled an embroidered midnight-blue kimono over her shorts and T-shirt. The contrast between delicate silk and sturdy cotton was interesting. It was a lot like Annie herself: the strength and stability of cotton underlying the delicate beauty of handwoven silk.

"As long as Ky thinks you're in this on your own, you're a target. Why should he go to the trouble of turning over two American nationals who will surely tell the world they've been held against their will, when the only thing that stands between him and the pearls—which is what he really wants—is you?" Simon shut the door behind him and walked across the room to the window. It was open to the night air but covered by an ornate cast-iron grillwork. It looked sturdy enough to keep out intruders. That was one point in their favor. He pulled the sheer curtains shut as lightning streaked across the sky.

"I don't know." He could tell she was considering the consequences of what he'd just told her.

"Neither do I." In case someone was watching them, Simon took a pack of cigarettes out of his pocket, lit one and stuck it in his mouth, as Leyton would do. "Maybe he isn't after anything but the pearls and he intends to honor his end of our bargain." He didn't believe that for a moment. Still, stranger things happened in the world. "Maybe I'm just getting paranoid." Simon heard himself say the words and was surprised. That particular nightmare, the fact that the pressure of his work would push him over the edge, was something he never talked about, not to his parents, his ex-wife, Micah, not anyone.

"No." Annie's tone was adamant. "You're not paranoid. You're worried about your brother and sister. And, I think, because it's hard for a man like you to stay so much in the background." She looked very earnest all of a sudden, her rich, cinnamon-colored hair loose on her shoulders, a riot of curls in the humid air. Thunder rumbled off in the distance, lightning flickered at the edge of his vision. "I'm doing my best, Simon." She looked as if she might begin to cry. He couldn't have that. She'd been a real trooper, but he couldn't let her break down now.

With a muffled curse he ground the cigarette to ashes in a bowl on the bedside table. "Annie, my God." This time he didn't listen to his brain telling him to back off, to take it slow, to keep away from this woman. Instead, he listened to his heart. He reached out and pulled her into his arms, against his chest. "Annie Simpson, you are a brave and remarkable woman. Now, turn out the light."

"What?" She laughed, but it was shaky and breathless. She didn't move into his embrace but neither did she pull away as he half expected she would. "I don't think we should be here alone, in the dark, together." It was the first indication she'd given him that she felt the same charge of electricity, of sexual tension, that he did whenever they touched.

"I do." He could feel the warmth of her fingers on his chest through the thin linen shirt. "Unbutton it." The roughness in his voice wasn't assumed. It was real. The tightness in his lower body, the surge of blood through his veins, the pounding of his heart against his ribs were just as real.

"Simon?" She tried to pull away. He covered her hands with his own, keeping her close.

"Just do it, Annie, please." He guided her stiff fingers upward to the second button. He held her within the circle of his arms with the strength of his gaze as well as his touch. "Trust me."

"You might be James Bond," Annie said, chewing her bottom lip, but working doggedly at the uncooperative buttons. She lowered her eyes, refusing to look at him. "I'm not Mata Hari. This is all new to me. Are you trying to seduce me?"

"No." *Don't tempt me, Annie love.* He lifted her stubborn chin with his finger, forcing her to look at him once more. "If Ky does have someone out in the garden watching this room, he's going to see just enough to convince him you're not alone in here. And won't be alone for the rest of the night."

"Oh." He felt her relax just a fraction. The last button slid free. She pulled his shirt from the waistband of his slacks. "I see. You want to give them enough of a show to ruin my reputation and probably save my life." She wound her arms around his neck, pressing against him, standing on tiptoe to fit her body into his. "I think that's a fair trade, don't you?"

Simon traced the outline of her lips with the tip of his finger. "They aren't going to think our little act is for real unless you kiss me." He lowered his mouth to hers.

When Simon's lips left hers Annie felt as if she'd just stepped off the edge of the earth. Or possibly that she'd been spirited to the dark side of the moon. She blinked, trying to adjust her eyesight to the sudden heavy darkness. Simon had reached up to pull the string of the single overhead bulb, cutting off the light. The hot flower-and-rain-scented night closed around them, sealing them away from the outside danger in the quiet shelter of her room.

"Do you think that was convincing enough for any voyeur out there in the garden?" She hoped she didn't sound as out of control as she felt. She'd thought Simon McKendrick was dangerous the first time she saw him. Now that she knew him better, had been held in his arms, pressed against his hard, lean body, kissed by him, she was even more certain of the fact. Making love with Mike had been good, more than good, great. Making love with Simon McKendrick could be heaven on earth, or a glimpse of hell. He could make a woman forget everything, make her long to be with him, even if it meant losing everything else in the world she held dear.

"I'm not sure if it looked convincing enough," Simon muttered, not letting her go even though their silhouettes were no longer visible through the transparent panels that draped the long, narrow window. "Another kiss."

He pulled her close again and Annie went, still in a daze of sensual awareness. It had been so long, years, since she'd been kissed like this. Since she'd felt like this, all woman, alive and whole and aching with needs and desires. Simon's mouth was moving over hers, tasting, caressing, insisting that she join his intimate exploration. Moving under her kimono, his hands splayed over her hips and teased the elastic of her panties just beneath the hem of her shorts. Then slid under her T-shirt to skim upward over her rib cage and cradle the soft heaviness of her breasts.

"Simon, please..." Annie never finished the sentence, never finished her thought, never knew if she meant to ask him to stop, or to go on making love to her. The doorknob rattled. Someone was trying to get in the room.

"Damn it, Ky's not wasting any time." Simon held her so tight she couldn't move. "There's no one out in the garden. They're already inside the hotel."

Annie's eyes had adjusted to the dark. She saw faint shadows pass across the narrow strip of light beneath her locked door. Simon clamped his hand over her mouth. She nodded, understanding his silent message to keep quiet. The hand was removed. As a key turned in the ornate, old-fashioned lock, a knife, slim and deadly, appeared in Simon's hand as if from nowhere. His voice was more sensation than sound. "Get behind the door and don't make a sound. Understand?" Annie nodded, her throat too dry to speak. "Where are the pearls?" She pointed to the suitcase at the foot of her bed. Simon nodded and moved to stand beside the door. With a grating click the lock gave to the outside pressure.

The door opened slightly. A man came into the room. He was carrying a gun, short-barreled and ugly. Simon moved almost as quickly as the flash of lightning that must have momentarily blinded the intruder so that he stood, irresolute, just inside the room. His hand came down on the gun arm of the stocky figure in the doorway with such strength that Annie clearly heard the snap of breaking bones. The man grunted in pain, dropped the gun and whirled to meet his attacker.

Simon was on him immediately. The fight was vicious and silent and over in a matter of seconds. Annie blinked trying to keep track of the writhing figures on the floor. Her vision was dazzled by the same lightning bolt that had blinded the intruder. She couldn't be sure what was happening.

"Annie, get the light." Simon's voice was harsh, strained. It took her a moment to find the swaying white cord above her head. She jerked it hard and it nearly came off in her hands, but blessed light flooded the room. Annie circled away from the two still-struggling figures and almost tripped over the gun. She picked it up and backed away from the man Simon had pinned to the floor. He wore a dark sports shirt and slacks, and his face was familiar. He was the soldier that Colonel Ky had ordered to escort Minister Chi home from the banquet earlier in the evening.

Simon spoke, low and viciously, in Vietnamese. The man spat out a reply that was clearly a curse. Simon pulled him to his knees, twisted his broken arm behind his back and pressed the knife blade tighter against his throat. He repeated the question. The man remained obstinately silent. Simon increased the pressure of the blade. A thin red stream of blood appeared on the soldier's neck.

"Simon! No!" The violence she'd always known was there in Simon had surfaced. He was lethal, a trained fighter, a killer if necessary. But she had also learned something about herself, holding the small deadly gun trained on their assailant. She, too, was capable of violence. If the intruder hurt Simon, or tried to hurt her, she could and would pull the trigger with no regret.

Simon looked at her, but she wasn't sure he saw her. He spoke to the man again. Annie recognized nothing that he said, only the threat of certain death implicit in his tone, in the menace of his brutal hold. Dragging the man to his feet, Simon gave him a shove that sent him stumbling into the hallway. Cradling his injured arm with his good hand, the man disappeared into the night.

"ARE YOU ALL RIGHT?" He heard Annie's voice as if from very far away. He'd never killed a man in anger, yet moments ago he would have done so without a qualm if it hadn't been for the horror, the revulsion he saw in Annie's eyes. She would never understand how close she'd come to death tonight. He didn't want her to know. Ky wanted the pearls. He would have killed her to obtain them. And when they were his, Micah and Rachel would have died also. But now Ky knew she was not alone, not unprotected, and he would be on his guard.

He would have killed Ky's henchman, and gladly, if he'd laid a hand on Annie. He had not, but in using the training that had become second nature to him over the years, he'd let Annie see the dark side of himself, and he wondered if she'd ever forget... or forgive.

She was staring at the gun in her hand as if it were a snake. How and when she had picked it up he had no idea. He took it from her shaking hands and shoved it into his belt, then closed and locked the door. As a last precaution he took the high-backed chair from the writing table in front of the window and jammed it under the doorknob.

"Does that really work?" Annie hadn't moved. He heard the quaver in her voice and it was almost his undoing. She was trying so hard to be brave and untouched by the madness she'd just witnessed.

"Sure. How do you think it got to be a murder mystery cliché?"

"In the movies the bad guys always seem to get in anyway." She was shaking so hard her teeth chattered. Would she let him take her in his arms, hold her close, warm her with his body, love her with all his bruised and battered heart and soul?

"It wouldn't be much of a story if they tried the lock, couldn't get in and skulked away into the night. Come here, Annie."

"I don't think you ever asked my permission to call me that."

Simon held his breath. If she turned away, walked toward the window or the bed or anywhere but straight into his arms, he didn't think he could stand it.

"Doesn't everybody call you Annie?" He stood very still, waiting for her to make the first move. She stayed where she was.

She sighed. "Yes. But I thought you might be different." The blue silk kimono slipped off her shoulder. She tugged it back into place. "I'm forty years old. It makes me think of rag dolls and little girls with big eyes and curly mops of orange hair. When I was a kid it made me mad."

"What did you do about it?" She was moving across the small room suddenly, moving into his arms.

Annie shrugged. "Got used to it. But not until after I broke Willy Pieracini's nose in the fifth grade for calling me Little Orphan Annie."

"Violent little thing, were you?"

"I can be when it's necessary." Was she telling him she could understand that violence and the passionate emotions that so closely resembled it were a very real part of life? Of his life? "Anyway," Annie continued, "after that no one at Dishop Elementary called me Annie without my permission."

He put his arm around her. "Do I have your permission?"

"Yes." She slid her arms around his waist. "I like the way you say my name. It makes me think of warm breezes and summer meadows. Silly things like that." She sniffed.

"Not silly, Annie. Wonderful." He nuzzled her temple and she turned her face up to his kiss. He could taste her tears, sweet and salty all mixed up together. "Don't cry, Annie. Tomorrow it will all be over."

"I'm scared, Simon. For you. For me. For Micah and Rachel. I'm not brave or even very smart sometimes. I might do the wrong thing, make it all go wrong. I owe Rachel so much. She stayed behind that last day and gave me a chance to get out of Saigon. She gave me my life, Simon." She was crying hard now. He picked her up in his arms, carried her to the bed and laid her on the lumpy mattress. Simon put the gun on the floor beside the bed, kicked off his shoes and lay down beside her. It had started raining sometime during his fight with Ky's hired thug. There wasn't a lot of thunder and lightning, just rain, torrents of it, as if the Flood had come again.

"Rachel knew what she was doing, Annie. She was over here a lot longer than you. Two tours of duty as an army nurse. Almost a year with Father Pieter at the orphanage. She knew."

"She gave me everything I have today. Chad and Doug, and Leah too, in a way. Mike..." She broke off for a moment and he could feel her fight to stop the tears. "She gave me my future. Now I have to do what I can to help her have her own."

"You've done a hell of a job so far."

"Like tonight?" Her tone was self-condemning. "I must have done something wrong, something to make Ky think I was an easy target."

"Ky's an opportunist. He saw a woman alone and took advantage of the situation. But he'd have tried something no matter who contacted him."

Annie snuggled closer and Simon sucked in his breath. The swell of her breasts pressed against his chest, her body curved into his. She went on talking and he let her, hoping she'd talk herself to sleep. "What if something goes wrong tomorrow? The children? Jacob's son and the others. It's enough of a blow to them that we can't bring the relatives out with us. I'd never forgive myself if the kids weren't allowed to leave."

She stiffened, turned in his arms. He couldn't see her face in the darkness but he sensed her anxiety.

"We can't afford any more procrastinating," she went on. "Most of these kids are almost adults. Some of them are, the boys thieves, the girls forced into prostitution. It's so much harder for them to adjust, to learn to fit into American life-styles as they get older. But they have so little chance of any kind of a decent future here. We should have been bringing them to the States ten years ago instead of pretending they didn't exist. I know how hard it will be for them. I can see it, a little, in my own kids. I don't want anything to interfere with the transfer, or any future negotiations. Oh, Simon, I don't think I can do it."

"Yes, you can." He smoothed his hand over her hair, rocking her in his arms. "Ky took his best shot tonight and came up short."

"What about that man? What if Ky knows who you are?"

"He doesn't." *At least not yet*. Simon wasn't certain how much longer he could remain in Vietnam without having his cover blown. His actions tonight had been totally out of character for Leyton. "All he knows is that Peter Leyton is spending the night with you."

"How will he explain the broken arm? And the knife cut?"

She sounded sleepier now, and Simon made his voice as low and monotonous as he could manage. "Let him explain to his boss. It's his neck on the line with Ky. He didn't get what he came after."

"I guess you're right."

She yawned, laying her head on his shoulder. Annie felt good in his arms, as if she belonged there, always had. Funny, he'd never slept with his ex-wife in his arms, at least not after the novelty of sharing the same bed had worn off. Somehow he'd be willing to bet just about anything that wouldn't happen with his Annie.

"Get some sleep. We have a long day ahead of us."

"I will." In moments she was asleep, deeply and dreamlessly. Simon held her close and waited for the dawn.

"COME TO BED, MY LOVE."

"I will, Hoang, soon. The rain keeps me awake." Le Thi smiled at her husband in the darkness. How she loved him. The day he returned to her from the war in the north had been the happiest in her life.

"You are thinking of the children who will go to the United States with the Americans."

"Yes." In a way she was. But her thoughts centered not on those children who would leave the country of their birth tomorrow but of one who had gone fourteen years before. Her daughter.

"They will do well. They have fathers who care, families to help them adjust to America and its ways."

"I know. It's the others my heart bleeds for, those the Americans seem to care so little about. They do not understand how hard it is in this land for a child who has no father."

"You've been thinking too much of the past since you lost the child." He crossed the room to take her in his arms. "Come to bed. We have a long day ahead of us. Are you sure you're up to it?"

"Yes. I want to go...to see the children off."

He kissed her lightly, softly, and she laid her head on his shoulder. God had given him back to her when she thought he was dead. Perhaps losing her baby, her tiny newborn daughter and the others that had followed, was the price she had to pay for having regained his love. Hoang was a hard man but just and kind. He would have loved her daughter as his own if she had been able to keep her, but she had not.

Le Thi did not speak idly of the plight of being a fatherless child in Vietnam. Her own father had been a French businessman forced to leave the country before her birth. She had spent time with him in Paris later, but never really knew him. Then she'd met Hoang and, though his politics frightened her, she had lost her heart to the young guerrilla leader. And when word had come that he was dead near the end of the Americans' involvement in the war, she had wanted to die, too.

Instead she had gone on caring for her ailing mother. When the money ran out and no more came from her father in Paris, she sold herself to an American diplomat who promised to care for her and her mother, get them out of Vietnam, to France or America to start a new life. Instead, he had made her pregnant and then abandoned her and their baby daughter in the chaos of a vanquished city.

She lay quietly beside her husband until his even breathing told her he slept, then slipped quietly out of their bed and returned to the window to watch the last of the rain wash the city clean as dawn broke on a new day.

She would never forget those last days of April fourteen years ago. Her mother had collapsed soon after the baby was born and never regained consciousness until just before she died. Le Thi could close her eyes still and feel the terror, see the panic and horror of a city besieged. She'd prayed to her father's Catholic God, to Buddha, to the spirits of her mother's ancestors, in vain. There was no one to help her, no one to turn to. She was alone.

She had been on her way to the orphanage of St. Dominic's, hoping the nuns might be able to find a place for her baby on one of the buses leaving the city. She had turned down a small street, less congested than the others, and nearly collided with a young American woman carrying two small boys. "Are you going to the embassy?" Le Thi's English had almost deserted her in her terror, but the woman seemed to understand.

"Yes. Is this the right direction?" Her Vietnamese was even worse.

Le Thi had nodded and before she could change her mind thrust the baby into the red-headed nurse's arms. "She is American, too. We are starving. Please take her with you." Then she turned and ran away.

For fourteen years she'd wondered about her child's fate. Then tonight, out of nowhere, out of the past, just as she'd appeared that long-ago day, Anne Simpson had walked back into her life. And it was Ky, that puffed-up, cruel tyrant of a man, who had given her the clues she needed to put all the pieces into place.

Now it would be easy. The impossible, the miracle she'd prayed for for so long, had happened. She knew where her daughter was. She knew who she was—the adopted child of Anne Simpson of Chicago, Illinois. It made no difference that the government of the Socialist Republic of Vietnam had no formal relations with the

United States. Somehow, she would find her way to Chicago. Somehow, she would make contact with her daughter, the baby she'd loved and lost so long ago. Somehow, she would make the child her own again.

CHAPTER FIVE

THE DOOR OPENED SUDDENLY and a blinding shaft of sunlight flooded the tiny, sweltering room. There were no windows in her latest prison, and Rachel's vision had grown accustomed to the darkness. She closed her eyes, filtering out the terror, filtering out the brightness. But a man's stocky body remained outlined against the insides of her eyelids and the uniform he wore was all too familiar. He was carrying a riding crop under his arm. He laid his hat on the small table, that, along with the stool on which she was sitting, made up the room's only furniture. She focused her attention on the whip handle so that she wouldn't have to look directly at Colonel Ha Thuck Ky.

A riding crop. She hadn't been horseback riding in years. She hadn't even seen a horse in years. Almost fifteen years, Micah had told her. So much time had passed, so much had happened in the world that she knew nothing about.

"Mrs. Phillips." Ky's tone was imperious. She sat up straighter. It seemed strangest of all, somehow, to be addressed by a title that held so little meaning to her now. Kyle Phillips had been dead for almost twenty years. They'd had so little time together, and sometimes she couldn't remember what he looked like or the color of his eyes.

"Yes, Colonel Ky." She was scared but she wasn't about to let him see her fear. Her English sounded forced and rusty. She hadn't used it in so long a span of time, she often found even her thoughts taking the form of the hill dialect she'd spoken for so many years.

"The exchange will be taking place very soon. I hope you have remembered everything I told you."

"If you mean that your soldiers found me and my brother wandering in the jungle and brought us safely to Saigon, I remember."

"And that because you have been living with a hill tribe of rebel clansmen for so many years my government, too, thought you dead...." he prompted.

"...or you would have returned me to my home and my loving family long before this. I know my lines, Colonel," Rachel said, daring her own terror. "Where is my brother?" If she didn't look directly at him, she wouldn't see the gold star on its red background on his uniform collar. She wouldn't have to remember the past, the pain and brutality she always associated with men wearing the Vietnamese army uniform. Men like this one.

"Your brother's whereabouts need not concern you. He is close by and will be brought to the exchange point later. You will not be noticed among the others, the *bui doi* and their families that my government is so graciously allowing to leave for the United States together."

So that was how he intended to camouflage her, among a group of refugees. She'd been wondering about that, about how he would manage the exchange without attracting attention. In her dark-colored, travel-stained *ao dai* and straw hat, she wouldn't be noticed in a crowd.

"I won't go without my brother." Rachel stood up, drawing herself to her full height. She looked Ky straight in the eye. Inside, her stomach knotted with fear and uncertainty. Defiance brought only pain and degradation. She had learned that lesson well. She was so close to freedom, so close to going home. *Going home.* It was a dream she'd forced to die years ago to preserve her sanity. It would truly kill her to give it up again. But regardless of the consequences, she wasn't leaving Vietnam alone. She wasn't going home without Micah.

The riding crop slammed down onto the rickety table with a sound like a pistol shot. Rachel jumped but she didn't cower. "You will do as I say." Ky's tone left no room for argument.

"When will my brother join us? I must know or I will not cooperate." Rachel was pleased her voice was steady. The trembling was all inside.

"You are as stubborn as those foolish and ignorant peasants who have sheltered you so unwisely all these years."

Rachel remained silent. The ignorant peasants he described with such derision were her friends. They had found her and Father Pieter wandering in the jungle, more dead than alive, after they'd escaped their North Vietnamese captors. The villagers had kept them hidden at the risk of their own lives, nursed Father Pieter through his last illness, tried with every small skill they possessed to save her child. *Her baby.* Rachel almost never let herself think about her son. A baby conceived in captivity, a child of rape, but hers all the same, loved and mourned though it had been years since the tiny premature infant's death.

When the dark times had passed and the countryside grew a little safer, the tribesmen began to trade among themselves, and eventually, so Micah had told her, he and Simon had come to hear that she was still alive. He had come to Laos to search for her, and because of that gallant and foolish gesture he was now a captive as well.

If only she'd been stronger, able to move more quickly through the thick jungle undergrowth, they might have made their rendezvous with a group of Laotian freedom fighters instead of being waylaid by a Vietnamese army patrol. If they had made it to the Thai border, Micah's old air force buddies would have gotten them safely across. Instead, they'd been captured almost immediately after coming down out of the hills. Since then there had been no opportunity to talk with Micah. She hadn't even seen him since they'd been brought to the south. She could only pray that he was alive and well, and that Ky would keep his word and let them go together.

Ky was speaking, ranting on about finding the village where she'd been sheltered, punishing the people, as a threat to keep her in line. She wasn't frightened by his rhetoric. The village was so remote, the jungle below it, the hills surrounding it, so rugged and inaccessible that not even Ky's soldiers would be able to find it.

"Who is this red-haired woman they have sent for you, this Anne Simpson?" Rachel forced her thoughts into order. She couldn't dwell on the past. She must concentrate on this man and his words. She had no doubt her freedom depended on it, as well as her brother's life.

"I don't know any woman by that name." That was true. The name held no meaning for her. "I am as puzzled as you that my family sent a woman to deal for us. I assumed my youngest brother would pay the ransom demanded for our release." She was guessing about the money but it made sense.

"Silence!" Ky was truly angry now. "There is no ransom. You are being returned to your people through the kindness of the government of the Socialist Republic of

Vietnam." He emphasized the words with a stroke of the whip handle against the palm of his hand. "If you do not do exactly as I tell you, you will never see your brother again."

Rachel's blood ran cold. She thought for a moment he might strike her with the riding crop. She sat down again, outwardly meek and compliant. "Yes, I understand." Defying him was a foolish and dangerous thing to do. Micah's fate rested in her hands. She let Ky see her cowed and submissive. What did it matter now, if she sacrificed her dignity? It was a small thing, of no importance. What was important was that she did not intend to leave this country without her brother.

Whoever this woman, this Anne Simpson, was, Rachel hoped she was prepared to put up a fight.

THE SUNLIGHT WAS BLINDING, the heat so intense it radiated up off the concrete runway at Tan Son Nhut in shimmering waves. Their journey was coming full circle, ending where it had begun. Annie had wanted to look nice for the final ceremony and she'd saved a white eyelet sundress for the occasion, but after only fifteen minutes outside in the oppressive heat and humidity, she felt—and looked, she suspected—as limp as an old dishrag.

She pushed straying curls of hair behind her ear and stifled a yawn that had its roots in tension as much as lack of sleep. It was mid-afternoon, the hottest time of the day, and she'd been awake since dawn. That morning Annie has surfaced from a deep and dreamless sleep to find herself wrapped in the comfort and safety of Simon's arms. Even now, in the noise and confusion of a large group of people, she could recall the touch of his body against hers, the pleasure of his embrace.

She hadn't awakened in bed with a man since Mike died. Of course she hadn't really been sleeping with Simon McKendrick, not in the sense that they'd made love together on the narrow, lumpy mattress, but she wished they had. He had saved her life, held her in his arms, comforted her, watched over her through the long dark hours of the night. He had been watching her when she woke, teased her gently because she snored, and then kissed her. And just as she had the night before, Annie found herself lost in that kiss, drowning in it, aching for more, yet afraid to face what her heart told her was happening.

Simon McKendrick was using her, albeit for a good cause, and she had to remember that. She couldn't risk falling in love with a man who let her know so little about himself. Even though she knew by now that they both liked baseball and Winslow Homer paintings and she'd confessed her addiction to old movies, she didn't think it was enough. They came from different worlds, life-styles that were separated by far more than the seven hundred miles that separated Washington, D.C., from Chicago, Illinois. Annie willed herself to stop thinking of what had passed between them that morning, although her traitorous pulse still raced with the sweet memory of his touch, the lingering excitement of his kisses. She had to let it go. She had no other choice—she needed all her wits about her to concentrate on the here and now.

A small brass band had been playing off to one side. Now they struck up a march as the limousine carrying Minister Chi and his wife raced down the runway toward Annie's group. The chartered plane that would take them all back to Thailand revved its motors to a higher, even more uncomfortable whine. A pungent wash of exhaust fumes assaulted her nose, making the faint variable breeze less welcome than usual.

The door of the corrugated metal hangar that Ky had been using as his headquarters during the ceremonies opened and the colonel came out, his small, stocky figure dwarfed by Jacob Paderwiski's bulk.

Simon was behind her, out of sight for the moment, but close enough to reach out and touch, to reassure her that the exchange would go well. So far there was no sign of Rachel or Micah. Actually, there were very few onlookers. Annie knew that the Amerasian teenagers had been separated from their mothers and relatives that morning. Jacob had returned to the hotel to pick up his luggage, angry and frustrated that his son's mother wouldn't be accompanying the boy, but he swallowed his disappointment in the best interests of the others. Annie's heart ached for him, for all of them.

"Nothing will go wrong," she whispered fiercely to herself. "It will go like clockwork." She opened her purse and looked at the pearls inside a plain white envelope. She ran her fingers over them one last time and said a prayer, short and fervent and to the point: "Dear Lord, don't let me screw up."

Colonel Ky was talking to Jacob as they walked toward the group. Billiup trailed them like a shadow. Annie couldn't hear a word, but Ky was smiling, a shark's smile. She glanced down at his hands. He was carrying a number of manila folders under his arms. Visas, birth certificates, Letters of Identity, all the documents the youngsters would need to start life in America.

Movement behind the three men caught her eye. Annie looked beyond them at the door of the hangar. The seven teens, each carrying a canvas satchel with everything they owned in the world inside, filed out of the building. Annie's heart began to beat faster than ever. The time had come.

Easy, Annie. Take it easy, love. Simon pretended to focus his camera on the group as a whole, but he continued to watch Annie's every move through the telephoto lens. Ky would have to produce Rachel and Micah within the next ten minutes. Or what? Simon considered his options. None of them was satisfactory. If the deal went sour he would have to let it. There was too much at stake. Every nerve in his body screamed for action. He wanted to drag Ky out of the hangar where he'd been waiting, screened from the sun, to choke Micah and Rachel's whereabouts out of him, beat him to a pulp if he didn't produce them whole and healthy in the next sixty seconds. Except that he couldn't do any of those things, not without risking all their lives.

It was up to Annie now. He had to accept that. He was nothing but an apparently disinterested bystander. He couldn't give Ky any more reason for suspicion. His behavior last night had been out of character enough for the ineffectual Leyton. He'd known that he'd have to play this charade through from the beginning. Nothing had changed. Nothing at all, except that he was falling in love with the courageous, fiery-haired courier he'd chosen to help bring his brother and sister out of Vietnam.

Simon lowered the camera and looked out across the concrete runway. Except for a small dilapidated wooden hut and the corrugated metal hangar, there were no other buildings nearby. There were no onlookers behind the high chain-link fence, just the members of the group, two or three military men with video equipment and several Vietnamese officials including Minister Chi and his wife. *Where the hell were Micah and Rachel?*

The flight crew opened the door of the plane. A portable stairway was wheeled alongside. Minister Chi started to speak, but the microphone, set up on a makeshift wooden dais, wasn't working very well. His words were garbled and indistinct. Simon continued to scan the area around the hangar. Two black Russian limousines sat alongside the building, each with darkened windows and a military chauffeur standing beside them.

If Micah and Rachel were inside one of the big, probably armor-plated cars, there was little chance of him getting to them without being intercepted by the guards. He couldn't take the chance. It would be a gallant but suicidal gesture. He wasn't Rambo, or even James Bond. Maybe that's why he'd survived in his line of business all these years. For the moment, at least, he'd have to rely on Ky's dubious integrity and Annie's courage and quick wits to get them all out safe and alive.

Jacob Paderwiski took the microphone, which suddenly decided to work perfectly. His voice boomed out over their heads. He spoke in halting Vietnamese, then English, thanking all those involved and vowing to help renew relations between the two countries. A polite round of applause followed his remarks. Members of the group shuffled restlessly from foot to foot, fanning themselves with pieces of paper, handkerchiefs, anything that came to hand. The teens stood stiffly in a row, both apprehension and excitement evident in their expressions. Ky stepped onto the dais and started to speak.

Simon paid little attention to his words at first. He watched a bus, painted in the colors of the Vietnamese army, as it rumbled out of a hangar two hundred yards away and began to move toward them. Tension tightened the muscles at the base of his skull. Something was up. He turned his attention back to Ky. There was a faint air of expectation about the man. The people standing around Simon also began to notice that something was about to happen. Heads turned toward the bus as it rolled to a halt between the dais and the chartered Air Vietnam plane. Ky made a sweeping gesture with his hand.

"Ladies and gentlemen. As a token of goodwill my government has decided, only this morning, to allow the families of these seven young people to accompany them to Bangkok." The door of the bus opened and twenty or twenty-five Vietnamese, some old, some middle-aged, several with young children, piled out carrying boxes, bundles tied up in cloth, battered suitcases, looking dazed and uncertain. "From this point forward it will be up to your government to follow through on this act of good faith by allowing these family members to journey with their loved ones all the way to America."

There was a moment of stunned silence before the members of Annie's group broke into shouts of joy. Applause and laughter filled the air. Jacob Paderwiski waded into the crowd of anxious Vietnamese and grabbed his son's mother, lifting her off her feet to wheel her around in an exuberant reunion. From that moment on pandemonium reigned. No one but Simon saw the door of the hut open. No one but Simon paid any attention to the small woman in a worn gray *ao dai* who emerged to walk, hesitantly, toward the fringes of the crowd.

Simon watched the female figure coming toward him with the unfamiliar tightness of tears in his throat. *Rachel.* He wanted to push past the knots of people who blocked his view and pull her into his arms. *Rachel. Alive and well, just as his mother had always believed.* Only once did she lift her head to look around her. Beneath the shabby conical hat, blue-gray eyes searched a sea of faces. For a moment her gaze seemed to settle on Annie's red hair before moving on, halting, passing him by only to return and capture his eyes with her own.

"Simon?" Disbelief and joy registered on her face before she wiped all expression from her features. He didn't have to hear her voice, he could read his name on her lips. "Micah?" She looked around, dazed. Simon sensed her fear as if it were a physical thing.

Don't worry. He gave Rachel a thumbs-up sign, just as they'd used to do as kids, then deliberately turned his back, lifting the camera to catch a shot of Annie bidding Minister Chi and Le Thi goodbye.

Where the hell was Micah?

THE INSIDE OF THE BIG Russian-made limousine was as hot as an oven, as hot as the small dark cell where he'd spent the past three months. The limo had windows, but that didn't make it any better. In fact it made it worse. Micah shut his eyes, trying to find the determination not to look out, but he couldn't summon the resolve. He was too tired, too bone weary to resist. Ky had won at last. Micah had no illusions as to why he was sitting on the runway at Tan Son Nhut. He was there because Ky wanted him to see Rachel leave, wanted him to see his sister and the mysterious red-haired woman who had somehow arranged for her release. Simon was behind all this and it helped to know his brother had taken charge. It had helped him control his temper as the martinet colonel had ranted and raved long into the night. It had helped when Ky had tried once more to intimidate Micah into revealing the location of Rachel's village.

Ky hadn't been able to force the information from him, but Micah had come damn close to breaking and they both knew it. That's why even though he was sitting less than a hundred yards away from his sister, he knew he'd never leave the ground. He was going to be a "guest" of the Socialist Republic of Vietnam for as long as Ky wanted him to remain there.

They hadn't even bothered to tie his hands. There wasn't any need. The driver was a mile away in the front, protected by a raised panel of bullet-proof glass. The gun the driver carried was equipped with a silencer, a not-too-subtle reminder of how easy it would be to dispose of him permanently. There were no locks, no handles on the door. He wasn't the first reluctant passenger Ky had entertained inside this car.

Micah shifted position on the hard, hot leather seat. His neck and shoulders ached with a fierceness that went clear through to the marrow of his bones. He wished he had an aspirin, a whole handful of them. Him, the guy who didn't even own a bottle of vitamin pills. His eyes burned from lack of sleep and the glare of the sun even though it's brilliance was filtered through the heavy smoked-glass windows.

He'd made it through three tours of duty in Laos without a scratch. He'd left a lot of friends behind, though, guys who'd only gone home in a box. But he'd always thought he was too damned lucky to die in Vietnam.

"Well, buddy," he said aloud, breaking the heavy, oppressive silence inside the armored limousine. "Looks like you're gonna get your chance to buy the farm in Nam after all. It's just takin' you twenty years longer to do it than all the rest."

"FAREWELL, MRS. SIMPSON." Colonel Ky was holding out his hand. Annie took it reluctantly.

"Goodbye."

"It seems Mr. Paderwiski is preoccupied with his new extended family." He nodded his head toward Jacob, his son and his son's mother, and an old man and woman, obviously the boy's grandparents. "Perhaps you can be persuaded to take charge of the documentation until he is free to accept it."

"I'd be happy to." The words nearly stuck in her throat.

Ky held out the manila folders. "Each family is represented." He spread them out in an arc. Annie counted eight. Her heart began to beat heavily, high up in her throat. "Rachel Phillips is there, just to your left, in the dark gray *ao dai* and the straw hat. I have kept my part of the bargain, Mrs. Simpson. Now it is time for you to keep yours."

Annie looked over her shoulder. The woman he described stood a little away from the others, her head slightly lowered, her face hidden in the shadow of her straw hat. She was small and slim like a great many Vietnamese women. Her dark hair, where it straggled out from under the hat, was liberally sprinkled with gray. Her age could be anywhere from forty to sixty. Annie hesitated. There was something about her, the set of her shoulders, the air of expectancy, that lifted the short hair at the back of her neck. As if sensing her interest, the woman looked up, directly at her. Blue-gray eyes met hers for a brief second and Annie was convinced the woman was indeed Rachel Phillips. Yet she was alone, conspicuously alone.

Annie clutched the envelope containing the pearls tightly to her breast. "No, Colonel Ky, I don't think you've fulfilled your part of the bargain. Where is Micah McKendrick?"

"He will board the plane just before it leaves. McKendrick entered our country illegally—he has no papers. Discretion is called for here and McKendrick would stand out in a crowd. You have my word." Ky's expression was passive but his eyes were filled with hate. It was funny—last night she'd been unable to read even a hint of his thoughts in those dark eyes. Today it was different. Perhaps it was because her senses were more alert, because she knew just how dangerous this man could be. She felt panic rise within her. She wanted to run screaming to Simon for help, but she did not. She could sense him in the background, knew he was somewhere nearby, and took comfort in that nearness.

Yet at the same time Annie knew that whatever she did next would be her own decision. Right or wrong, she'd have to live with the consequences for the rest of her life. Could she hand over the pearls, walk away and trust Ky to honor his word? She recalled for one vivid, heart-stopping moment the cruel face of the man who'd broken into her room last night, a man sent to kill her by Ha Thuck Ky.

"No, Colonel." Annie wasn't certain where she got the courage to say the words, but it came from somewhere deep inside. "I don't think your word is good enough. I'm afraid I can't turn over the pearls until I know Micah McKendrick is safely aboard the airplane." She knew Simon wouldn't blame her if she took the eight folders of precious documents she'd been offered and cut her losses. He wouldn't blame her but she'd blame herself.

Annie couldn't turn tail and run. She would stand her ground and risk destroying everything they'd worked for as well as endangering each and every one of their lives. She would do that because it was the only chance she had of winning Micah McKendrick's freedom.

Jacob and Billiup were beginning to urge the Vietnamese toward the aircraft. She shifted position slightly, still holding the envelope containing the pearls in full view of Ky's increasingly avaricious gaze. "Time is growing short, Colonel," she heard herself say in a cool, calculated tone that sounded nothing like her usual voice. "Surely one American is not worth losing the pearls over. I can assure you the McKendrick family has no more money. If you plan to hold Micah McKendrick for ransom, also, you have made an error in judgment."

She could see Ky turning over the possibilities in his mind. The reality of the pearls here and now, within reach, against the not-so-certain possibility of more money in the future. Minister Chi walked toward them. Ky spoke a single sharp word in Vietnamese. Annie didn't recognize it but she had no difficulty determining its meaning by the look of pure hatred that twisted Ky's features. "You win, for the moment, Mrs. Simpson. McKendrick will accompany his sister out of my country."

"I'm glad you see things my way, Colonel." She turned pointedly to include Minister Chi and Le Thi in the conversation, but the qualifying rider in Ky's last remarks left her cold with fear.

"A safe journey home, Mrs. Simpson." Ky gave a slight bow and motioned to one of his guards. The man moved away at a brisk walk. Annie said something appropriate to Le Thi, listened to her response, made a reply. Later, she would not recall a word of the conversation. As she watched, the guard halted before one of two limousines parked by the hangar, said something to the driver and opened the door. A big man got out of the rear door of the car. Even from a distance he looked very much like Simon. He was older, of course, broader in the shoulders, heavier, with gray in his night-black hair and beard. He moved forward awkwardly, stumbling a little when the guard pushed him roughly from behind. He was limping and his khaki shirt and pants were torn and filthy.

Annie kept on talking, kept on moving casually toward the plane, but her attention was focused on Micah. She shivered despite the heat. At that moment she realized how cruel a man Ha Thuck Ky actually was. He had intended for Micah McKendrick to watch his sister's release, watch her board the plane for home, all the time aware that he, Micah, would probably never leave this country alive. She pretended she had all the time in the world to say her goodbyes, while silently she screamed at Micah to hurry onto the plane. Only when she saw him disappear inside the open hatchway did she allow herself to believe that everything was going to turn out all right.

A hundred feet away from the plane she stopped, watched Rachel climb the steps with three other Vietnamese, saw Simon follow her and turn to wait at the top of the steps. She began to breathe normally again. It was almost over. She'd gambled that Ky's desire to possess the pearls was stronger than his desire to keep Micah captive, and she had won.

"Goodbye, Mrs. Simpson." Ky was at her elbow. He held out his hand, eyes gleaming with malice. "I'm sure you will describe your trip and the happy circumstances of the rescue of Mrs. Phillips and Mr. McKendrick to the authorities with the appropriate gratitude for my country's cooperation in arranging for their return."

This time the threat was more in his tone than in the words he spoke.

"And what if I choose to tell the truth, Colonel? All the truth?" Annie held the envelope toward him. She was being foolish to bait the man this way. His next words convinced her of that folly. As they slashed into her brain and her heart she knew they would stay with her the rest of her life.

"Because if you do that, you would never see alive any others that might possibly, like Mrs. Phillips, have been left behind." He held out his hand for the envelope. Annie let it drop from nerveless fingers.

"Have a safe flight, Mrs. Simpson."

Annie turned without a backward glance and started climbing the steps toward Simon, toward home.

CHAPTER SIX

"SIMON?" ANNIE OPENED her eyes, surprised to find she had them squeezed tight shut. Her fingers were curled just as tightly around the armrests of her seat. Deliberately she relaxed, taking a deep breath, letting it out in a ragged little sigh of relief and thanksgiving.

"Are you okay?" Simon's voice was rough-edged but wonderfully matter-of-fact. Everything must be fine.

Annie tried to smile. "Are we really in the air?" The few interminable minutes they'd waited on the runway before takeoff had been the longest in her life.

Simon touched her cheek very lightly with the tip of his finger. "It's all over. We made it. Look for yourself."

Annie unfastened her seat belt and looked out the window. A patchwork of green and gold fields, trees and water stretched away beneath the wing of the aircraft. "When I was stationed in Manila we worked on some pretty badly shot-up guys," Annie spoke softly, almost in a whisper. Her thoughts were chaotic, unfocused, but the emotions she was attempting to describe were strong and vivid. "Most of them always had the same comment about Vietnam. They said it sucks." She shrugged and tried to smile, but it came out twisted and sad and she gave up the attempt. "I thought they meant it the way you usually mean that phrase and never paid much attention. Even when I escaped with the children I still couldn't understand what they'd been trying to tell me because it was all over with so quickly and I was so scared I couldn't feel anything at all. But now I know." Her voice faded into a whisper. "I felt it today, the pull of the earth beneath us. The war's been over for fourteen years and I still felt something, some force...." She stopped talking for a moment, looked down at her hands folded in her lap, the knuckles white beneath the pale gold of her skin. "I felt as if we could be swallowed up by this place and no one would ever hear from us again."

Simon hunkered down in the aisle, bracing himself with one arm on the back of her seat, and took her hand in his. "No, Annie," he said quietly, "you're wrong."

"But I did feel it," she insisted with the obstinacy of fatigue and reaction. Tears filled her eyes. She blinked them back. "I felt as if Vietnam would reach up and pull us down out of the sky."

"Not Vietnam," Simon repeated patiently. "Evil." His hazel eyes were level with hers. She stared into the gold-flecked depths and saw great strength and integrity and something more, something dark and exciting that her confused senses refused to acknowledge at the moment.

"Evil?"

"What those boys were telling you was true in a sense. But it was the war that was wrong, not the place. The evil of war, any war, can be felt even when you're no longer directly involved. And today you dealt with evil again, on a smaller scale I grant you, but evil still."

"Ky." Annie bit her lip. If she closed her eyes she could see his face sharp and clear, his expression triumphant as he held the pearls at last. She remembered his words and squeezed Simon's hand tighter than ever. "He is evil."

"There have always been men like him in this world. There always will be."

"He threatened me, Simon. He threatened all of us. He said if anyone learned of his part in Rachel's imprisonment, if any mention was made of the pearls, that...others...might not be as lucky as she was."

"Others." Simon's breath hissed between his teeth. His expression hardened, steel edged his words. "The bastard."

Annie shivered at the cold rage that flared in his eyes. "All these years I've listened to the reports, I've been active in the MIA/POW groups, but I've never been convinced that any of our soldiers were still alive. I...I just wanted them to be accounted for, so that their families could have peace. Then you came to me about Rachel." She stopped talking, swallowed hard and took a deep breath. "I began to doubt again. And now..." Two bright tears traced a path down her cheeks. "Simon, what if he was telling the truth?"

"We can't discount the possibility that some American soldiers might still be alive in Southeast Asia. After all, if Rachel survived, so might others. But one thing's certain. Ky doesn't have any more proof of their existence than we do."

"Are you sure?" She wanted very much to be convinced of that. Her defenses were so battered, her emotions so close to the surface, she didn't think she could cope with the pain if she believed what Ky told her was the truth.

"I told you last night, Ky's an opportunist. He threatened Rachel and Micah, too. And just as convincingly." Simon stood up, keeping his head bent slightly to accommodate the low ceiling of the plane. "I'll take you to them. You can hear Rachel's story firsthand. She'll want to thank you, and so will Micah, for what you've done for the McKendrick family. But first I think we're going to have to run the gauntlet of your friends and admirers."

They moved up the aisle. For the first time since she'd boarded the plane, Annie was totally aware of what was going on around her. English and Vietnamese mixed and collided in conversations on all sides. Members of the group reached out as she passed to stop her and introduce her to aunts, uncles, brothers and sisters of the seven teenagers. Jacob Paderwiski, beaming with pride, wrapped her in an enormous bear hug without even getting out of his seat. He, too, was anxious for her to meet his son's relatives. Annie smiled and nodded and hugged Jacob back. She wondered if Simon realized the pearls not only had ransomed Rachel and Micah but had allowed seven other families to remain intact? She looked at him over Jacob's shoulder, saw him smile, and knew he had read her thoughts.

Annie finally managed to disengage herself from Jacob's embrace. Two rows farther on they passed Billiup's seat. He leaned out into the aisle. "Don't worry." He gestured toward the front of the plane. "I'll see to it that you're not disturbed." His pale eyes met and held with Simon's dark gaze.

Simon nodded once. "Thanks." Turning away, he pulled back the curtain that separated the two sections of the aircraft and held it aside for Annie to enter. She took a deep breath, suddenly reluctant to meet Rachel and Micah face-to-face. Simon held out his hand. "Come on. The hard part's over, remember." He smiled and Annie smiled in return.

"I know. From now on everything will go like clockwork."

RACHEL PERCHED ON THE ARM of an aisle seat and opened the lid on the first-aid box she'd asked the stewardess to bring her when she'd noticed the ugly abrasion on Micah's forehead.

"Turn your head this way." He was still her younger brother even if he stood a foot taller and outweighed her by almost a hundred pounds. He leaned his body out into the aisle, accepting her ministrations with the same barely restrained impatience he'd always shown when confronted with physical weakness, his own or anyone else's.

"It's just a scrape, Rachel. Clean it off and forget it."

She frowned and pulled her lower lip between her teeth. "I'm afraid it'll get infected. Every little cut or scratch gets infected over here—you know that." Rachel frowned harder, rummaging through the first-aid supplies for a cream or ointment to cover the wound. She was glad to have something to do. Sitting idly in her seat left her too much time to think of the future. For years, so many years, she'd had no future to contemplate. Now that the possibility was staring her in the face she was scared to death. "Micah. Hold still." He reluctantly did as he was told.

Rachel worked quickly. Somehow she always felt better when she was working. The familiar look and feel and smell of gauze bandages and antiseptic helped, too. For a minute or so she'd even been afraid to open the kit. She'd been away from the modern world for so long. What if everything was different? What if so much had changed, so many things passed her by that she could never hope to catch up to the medical profession? She began gently, automatically, to swab the raw, bruised skin above Micah's left eye. What would she do with the rest of her life if she were so out of step, so outdated, that she couldn't function as a contributing member of society again?

"Hey, Sis," Micah protested. "Take it easy, will ya? It's only a scrape. I tripped and bumped into a door, that's all. It doesn't require major surgery." Rachel didn't believe for a moment that he'd just "tripped." Ky's men were probably responsible for the injury. "Rachel." Micah wrapped his big hand firmly around her wrist. "If it gets infected—and it won't—I'll get a prescription for some antibiotics when we get back to the States."

"Antibiotics." Rachel said the word wonderingly as if she'd half forgotten its meaning. "That's right." She smiled, almost laughed aloud. "Just pick up a phone, dial the doctor and run down the block to the drugstore to pick up a bottle of penicillin or anything else you need."

"Anything at all." Micah grinned, too. His teeth were white and straight, his smile as compelling as ever. Rachel found herself staring at him. He was still very much the Micah she'd grown up with, but very different, too. The brother she remembered had rushed to meet life head-on, to experience new things, defy convention, take any risk. This Micah was older, to be sure. After all, more than fifteen years had passed since they'd last seen each other. But there were other changes, too, deeper, more significant ones than graying hair and a few new lines around his mouth and eyes. Something had happened to chain Micah's spirit as surely as she herself had been physically confined.

"It's the beard," he said waving his hand in front of her eyes.

"What?" Rachel blinked in confusion.

"I never wore a beard when we were kids."

"No. But you used to have long hair with sideburns down to here." She reached up and touched his cheek.

Micah didn't pull away from her touch, but she felt him stiffen as the tips of her fingers grazed his skin. "I need a haircut," he said, his low, deep voice gruff and strained. "I haven't seen a barber or a barbershop since I left Bangkok. And that was back in June." He ran his hand through his shaggy salt-and-pepper hair. "I feel like one of those old mountain men just come down from the hills."

"I feel like Rip Van Winkle," Rachel said, unable to keep a quiver out of her voice. "Everything will be so different when we get home. Oh, Micah, maybe you shouldn't have come after me." Tears welled up in her eyes. She sniffed, determined not to cry. If she let the tears start she was afraid they'd never stop.

"The hell I shouldn't. We're just lucky we had good ol' Simon to bail us both out as usual." He grinned again, inviting her to recall any number of childhood scrapes.

"Did I hear someone about to take my name in vain?" The curtain parted and the red-headed woman she'd noticed earlier preceded Simon into the first-class section of the plane. Rachel closed the lid on the first-aid box. *Don't panic. Smile, act normal.* She looked down at her hands. Her nails were broken and dirty but at least she'd stopped shaking. She took a deep breath. She might as well get used to meeting people again.

"Rachel. Micah. I want you to meet someone." Simon's voice sounded very much like their father's, Rachel decided, her mind darting from one subject to the next, even as she tried very hard to concentrate on what her brother was saying. "This is Anne Simpson. Formerly Lieutenant Anne Norton," Simon added quietly, obviously for her benefit.

"Anne Norton?" Rachel felt an unwelcome tug of memory. She looked hesitantly at the woman standing in the open space in front of the plane's galley.

"Hello, Rachel." She tilted her head and smiled. Red curls brushed across her shoulder.

Rachel's memories became more sharply focused. Her breath quickened and she clutched the first-aid box more tightly. *Careful, she had to be careful not to let the memories of the bad times get too close to the surface.* "Annie?" The name came out a rough-edged whisper. She cleared her throat and tried again. "Annie Norton?"

"Yes, Rachel. Welcome home." Tears slipped down Annie's cheeks. Rachel felt tears in her own eyes and tried once more to hold them back.

"You made it safely to the embassy that day?"

Annie nodded, following her ricocheting line of thought without any trouble. "I kept the two little boys with me. Do you remember them? They're my sons." She looked as if she were going to say more, then decided against it. "Do you remember, Rachel?"

"Yes." She looked past Annie into another time and place. It had been imperative that Annie get out of the city when she did. She was a member of the U.S. military, and doubly at risk. "After we got separated I made my way back to the bus. The sisters and I managed to commandeer a truck." She had to be very careful how much she let herself remember about those last days in Saigon. The fear and terror, the pain, were too close behind them to linger very long with the memories. "The next day Sister Angela and Sister Michelle and the last of the children were taken away to a boat on the river, or a plane... I don't remember... by a Dutch embassy official. I... I never knew if they made it safely or not."

"They did," Simon assured her.

Rachel looked at him, but she didn't know what to say. *He had failed her when she needed him most. She'd counted on him to warn her when it was time to leave Saigon. She'd never received any word from him. That's why she and Father Pieter had remained behind. She had no way of knowing the end was so near. Surely there had been time for him to get a message to her, as safe as he was in the embassy in Bangkok?*

"And Father Pieter?" Annie asked very softly. Rachel turned her head. Annie was still crying, but silently, the same way Rachel herself had learned to cry when she was alone in the darkness of the jungle night. Teardrops were making dark spots on the bodice of Annie's white eyelet sundress. Rachel hadn't worn white eyelet since she was seventeen years old.

"He's dead." She said it quickly so that the pain would be over sooner. "He died five rainy seasons past." She shrugged, and the gesture was no less poignant for the abrupt way in which she spoke. "I lost track of the years a long time ago."

"Where have you been, Rachel?" It was Annie who asked the question.

"With friends." Rachel gripped the box so tightly her knuckles showed white beneath the skin.

Simon and Micah exchanged glances. Annie moved to take the heavy box and put it on the floor. Rachel remained where she was, suddenly so tired she could barely keep her eyes open. Annie put her arms around her. Rachel didn't protest when Annie urged her down into the seat, adjusted the back and covered her with a blanket Simon had pulled out of one of the overhead bins.

"I'm tired." It was good to have someone fuss over her again. She let Annie tuck her in like a child. If she could sleep she wouldn't have to remember anything she didn't want to. She never dreamed about the bad times, at least not that she ever recalled. Annie bent to place a small pillow behind her head. Rachel waved it away. "I'll just rest my eyes for a few minutes. You'll wake me before we land in Bangkok? I...I need to wash up and I have to do something with my hair." She reached up to smooth her hand over the bun at the nape of her neck. "I haven't even looked in a mirror in . . . years."

"I'll wake you in plenty of time. Go ahead and sleep."

Annie's voice was low, soothing to Rachel. It was good to hear her American accent again. When they got back to the States everyone would sound like that. Rachel drifted off to sleep. For the first time she could really believe she was going home.

"SHE'S BEEN WITH THE Hlông, I can tell you that much." Micah stood up, or tried to. The plane's low ceiling kept him from standing upright, as it did Simon. By unspoken consent the three of them moved to the front of the deserted first-class cabin so that their voices wouldn't disturb Rachel's rest. "They're a tribe of hill people in Laos," he explained for Annie's benefit. "We fought alongside them in the war when I was with the Ravens."

Annie held out her hand. "I'm pleased to meet you, Micah McKendrick." Micah stared down at her outstretched hand. After a long moment he wrapped his big callused palm around it.

"I'd like to add my thanks to Rachel's. From the little Simon's had time to tell us about what went on, I take it you saved my worthless hide back there at Tan Son Nhut."

"You saw the whole thing, didn't you?" Annie's great brown eyes still glistened with tears. She held on to Micah with both hands as if assuring herself that he was real.

"Yeah." Micah stared at her bent head, seemingly at a loss. "It hasn't been one of my better days." He didn't pull away from Annie's grasp and Simon was surprised. Since his wife had died twelve years earlier, Micah had had very little to do with women. Misogynist was perhaps too strong a word to use to describe his attitude toward the opposite sex, but just barely.

"Ky wasn't going to let you go." Annie's voice trembled with reaction. "I didn't know what to do, but I couldn't just walk away and leave you behind. I told Ky, 'No Micah McKendrick, no pearls.' He didn't call my bluff."

"Were you bluffing?" Micah's lips curled into a wry smile. Simon's surprise turned to astonishment. His taciturn brother was actually carrying on a conversation of his own free will.

"I don't know," Annie replied wonderingly. "I was too scared to think at all. I...I just did what I had to do."

"I think you could do just about anything you set your mind to, Mrs. Simpson." He gazed down at Annie and she tilted her head back to give him a brilliant though lopsided smile in return.

"Please, call me Annie. Simon does." She looked over Micah's shoulder and smiled at him, too. The smile hit Simon with the force of an exploding grenade. *Lord, she was something special.* She even had Micah eating out of her hand and they'd known each other less than thirty minutes. Micah, the man who avoided women like the plague. "Your brother deserves all the credit."

Simon discovered he didn't like the idea of his brother holding hands with Annie Simpson. "We were in this together, remember?" He tried to smile, too, hoping it would take the sting out of his gruff words.

"I spotted Simon in the crowd," Micah said, disengaging his hand from Annie's grasp as though he might have read Simon's thoughts. Or, more likely, his body language. Micah was pretty much of a hermit when it came to people, but no one knew more about birds and animals than he did. And underneath all the civilized posturing, people still acted pretty much like animals. "I knew if there was any way out of that mess he'd come up with the solution. I just never thought his solution would be you." He smiled at Annie. Again.

"I was only a go-between," she insisted. "Tell me about the Hlông," she requested suddenly, shifting attention away from herself as neatly as Micah had.

"Back during the war we referred to them as the *meo*. They flew with us in Laos, as our guides. They call themselves the Hlông. It means 'mankind' in their language. They're proud and loyal, good fighters, and they know the mountains like the backs of their hands. Being taken in by them was probably the only good thing that happened to Rachel over here. Evidently they've been hiding her, and Father Pieter while he lived, for almost eight years."

"And before that?" Simon's expression was as grim as the tone of his voice.

"A work camp somewhere up north. Other than that she wouldn't tell me."

They were sitting in three aisle seats, their voices lowered almost to whispers. Annie turned her head but apparently couldn't see Rachel's face. From across the aisle Micah noticed her attempt to check on their sister. He looked back, too. "She's still asleep."

"Good. Rest is the best thing for her at the moment." She gave a satisfied little nod. Looking thoughtful, she leaned forward, her elbows resting on the seat arm, her chin cupped in her hands. "Simon?"

"Yes," *Love*, he almost added before remembering to stop himself.

"I don't know anything about government procedure in a case like this." She seemed to be searching for just the right words to convey her obvious uneasiness.

"Don't worry. I'll see to it that no hotshot pencil pushers from State get to her until she's ready for them."

"She needs a doctor." Micah shook his great shaggy head. "She can't weigh more than ninety pounds."

Simon's hazel eyes caught and held his brother's. Micah's eyes were blue-gray like his sister's; otherwise Simon knew they looked a lot alike. "She'll have the best." That much he could promise his brother. They hadn't been close, not for a lot of years, but then Micah let no one close to him. And in his heart Simon realized he was the same.

"Damn right she will." Micah turned away to look out the window. Simon let him. They both needed time alone with their thoughts. And he had to talk to Annie.

He moved out of his seat to kneel beside her. She was asleep, her head resting on her hand. Simon felt the corners of his mouth turn up in a smile. He eased her back against the seat into a more comfortable position. She didn't stir. Fatigue had etched fine new lines from her nose to her mouth. She was almost as close to the edge of exhaustion as Rachel was. Regretfully he decided she needed rest more than he needed to hear the sound of her voice.

Simon glanced at his watch. More than an hour until they landed in Bangkok. He'd use the time to start formulating some kind of plan. It was essential he notify his parents as soon as possible. He sure as hell didn't want them hearing about Rachel's return on the six o'clock news. He'd have to brief Micah on what to say to the hordes of press and bureaucrats that would descend on them almost as soon as they landed in Thailand. And somehow, some way, he needed to find time alone with Annie.

"WAKE UP, LOVE." It was Simon's hand on her shoulder, Simon's voice calling her love, tempting her out of the hazy dream world that she'd been inhabiting. "Wake up, Red."

"Red." Annie sat up straight, surprised to find her seat belt fastened snugly around her middle. "I was just resting my eyes." She blinked at the bright sunlight outside the plane window. "Don't call me Red. Have we landed?"

"Safe and sound," Simon informed her with a half grin. "You really were out of it." For the first time Annie realized the aircraft was standing still. "We have to talk."

"Yes." Annie put her hands to her face and pressed her fingers against her eyelids. "I must look a mess." She pushed helplessly at the red curls framing her face. "I'm sorry. I didn't mean to fall asleep on you."

Simon reached out to touch her cheek. "Annie, we've only got a few minutes. You understand you have to go along with what Ky told you, whether we believe his story about other Americans still being held in Vietnam, or not. When the authorities start asking you questions just tell them the truth as far as you can. They won't know anything about the pearls, so you won't have to mention them. All you know is that when you got to Tan Son

Nhut to pick up the kids, all these relatives popped out of a bus. . . ."

"And Rachel and Micah were with them. Where are they now?"

"In the lavatories getting cleaned up a bit." He took her hand and Annie held on tight. "I'm still not supposed to be here. I have to continue playing Leyton until I get back to the States."

"I understand." Annie swallowed a lump in her throat. Her skin felt tight and stretched when she tried to smile to show herself, and him, that she was going to get through this without causing a scene. She just wasn't ready for it to end this quickly. "Will I see you again?" Annie couldn't stop herself from asking the question.

"Sure." He smiled and her heart flip-flopped inside her. She went hot, then cold, then liquid inside. Mike had never affected her like this. She'd felt safe and secure and happy with him, but Simon made her feel like she was sixteen again and the man with her was the sexiest mortal she'd ever seen.

"When?" Annie was amazed at her own daring. She'd wait a hundred years if he asked her to.

"In about half an hour. After we get through customs."

"Oh." Annie couldn't subdue the small relieved sigh that accompanied the word.

Simon laughed out loud and she realized it was the first time she'd heard him do so. He laid his hand along the side of her face. "Don't look as if this is the airport scene from *Casablanca*, okay? I'm not about to tell you our problems don't amount to a hill of beans and watch you get onto another plane with Victor Laszlo."

"I should never have told you *Casablanca* was my favorite movie. And anyway, you're probably going to be the one to get on another plane and fly off into the sunset. We'll probably be held up here for days taking care of the paperwork." She was determined to be as brave and noble as Ingrid Bergman if it killed her. "Did I ever tell you I hate the ending of that movie?"

"Good. Because the last thing I intend to do is walk off into the fog with Claude Rains. I'll be here."

"Don't count on it, McKendrick." Annie looked over her shoulder with a gasp. Billiup was standing in the open space at the rear of the first-class section. He made a slight, awkward bow in her direction. Simon stood up, hands loose at his side. Still, Annie had the distinct impression she was witnessing a showdown. "I hope you don't expect me to come up with some ID, McKendrick." Billiup shoved his hands in the pockets of his baggy gray pants. "But I have orders to take you out of Thailand with me."

"Since when does CIA carry ID in the first place?" Simon growled. His expression was murderous.

Billiup looked more interested than menacing. He ignored Simon's belligerent tone. "When did you catch on?"

"Just now, damn it," Simon admitted in disgust. "I should have known there'd be somebody from the Company planted in the group. Congratulations. I never would have pegged you."

Billiup bowed again. "I'll take that as a compliment." He waved toward the front of the aircraft where the flight crew was getting ready to deplane through the forward exit. "Come on, McKendrick. I have orders to get you out of here damn fast."

"Get off my back, Billiup." The expression on the smaller man's face remained affable but a small, deadly gun appeared in his hand.

"No way, McKendrick. You're a walking international incident. You three-piece-suit types that play by the rules don't belong in this game. Hell, State probably doesn't even know you're gone. I only got word from one of our contacts when the plane landed, myself. You sure as hell could screw up everything over here, and my butt's on the line right along with yours." He gestured forward once more. "Start walking. I don't want to be standing here like a sitting duck when that bull moose of a brother of yours gets out of the john."

Simon took a menacing step toward Billiup. Annie flew out of her seat. "Simon. No." She was remembering the fight in her hotel room. Her heart hammered against her rib cage. Dangerous. Lethal. Capable of real violence. She didn't want to see that part of Simon again. She didn't want to feel the fear for him she'd experienced on that stormy night. She put both hands on his chest and pushed. He didn't budge an inch.

"Get out of my way, Annie." His voice was a low growl that raised the short hairs at the nape of her neck.

"Be reasonable, McKendrick," Billiup said, still in the same friendly tone he'd been using. But he'd taken a prudent step backward. "You're one of the best we've got. Your brother and sister are safe. The kids and their families are on their way to the States. Annie and Paderwiski can handle the media and the paper pushers. Let's cut our losses and get the hell out of here before the whole deal blows up in our faces."

"Listen to him, Simon." Annie felt the muscles of his chest and shoulders relax slightly. He looked down at her—at her, not through her. He reached up to cover her hands with his own. "You win, Billiup. I'll be in touch, Annie love. I promise."

"Sure." Annie wished she could believe what he said, but she knew real life didn't always work out the way you wanted it to. She wished Simon would kiss her goodbye. He didn't, so Annie reached up on tiptoe and kissed him instead. His mouth was warm and hard on hers, arousing, caressing, a promise. "Goodbye, Simon."

"Here's lookin' at you, kid." The corner of his mouth curved into a half smile that never quite reached his eyes. "I've always wanted to use that line." He turned on his heel and walked out of the plane without a backward glance.

CHAPTER SEVEN

ANNIE STOPPED WITH HER HAND in midair, a thermometer poised six inches away from the wide-open mouth of the feverish, fretful seven-year-old she was examining. The all-music FM radio station they usually listened to at the clinic was playing "As Time Goes By." Annie groaned softly under her breath.

Elbert Nathanial Woods shut his mouth with a snap. "You sick, too, Mrs. Simpson?" he asked suspiciously. He squirmed, rustling the thin paper covering the high examination table. His skinny legs stuck straight out in front of him, the toes of his scuffed running shoes pointing straight at the ceiling, the knees of his jeans worn almost through. "Maybe you need a shot worse than me." Elbert had been vehemently and vociferously admonishing Annie not to give him an injection since the memory of his last school inoculation booster was still very fresh in his mind.

"No shots." Annie crossed her heart.

"Promise?" Elbert demanded, still not convinced.

"Promise." Annie smiled as teeth, tongue and pink tonsils were presented to view. She popped the electronic thermometer under Elbert's tongue. "Close," she ordered, leaving nothing to chance. Elbert did as he was told. The music ended and a commercial for a florist came on. Annie breathed a sigh of relief, put the tantalizing mental image of Simon McKendrick's smile from her mind and forced herself to concentrate on Mrs. Woods's questions about her son's illness.

"He's got all the symptoms of the flu bug that's going around," Annie explained to the harassed young black woman who had three more just like Elbert at home. The thermometer beeped and Annie read the numbers on the monitor before ejecting the soiled plastic sleeve into the wastebasket. "101.2. Yes, Elbert," she announced, holding out the monitor so he could see it, too, "you're sick."

"I knew that." Elbert scratched his bare tummy. "I ache." He looked as though he might cry.

"Your mom can give you some Tylenol for that," Annie told him with a pat on the knee. She directed her next words to Mrs. Woods. "I'll confer with Dr. Montoya and see if she feels Elbert should have an antibiotic."

Annie employed Dr. Maria Montoya at the clinic to enable herself, and the other nurse practitioners, to provide more complete care for their patients. Annie on her own wouldn't have been able, legally, to prescribe any medication for Elbert's symptoms. His mother would have been forced to take him to a doctor's office with much higher overhead and correspondingly higher fees. With Dr. Montoya on the premises that problem was avoided. Having a doctor on staff at the clinics raised Annie's overhead, too, but until the American Medical Association and the State of Illinois recognized the expertise of nurse practitioners and allowed them to prescribe simple medications on their own, it was the only solution.

"I hate pills," Elbert warned, folding his hands over his chest, preparing to do battle. His dark eyes were dull with fever, but his small face was set in determined lines.

"Okay," Annie said, pretending to consider her options. "I could ask Dr. Montoya to write the prescription for a nice cherry liquid."

"Don't like cherry."

"Orange?" Thankfully the manufacturer produced the medication in two different flavors.

"Okay." Elbert smiled. "I like orange."

"Then it's settled." Annie lifted Elbert down off the high exam table and deposited him in his mother's lap. "I'll talk to Dr. Montoya right now while Elbert gets dressed. You can pick up the prescription at the desk on your way out."

"Thanks, Mrs. Simpson. I sure hope the rest of the kids don't come down with this."

"I do, too, Mrs. Woods. But if they do, we'll be right here to help you out."

"Amen," said Elbert's mother.

"Amen," Elbert echoed as his head popped out of the neck of his Chicago Bears sweatshirt.

"Come on, El honey. Your brother will be home from school soon. We got to get goin' or we'll miss our bus."

"Goodbye, Elbert. You have a happy Thanksgiving." The holiday was two days away. Chad was picking up the turkey on his way home from school that evening. Annie's parents were coming to spend the weekend on their way from Annie's hometown in Michigan to their winter home in Phoenix. This year they would spend Christmas with her two younger sisters in California. It would be the first holiday season she and the kids had spent entirely alone since Mike died.

"Turkey and dressing and everything. My dad will be home, too." Elbert's father drove a transcontinental bus and was usually gone for a week or more at a time.

"That's nice, Elbert." Annie smiled, but already her mind was on the patient in the next cubicle. And if she were totally honest with herself, more than a few thoughts were taken up with Rachel, Micah and Simon McKendrick.

The story of Rachel's captivity and return to the States more than likely would be released on the national news broadcasts that evening. She knew because earlier that day she'd fielded two calls from the TV networks wanting verification of her part in the rescue. Annie stuck to her story, the same one she'd given the State Department people in Bangkok two weeks earlier.

She had said she'd known nothing about Rachel or Micah McKendrick being in the hands of the Vietnamese until she was given their papers along with those of the rest of the Amerasian teenagers' relatives. She'd only spoken to Rachel briefly on the plane to Bangkok. She hadn't seen her since. She hoped the phrases didn't sound as rehearsed to the TV reporters as they did to her own ears. When asked if she believed there were other Americans still being held captive in the jungles of Southeast Asia, Annie told the truth: if there were, she hoped they would be released immediately, but of any captured Americans, she herself had no proof. Her main interest, she repeated, was in the well-being of the thousands of half-American orphans left behind.

One of the reporters appeared slightly interested in what she had to say, but only slightly. He asked if she would agree to be interviewed at a later date if he decided to do a feature on the Amerasians' plight. Annie said that she would be more than willing, eager, but she seriously doubted if the man would follow through. Two weeks earlier the groups' return from Vietnam had stirred barely a ripple in the media. The second network representative hadn't even bothered to ask about the Amerasian orphans.

No one was aware she'd known Rachel fourteen years ago in Saigon. She didn't intend to offer the information, either. Annie just hoped the media wouldn't hound Rachel unmercifully; her adjustment would be difficult enough without unwanted publicity. But she had a feeling that hope was in vain.

"I DON'T THINK ANYONE WILL find us here." Simon settled back in the rattan chair. It creaked in protest and he made a face. "These things are damned uncomfortable."

"But they go so well with the decor." Rachel waved her hand in an expansive gesture. The restaurant's interior was a cross between a beachcomber's heaven and a gardener's nightmare. There were plants hanging from the ceiling, sitting in huge pots on the floor, even small potted ferns on the glass-topped tables that matched the high-back chairs. In the few places where there were no plants, there were fishing nets and glass floats and seashells. One entire wall was taken up by an immense aquarium filled with colorful and exotic tropical fish. A "yuppie" bar, Simon had called it and then explained the unfamiliar term.

There were so many unfamiliar things. Her head whirled when she tried to remember them all. How to run the microwave oven and the VCR; what a compact disc was and why it was better than a record album or cassette tape; Iran and Iraq, Contras and Sandinistas, Reagan and Gorbachev; Star Wars—the movies and the weapon; artificial hearts and AIDS. The list was endless. She was afraid she'd never catch up.

"This place has a great view of the sunset, I've been told," Simon broke into her thoughts. "At least it would have if it weren't pouring rain." His tone was as ironic as her own. He looked out the window. Breakers rushed toward the shore, pushed along by an angry wind that sent low gray clouds, heavy with rain, lumbering across the sky.

"So much for Florida's sunny Gulf Coast." Rachel grinned. Her brother was scowling as if he intended to chase away the rain with his bare hands, or the force of his will. Simon had always been that way, quietly determined. She wondered for a brief, bleak moment why he hadn't come for her, or warned her in time for her and Father Pieter to escape that long ago April, but resolutely put the question from her mind. Time later to confront old ghosts. This evening she intended to enjoy herself. She was wearing a new mint-green blouse and long full skirt. She'd had her hair cut and permed. She'd gained eleven pounds. She was clean and dry and knew where her next meal was coming from. Best of all, when she looked in the mirror, someone familiar, not herself yet really, but not the hundred-year-old crone she'd resembled those first few days, stared back at her.

The waiter brought their drinks. Rachel stirred her club soda and lime with a red swizzle stick and studied the oversized menu. She was feeling a lot better but her stomach still wouldn't tolerate alcohol. It would, however, tolerate a huge baked potato with butter and sour cream. She told Simon so.

He took a swallow of his beer while she continued to read. "Actually, this isn't typical weather for Sarasota in the middle of December. Dad assures me it's usually great this time of year. That's why they moved down here when they sold the hardware back in Pennsylvania." He looked out the window again, scowling at the downpour once more.

"I'll have to go back there," she said thoughtfully. "See the aunts and uncles, the cousins. I'll have to face Kyle's mom and dad sometime."

"Slow down." Simon grinned but his eyes and expression were serious. "You've got the rest of your life to do all those things. Don't try to make up for all the lost years at once."

Rachel nodded, relieved to hear her wishes spoken aloud. "There's plenty of time to go back home." She changed the subject abruptly. "I hate leaving the folks at the mercy of those reporters tonight."

"They'll do fine." Simon signaled to the waiter that they were ready to order. "Mom unplugged the phone before we left and tonight's their bridge night. They'll be out of the condo in an hour. We'll have a nice quiet dinner—how about the stone crab legs? They're out of this world." Rachel nodded agreement. He gave the order to the waiter and settled back to continue their talk. "Even if we dawdle over dessert and coffee, I'll still have you home by nine-thirty. Bedtime."

"Eleven-year-old children go to bed at nine-thirty," Rachel complained.

"All right." Simon held up his hand to show he had no intention of starting an argument. "You can stay up till ten, but don't expect me to take the blame when Mom and Dad walk in and find you still awake."

"Simon." Rachel studied the bubbles rushing to the top of her glass. He was joking. She was serious. "They're driving me crazy." She looked up and knew her eyes were bright with tears. She blinked them away, disgusted with her own weakness. Her brother was watching her carefully as she knew he would be, as they all did, his hazel eyes narrowed in concern.

"They love you, Rachel." He ran his thumb up and down the side of the beer bottle, avoiding looking directly at her. "We all do. Mom and Dad are trying, maybe too hard, to make it all up to you."

"You can't." Rachel didn't mean to speak so harshly but she couldn't help herself. She stopped, took a deep breath and went on. "I love all of you, too. I know everyone means well. Mom and Dad . . . they're just too close." She broke off, unable to put her feelings into words. She had to be careful. She cried so easily. Everything, anything, a look, a touch, a few bars of music from some half-remembered song, brought tears. How could she explain? Did Simon realize how important the paper-thin shell of composure she'd created for herself was to her sanity, her very fragile peace of mind? She reached out, touched his wrist, tentatively, fleetingly, then pulled back. "Simon, I'm not used to love."

"Do you want to come and stay at my place?" Rachel blessed his matter-of-fact tone of voice, his lack of emotional reaction to her outburst. He understood, he loved her, too, but he wouldn't crowd her, wouldn't suffocate her with emotions she couldn't yet return. "You'd be alone most of the time. I'll be out of the country on an...assignment...again soon. I don't think you're ready to drive in D.C. traffic. Are you up to tackling public transit?"

Rachel shook her head. Crowds terrified her. "I never did like taking the bus. And I'll never be ready to drive in D.C. traffic. I'd feel safer driving the pace car at the Indianapolis 500." She shuddered, only slightly exaggerating the anxiety speeding along the Beltway had produced in her those first few days back in civilization.

"You'd be lonely and at loose ends and Mom and Dad would be worried sick." Simon summed up the situation in a nutshell.

"I know." Rachel felt fatigue wash over her. She raised her hand to her temple to massage away the tension, then deliberately lowered it to her lap. It was still so hard to concentrate sometimes. The doctors had told her that her difficulty concentrating, like her fear of crowds and occasional anxiety attacks, would diminish as she grew stronger, more able to cope with the high-tech world she'd so suddenly been thrust back into. But it hadn't happened as yet, and she'd been back nearly a month. "I was going to ask Micah to take me north with him. His work sounds fascinating. I thought I might be able to help him correlate his research, file, type. I can still do that. But he left in such a hurry I never got a chance."

Micah had disappeared the day after Thanksgiving, saying he'd been away from his work and his research far too long. He hadn't asked her to go with him. He'd had his fill of newspaper and television reporters, pencil pushers from State and Army Intelligence and even a few she suspected of being with the CIA. Micah had changed so much, became taciturn and moody. He was far more a stranger to her than Simon, although her youngest brother, too, seemed to have a lot to hide at times.

"If you go back to D.C. with me you'll be alone a great deal of the time. Is that what you want?" His question interrupted her thoughts.

"No." She spoke too loudly, too quickly. Her hands trembled. She set the glass down on the glass-topped table very carefully. "I... I don't want to be alone, either. Alone with nothing to do." She wasn't able to hide the sheer terror the thought produced; too many hours of solitude to think about the past, to think about what was, what might have been, what was to come.

"Would you like to spend some time with Annie Simpson?" The question surprised her. From the look on Simon's face she suspected he'd surprised himself with the question. The waiter arrived with their salads. Rachel welcomed the interruption. Did she want to see Annie again? She had known Annie right before the bad times. She thought about it while the young man with a blond crew cut and two earrings in his left ear asked if they wanted fresh-ground pepper on their salads. They both declined and he bowed himself away from the table.

Annie, smiling and easygoing, full of common sense and a heart as big as all outdoors. She was a link with the darkness of the past, it was true, but Rachel sensed her friend could also be a bridge to the future.

"Yes." Rachel spoke before she could have second thoughts. She was amazed by the surety she could hear in her voice. "I'd like to see Annie again."

"ANNIE SIMPSON, PLEASE."

The voice on the other end of the phone line was achingly familiar. Annie had heard it in her thoughts, in her dreams, a hundred times since she'd last seen Simon on the plane in Bangkok. "Simon." His name sifted past her lips, emerging as more of a sigh than a spoken word. Annie straightened her shoulders, ran her fingers through her hair and sat up straighter in her chair. "How did you know to find me here?"

"I have my sources."

Annie swiveled her chair to look out the window of the storefront clinic. It was a dreary sight; trash littered the little-traveled side street of the less than affluent neighborhood. It was raining and cold and the weather report said the rain would soon turn to sleet. "I bet you do." Annie turned away from the depressing scene outside and her eyes were caught and held by the twinkling lights of the small Christmas tree sitting on the corner of the receptionist's desk. She smiled, she couldn't help herself; it was so good to hear his voice. "Phone taps, spy satellites, people listening at keyholes."

"I hate to disappoint you, but I called Chicago information and got your home listing. Your daughter answered and told me you'd be at this number until six."

"At least." It had been a long day filled with house calls and whining, croupy toddlers. She was tired and it must have been apparent in her voice.

"Is this a bad time to call?"

"No." Even if there were sixty people still sitting on the row of folding chairs along the wall that served as the waiting room, instead of six, she wouldn't have wanted him to hang up. "How is Rachel?" *How are you?* is what she wanted to ask, but she couldn't seem to find the courage. If she closed her eyes she could see his face, remember the touch of his long, strong fingers, the clean, spicy scent of his skin.

"Physically she's doing fine. The doctors have the malaria under control. She's gaining weight, too fast as far as she's concerned, and all things considered, she's in pretty good shape."

"I'm glad." Annie wasn't surprised to hear that Rachel had contracted malaria during her years in Southeast Asia. The disease was, after all, endemic to the region, but in most cases treatment was effective in controlling the infection. "I think of her...of all of you...often." It was as close as she could come to saying how much she had missed him.

"Annie." The name she'd always disliked sounded natural and right coming from Simon.

"Yes?"

"I have a favor to ask of you."

"Anything," Annie replied, and meant it with all her heart.

"Could you find room for Rachel in your house for a couple of weeks?"

"Of course." Annie didn't hesitate, although it would mean shuffling bedrooms around, moving Doug's things into the sparsely furnished spare room in the attic where Chad now slept when he was home. There would be an argument but Doug would understand. She hoped. "When will she be here?"

Simon laughed softly and Annie felt her stomach somersault. A slow, melting heat began low in her middle and spread even lower. His laughter was unforced and natural and very, very sexy. Her body reacted to the stimulus even if she didn't allow her heart and brain to do so. "You don't have to make up your mind this minute, you know."

"I know that. When will she be arriving?" Annie repeated the question, tucking the phone onto her shoulder so that she could initial a patient's chart that the other nurse practitioner on duty had just handed her.

"As soon as we can get a seat on a plane. It's a little easier to fly out of Florida during the holiday rush than it is to fly down here."

"Florida?" Annie had assumed he was calling from Washington. Maybe even from jail. What did they do with spies who disobeyed orders the way he had?

"Our folks have a condo in Sarasota. We hoped the media wouldn't be as much trouble down here. We were wrong. It did take them a couple of days to ferret us out but that was all."

"I'm sorry. I see Rachel's face on every tabloid in the rack at the supermarket. Not to mention *Time* and *Newsweek*."

"It's been a hassle."

"Is that the only reason she needs to get away?" Annie didn't know why she felt compelled to ask that question, but she did.

"No." Simon was silent for a long moment as though choosing his words very carefully. Again Annie had no trouble picturing his expression, the furrow between his dark brows, the strong, clean line of his jaw. "She needs some time and space to find herself, to find a new direction for her life. She has to think beyond day-to-day survival for the first time in a lot of years. She's scared, Annie. She needs someone to talk to who's got a better perspective than my parents. Or Micah and me for that matter. I know it's asking a lot, especially over the holidays...."

Annie didn't let him finish. "I'll do everything I can. Just call and let me know when her plane gets in." A baby started crying beyond the partition that separated the office from the examination cubicles. Someone coughed and shifted restlessly on the squeaky wooden folding chair. Annie didn't want to hang up, but she had to. There was too much work for the other nurse to finish on her own if they were both going to get home at a reasonable hour. It seemed there was never enough time or enough skilled hands to handle the volume of patients, especially at this location, a transitional neighborhood of low-income families and elderly of various ethnic groups. "I have to go, Simon." There was so much more she wanted to say.

"I understand." Was there reluctance in his voice also? She couldn't be sure. "I'll be in touch."

"Simon." She had to know. "Will you be coming with Rachel?" How did you go about renewing a relationship that had never really been? If she hadn't seen Rachel's face on TV or in a newspaper or magazine every few days, she might have come to believe the things that happened in Vietnam had been some kind of strange and exotic dream. She didn't know how to describe her feelings for this enigmatic man. She just knew she wanted very much to see him again.

"No."

"Are you spending the holidays alone?"

"I'll be out of the country." Simon's tone was neutral, without inflection.

"Where?" Annie knew she was out of bounds but didn't care.

"I'm not at liberty to say."

"Of course, I'm sorry." This was why it would never have worked between them. He wasn't at liberty to say and she couldn't keep from asking. "Then I'll wish you a merry Christmas right now."

"Merry Christmas, Annie love." The line went dead.

SIMON LOOKED DOWN at the phone. His hand still rested on the receiver. Why in hell had he said that? "Merry Christmas, Annie love." *Damn it, he had no business saying something like that to her.* It wasn't fair to either of them. It was just that the sound of her voice, warm and sweet like honey in the sunshine, had caught him off guard. Simon turned away from the phone and crossed the high-ceilinged main room of the condo. He opened the sliding glass doors and stepped onto the small wooden patio overhanging the canal that ran to the Gulf of Mexico a quarter of a mile away.

He raked his fingers through his hair, then shoved his hands into the back pockets of his jeans. The wind had been blowing steadily from the west for the past three days and he could hear the breakers washing ashore in the distance. The rain was over, the sun warm and golden bright as it dipped toward the horizon. Behind him the small, ultramodern condominium was silent and deserted. His parents and Rachel had taken advantage of the improved weather to drive down the coast to Venice and comb the sand around the Venice pier for sharks' teeth, the main tourist activity along that stretch of beach.

Simon had declined the invitation to accompany them. He needed solitude almost as badly as Rachel. He'd been trying to tell himself for the past five weeks that he wasn't in love with Annie Simpson. He'd almost convinced himself, too. Until today. Until five minutes ago when he'd spoken with her, heard the caring and longing in her voice.

It was probably a good thing he was leaving for Nicaragua the day after tomorrow. Things were heating up down there again. State didn't always trust the information they got from the CIA operatives. Hell, they almost never trusted it. They wanted their own observer and they'd called him. The thing was, he could have turned down the assignment if he'd wanted to. There were plenty of young hotshots who'd have jumped at the chance. The truth was he wasn't ready to retire. Not yet. He still enjoyed the game of cat and mouse. And the danger, he might as well admit it.

He needed all his wits about him on this jaunt. He couldn't take the chance of seeing Annie again, of talking to her, laughing with her, touching her. All the excuses he'd made to himself, that what he felt for her was nothing more than friendship, gratitude, a sense of responsibility for placing her in a dangerous situation, were arguments no more substantial than the last of the rain clouds in the blue Florida sky overhead.

He'd have to face the truth if he saw her—all of it. He loved Annie Simpson. He thought she might be falling in love with him as well. Except that it wasn't that simple. Few things were. Love and marriage and his line of work just didn't mix. He'd tried it once before and watched love die. Jenna, his wife, had tried. So had he, but their love wasn't strong enough to withstand the pressures of his unexplained absences and inability to confide in his wife just why the long separations were necessary.

When he was gone, out of touch, it was as if he'd never existed, as if he were dead, Jenna had told him tearfully. She also told him she didn't intend to stick around until that really happened. That had been eight years ago. He didn't work the same way now, but his job was still dangerous. If he got caught in Nicaragua he'd most likely end up in a jail cell, not in front of a firing squad, but State would deny they had anything to do with him and he'd be left to fend for himself in a Central American jail.

As good as dead to his family and friends.

He couldn't ask Annie to be part of that kind of life. He didn't want to watch love die the way it had with Jenna. He was who he was, and what he was. He couldn't change that. He didn't have the kind of skills that looked good on a corporate résumé. He wasn't altogether certain he wanted to. That was the stalemate. So for both their sakes, he wasn't going to fall any further in love with Annie Simpson. And he was going to do his damnedest to see that she didn't fall the rest of the way in love with him.

CHAPTER EIGHT

"BÂY GIO MÂY GIO RÔI?"

Leah looked at the clock on the mantelpiece. *"Bây gio là chín gio."*

"Cám on ông." Rachel placed her hands together and made a polite little bow of thanks.

"What did you say? What did you say?" Mike demanded, throwing a handful of tinsel at the Christmas tree. These impromptu lessons in Vietnamese had been going on since Rachel's arrival three days earlier.

"She asked me what time it is," Leah explained, plucking half the tinsel from the spot where it had landed and redistributing it more evenly along the branches above the twins' heads. Earlier that evening Chad and Doug had set the seven-foot fir in its customary place in front of the big window in the living room before leaving to drop Doug off at the fast-food restaurant where he was working the late shift. "I said it was nine o'clock. How was my accent, Rachel?"

"Very good. You learn quickly."

"It's fun." Leah plugged in the colored Christmas lights. Somewhat to Annie's surprise, they all worked.

"Way to go, Leah," Mike said. "Mom always makes a mess of the lights."

"I do not," Annie said, but without much conviction. It seemed that no matter how carefully she packed the lights and decorations after the holidays each year, when it came time to get them out of storage again, some strange electrical malaise seemed to infect each and every string.

"Yes you do, Mom," Leah said kindly but firmly. "You're hopeless with Christmas lights."

"They twinkle," Rachel said, reaching out to touch a blue one near her hand. There were stress lines around her eyes and a small furrow of tension between her brows, but she was smiling and seemed to be enjoying herself. Annie leaned back in the big wing chair by the fireplace and put her feet up on the hassock Leah had pulled into place for her. It had been a long, hard week at the clinics and she was so tired she didn't even have enough energy to help decorate the tree. Contentedly she watched her youngest sons, her daughter and Rachel as they worked. Other people might have prettier and more sophisticated, color-coordinated, theme-oriented trees in their homes, but each and every ornament of theirs, however shabby, held precious memories of holidays past.

"They're called chaser lights," Jon explained. "Let's see. I don't know the word for chaser but light is *môk cái dèn*."

"Very good." Rachel looked impressed as she added another handful of tinsel strands to the tree.

"I know some Vietnamese, too," Mike said with an air of bravado. So far he'd paid little attention to the language lessons. "I can say good morning, good afternoon, good evening and goodbye."

"Big deal," Jon scoffed, balancing a battered papier-mâché angel Doug had made in the second or third grade—Annie couldn't remember which—on a branch six inches above his head. "*Chào ông*. They're all the same words. *Chào ông*, Mike. *Chào ông*, Mom."

"Wrong," Mike chortled with something other than the Christmas spirit evident in his tone. "Not 'Mom.' It's *me*. That's the word for mom." He pronounced the Vietnamese word as though he was saying *map* and couldn't manage the *p* sound. Annie recognized his earnest attempt at duplicating Rachel's pronunciation and accent and was proud of his effort. "Isn't that right, Rachel?"

"Close enough." Rachel looked as if she were trying not to laugh. "*Chào ông* is a lot like the Hawaiian word *aloha*. It has different meanings in different situations."

"I think that's a stupid way to talk," Mike said.

"You think everything's stupid," Jon shot back.

"*I* think this tree looks great," Rachel interrupted, averting an argument. "It's the first Christmas tree I've seen in..." Her voice trailed off into silence. She busied herself, placing a candy cane on a branch just so.

"Hey, guys," Annie said, before the lull in the conversation could stretch out long enough to be noticed. "I'm hungry. How about you?"

"Yeah," the twins chorused. Their minds were always perfectly attuned when it came to the subject of food. "Pepperoni and green-olive pizza from the Pizza Joint."

"Now why did I know that's what you would want?" Annie laughed delightedly. They were such lovable imps.

"Because it's Christmas pizza," Mike said, shaking his head as if to indicate Annie must have lost her mind to have forgotten something that important. "We always have green-olive and pepperoni pizza when we finish putting up the Christmas tree."

"It's tradition," Jon explained helpfully for Rachel's sake. "At least it's our family tradition."

"I heard Chad come in the back door. Why don't you get some money out of my purse and see if he'll drive you over to the Pizza Joint. There's no school tomorrow so you can play video games while you're waiting for our order."

"Rad," Mike said, kicking out of his way the empty cardboard box for the mantelpiece decorations that Annie had put up earlier.

"You get our coats, Mike," suggested his more practical brother. "I'll tell Chad Mom said he had to take us now."

"Not tell," Annie said, despairing of ever teaching the two boys manners. "Ask."

"Right, Mom." Two pairs of brown eyes met in understanding. It was only five days until Christmas, after all, and it wasn't smart to antagonize present-buying parents this close to the big day. "We'll ask."

"Politely," Mike added for good measure, drawing the syllables out to inordinate length to emphasize his point.

His twin elbowed him in the stomach for his pains.

"Mom, he hit me." Mike looked on the verge of retaliating in kind.

"Enough! Go!" Annie laid her head against the back of the chair in mock defeat. "I'm raising barbarians," she moaned, shaking her head.

"They're great kids." Rachel put the lid on the ornament box and stacked the empty lights box on top. "All done."

"It is a radical tree," Leah said, standing back to admire their handiwork.

"When I was your age radical meant someone burning his draft card or the ROTC building on campus," Rachel said with a small, puzzled laugh. "Now it means 'far out.'"

"Far out?" Leah laughed, too. "That's weird. I guess I should say it's a lovely tree. That's what I really meant." She adjusted the papier-mâché angel and moved two glass ornaments from a cluster of four or five that Mike claimed as his own and had bunched together on two adjoining branches. "That's better." Leah nodded, satisfied. "I'll take the boxes down to the basement," she offered.

"Thanks for taking care of the mess, honey."

"I'll be in my room. Call me when the pizza gets here."

"Okay." Annie closed her eyes a moment and savored the sudden quiet in the room. The fire popped and crackled behind a wire screen on her left, the tree blinked and sparkled, and the faint aroma of fresh-cut pine lingered in the air. Annie smiled at Leah's slim back as she disappeared toward the kitchen and the basement stairs at the end of the hall. She was growing into such a beautiful and intelligent young woman.

Rachel curled up in a corner of the couch, tucking her feet under her. Annie watched her from half-closed eyes. The Christmas tree was directly behind her, outlining her slender figure with a halo of twinkling colored lights. Rachel, who had been studying the fire, glanced in Annie's direction and saw her watching her.

"I've been dreading the holidays," she said in a rush, reluctantly, as if she felt guilty for making the admission. "But now..." Rachel made a sweeping gesture with her hand that included the tree, the candles and pine garland on the mantel, the Christmas cards taped to the mirror in the hall. "It's all so much like I remember when I was a little girl back in Pennsylvania." She rested her cheek on her hand and stared into the fire thoughtfully.

"What's wrong, Rachel?" Annie held her breath. She'd been very careful not to put Rachel on the spot by asking questions that she wouldn't feel comfortable answering. After all, she'd offered the woman a sanctuary from publicity and from her parents' overprotectiveness. She didn't want to be guilty of the same behavior. Annie knew Rachel's adjustment to being back home would take time. She wanted to help, but she felt it was important for Rachel to move into the mainstream at her own speed.

"I feel dreadfully guilty for leaving my parents alone in Florida at Christmas time. This is the first Christmas in twenty years we could have spent together as a family. Now Micah is back in Michigan with his birds and Simon is God knows where. My parents are both in their seventies. How many more Christmases will they have?" She made a steeple of her hands and placed them against her lips for a moment, as if trying to find the words she wanted to speak. Annie had noticed the same thing once or twice before and realized that Rachel must be searching for English words that she'd nearly forgotten after so many years of disuse.

"I'm sure they understand how you feel, Rachel." Annie wasn't even certain Rachel heard what she said.

"You can't imagine what the reporters were like," Rachel continued. "And Mom and Dad meant well but they hovered so closely. The happiness..." Rachel laughed self-consciously. "I've had to adjust to so many things these past years, Annie." She stared into the fire, but Annie knew the images she saw in the dancing flames were of far away and long away. "Heat and cold in the mountains, snakes, monsoons, diseases there aren't even names for." She shrugged, a gesture that conveyed her inability to describe what she had seen and experienced. "Prison..." Her voice faltered, faded, then grew strong. "I wouldn't allow myself to believe I'd ever see my brothers or my parents again. Then, overnight, everything changed and the one thing I've found I can't deal with yet is happiness. It's just too difficult to handle."

"Christmas is a time for families," Annie said thoughtfully, a germ of an idea taking root in her thoughts. In the space of a heartbeat she pushed the thought aside to concentrate on what Rachel was saying. Later there would be time to plan for Christmas surprises. Now she had to give Rachel all her attention.

Annie didn't know how to answer the more difficult questions Rachel's confession had sparked in her mind. She didn't feel qualified to counsel the other woman. Her life, except for her air force tour of duty in Southeast Asia and her escape from Saigon with the children, had been free of trauma.

Until Mike's death.

She rubbed the bare third finger of her left hand. She'd stopped wearing her wedding ring soon after she'd returned from Vietnam. Her husband, no matter how much she loved him and still cherished his memory, was dead and she was not. Life went on and you made the most of it. The words sounded too simplistic, too clichéd to say aloud, no matter how profound the truths behind them were. Still, being unable to find just the right combination of words didn't deter Annie from wanting to say them.

"I can imagine a little of what you've been through. I understand about being afraid of happiness, a little, too. When my life is going along smoothly, everything working out just as it should, I always wonder what's going to go wrong. What crisis will be next on the cosmic agenda? Mike always said I was never happy unless I had something to worry about. Then he died and I learned what true unhappiness really was. If there's one thing I've worked hard at since his death, it's trying not to worry so much about what might be."

"Or what was," Rachel said very quietly, almost as if she were talking to herself.

"Or what was." Annie knelt on the hassock in front of the wing chair. She put her hand over Rachel's where it rested on her knee. "You didn't let anything you went through in Vietnam break your spirit. Don't let fear rob you of your future."

"What if I lose it all again?" There was anguish in Rachel's voice, dread in her eyes. Annie felt tears push against the back of her throat, but she swallowed them. "What if I never feel whole again inside?"

"You will, Rachel. Believe that. You have to be strong. You'll want to love again, to reach out again, I promise you." Tears replaced the fear in Rachel's eyes but she blinked them away, not allowing them to fall. She hadn't cried at all that Annie was aware of. For Rachel, Annie suspected, tears represented a loss of control that she didn't feel strong enough to deal with.

"Don't expect too much of me, Annie." Rachel's voice was low, made ragged at the edges by unshed tears. She didn't look directly at Annie but just past her left shoulder.

Annie pressed Rachel's knee, forcing her to look into her eyes. "Don't ask too little of yourself."

Rachel was silent but nodded once, reluctantly, and smiled.

A car door slammed in the driveway. Chad and the twins had returned from the Pizza Joint. Upstairs she heard Leah's bedroom door open and close. There was so much more she wanted to say, so many more things she knew within her woman's heart that Rachel needed and wanted to say in return. But Rachel also needed the two or three minutes of peace and quiet they had left to pull herself together. "I could use a glass of wine," Annie said a shade too brightly. "How about you? I have a jug of rosé in the refrigerator that isn't half-bad."

"I'd like that." Rachel sat upright on the couch, lifting her hands to run her fingers through the shoulder-length curls of black hair, the gray in it now skillfully hidden by Leah's favorite stylist. Annie thought Rachel looked years younger.

Annie touched her own hair in a reflexive gesture. There were more and more gray hairs showing up in the unruly red mane these days, too, but if the truth be told she almost welcomed them. Anything that toned down the abominable carroty red was an improvement in her eyes. Anyway, in three months she'd be forty years old and heaven knew she'd earned each and every one of them. She wondered if Simon would notice the gray. If she ever saw the man again, that was. Right now that didn't seem to be much of a possibility. With a sigh Annie headed for the kitchen.

MICHAEL AND JONATHON CAME racing into the living room like twin cyclones. "I'll put on the Christmas albums," Mike shouted.

"I'll light the candles and turn off the lamps," Jon called back just as loudly. Rachel never failed to marvel at their energy level. It always seemed to be hovering somewhere just below a state of volcanic eruption. They were so very different from the children of her village. Not only because they were born into a civilization half a world away and light-years more advanced than the simple hill people who had taken her into their homes, but because they were allowed to be children.

The war in Vietnam had been fought in Laos, too, secretly for the most part, she now knew, and the Hlông people had been loyal and fierce warriors. But the long years of fighting, the strife that followed the end of the Americans' involvement in the region, had drained them of their strong young men. There were almost no able-bodied adult males in the village when she first arrived with Father Pieter, only very old men and baby boys. A blessing in disguise perhaps, she'd since discovered, because in their secluded mountain valley they'd been left alone, too isolated and of too little value to be bothered with. But when she left, some of the oldest of those little boys were growing into manhood and going off to fight in small marauding bands that harassed the Vietnamese army units that patrolled the hills and jungle trails and would eventually bring the wrath of the conquerors down on them once again.

"Isn't Christmas great, Rachel?" Mike asked ingenuously as he sat down on the sofa beside her. "We always have pepperoni and green-olive pizza after we trim the tree."

Rachel smiled. "You're a very lucky boy."

"I know." He cocked his head. "Did they have Christmas where you've been?" Rachel wondered just how much Annie had told her youngest sons about their houseguest.

"No. Christmas is a Christian holiday. Where I lived the people worshiped Buddha and spirits called *phi* they believe live in everything and everybody."

"Evil spirits. Radical," Mike said, impressed.

Rachel didn't feel up to explaining the villagers' religion, a blend of Buddhism and animist beliefs, in great detail. "Do you know who Buddha was?" she asked, uncertain what ten-year-olds were taught these days.

"In social studies class we learned that a lot of people worship him in China and Japan and India. Places like that," Jon said with a frown that showed how hard he was trying to remember what he had been taught about the strange religion.

"His statues are always round fat guys with jewels in the bellies," Mike added helpfully. "I've seen pictures. Remember in the book Mom brought back from Thailand, Jon?"

"I read it," Jon announced proudly. "You only looked at the pictures."

Rachel laughed. She couldn't help it. Mike grinned, pleased that their byplay had produced such a response.

"I guess most of Buddha's statues are pretty roly-poly," she admitted. "But he was a very great and good man and someday I'll tell you how the Hlông celebrate their holidays. Right now I think the pizza is on its way."

Leah came into the room with plates, napkins and silver on a tray. Annie also carried a tray with goblets of soft drinks for the boys and Leah and wine for the adults. A few steps behind her, Chad appeared with the biggest pizza Rachel had ever seen. The twins sat cross-legged on the floor in front of the coffee table. Annie pulled a pillow off the couch and did the same. Leah sat on the couch next to Rachel and Chad took his place in the wing chair by the fire. Annie served the pizza with a great deal of flair and much kibitzing from the audience.

Rachel accepted a slice of pizza presented to her on a china plate. The napkins were linen and the silver old and heavy. Chad caught her looking at the beautiful, intricate pattern on the handle of her fork.

"We always use Mom's good china for Christmas pizza," he said with a crooked smile that Rachel couldn't help but return. "It's tradition."

"I have no idea how it got started." Annie's tone was rueful but her eyes sparkled with merriment. "All I know is five years ago I had a china service for sixteen. Today it's down to twelve and almost all the casualties occurred at Christmas time."

"Pepperoni and olive pizza should be on everyone's list of holiday goodies," Rachel decreed, wiping tomato sauce off her chin.

"Yeah," Mike said, attacking his second piece with relish. "Pizza is nature's most perfect food."

"That's milk, dummy." Jon shook his head in disgust. "You're ignorant." He too took a second piece of pizza.

"Am not." Mike looked mutinous.

"Are too."

"Boys. Enough," Annie interjected. "It's too close to Christmas for arguments."

"I'll be glad when the dorm reopens and I can go back to the peace and quiet of academic life," Chad remarked.

"Peace and quiet," Mike hooted. "In your dorm? I've been there when you were playing your stereo loud enough to rattle the window."

"He's right, Chad," Leah said with a smile and a toss of her head. "It's a wonder you're not deaf."

"Look who's talking." Chad wasn't so grown-up he could ignore such a concentrated attack of sibling insults. "You're going to fry your brains with all the hot rollers and curling irons you use on your hair."

"Children. Children." Annie tapped her goblet with the handle of a fork to draw their attention. "Let us remember that Santa and his elves are watching all the boys and girls to see who is naughty and who's nice. We wouldn't want to find our stockings empty on Christmas morning because we'd misbehaved, now would we?"

The twins sat up straight, looking angelic. "No, ma'am."

"And of course that goes for older children, too."

"I'm always good, Mom," Chad said with a wicked grin. "And if I can't be good, I'm careful."

"Chad!" Annie almost choked on a swallow of wine.

"Got ya, Mom." Chad stood up and bent down to give Annie a quick hug. "I'm going over to Roger Carmine's to listen to his new CD player. Don't wait up for me. Doug's got a ride home from work, so don't worry about him, either," he added, anticipating his mother's next question.

"Drive carefully." Annie smiled up at her tall, handsome son. Rachel felt her heart twist inside her. Somehow she knew her son would have grown to be just as strong and handsome as Chad.

"Good night, Rachel. Night, Leah."

"What about us?" Mike demanded.

"Get to bed on time. And save some of that pizza for Doug. You know he's always hungry when he gets home from work." Chad faked a punch in the air at the twins.

They groaned and went back to eating pizza as if they might never get another meal. "I can't wait until I'm old enough to drive a car," Mike said under his breath. "I'm going to stay out as late as I want, whenever I want."

Annie, overhearing the remark as Rachel had, just shook her head as if to say, "What can I do with those two?"

Rachel looked into the dying embers of the fire. In a way because she had stayed behind that day in Saigon, she felt a special closeness to Annie and her children. Without her there would be no happy gathering in Annie's comfortable living room. It helped, a little, to know that her sacrifice hadn't been completely in vain.

But she also couldn't help wondering what life would have been like for herself and her brothers if they had never been involved in the Vietnam conflict. What would Christmas in her parents' home be like with a gaggle of noisy, happy grandchildren laughing and arguing around their tree? Would she have liked her sisters-in-law? Would she be thinking of what to buy for her nieces and nephews, deciding if her own children were old enough for a stereo and a telephone of their own, instead of sitting at the very edge of Annie's family circle sharing the warmth only from a distance, and mourning what might have been?

No, not mourning. Rachel was enough of a survivor to know that way lay madness. Annie was right. She couldn't let what was over and done with dominate her thoughts or she'd be paralyzed with fear and regrets and never get on with the business of her life. She wasn't as optimistic as Annie. She didn't think she could love again, not one to one, not as a man and woman should love one another. But she could give of herself in other ways, and as soon as the holidays were over, she'd begin to search out opportunities to do just that.

Perhaps she shouldn't have run away from the reporters, left her parents alone for the holidays in Florida. The press would have grown tired of hounding her soon enough if she'd simply ignored them. If she'd had the courage to do that, her scattered family might be together today. But she'd let her uncertainty overwhelm her, and now she was alone. Among friends but alone nonetheless. It was a familiar feeling but one that was no longer forced upon her by circumstances she couldn't control.

Her own choice. It had been so many years since she had had the luxury of freedom. Rachel smiled to herself. From this day forward, no matter what happened, she controlled her own fate. She was free merely to enjoy the holidays. Tomorrow there would be snow, the television weatherman had said. Snow. She hadn't seen snow in years and years. Even without her family beside her to help her celebrate, it was going to be a very merry Christmas and, God willing, a happy New Year.

LE THI LOOKED UP FROM the book she was reading. Her husband had just entered their small apartment near what had once been the embassy district of the city. She'd closed the shutters on the windows to keep out the hot afternoon sunlight and the room was dusky and cool, the scent of flowers heavy in the air.

"You look tired, Hoang." He had been working too hard in the weeks since the American delegation had gone. She feared for his health.

"Meetings, arguments, endless, fruitless discussions," he said with a great deal of irony in his voice. He loosened his tie and pulled it from the collar of his shirt, undoing the top buttons. Even after all these years she still could not get used to seeing him in Western dress. "The Americans did not win the war. But neither did we. The bureaucrats from Hanoi and their Soviet counterparts have triumphed over us all."

"You do your best." Le Thi placed the book on a small table near her chair and walked into her husband's arms. He bent his head to nuzzle her hair.

"My best is not good enough. We must be allowed to trade with the rest of the world once again. Those in power are too blind to see." He held her tightly for a moment, then let her go with a sigh. "I am a soldier, not a diplomat, but I do what I must do."

"There is more than the usual bickering among the Council of State and the ministers?"

"There is new pressure from the Americans to return their dead and locate the missing. Since Mrs. Phillips was found by that madman, Ky, they are more than ever certain we are withholding information from them."

"Are you, Hoang?" Only in the privacy of their home dared she ask such a question.

"I cannot be certain what information those at the highest levels are privy to." He walked across the small room to open the wooden shutters and stare out the window at the crowded street below. "I do not know."

"I will make you some tea," Le Thi said quickly, hoping to take his mind off the problems he faced daily in his work. "You'll feel better after that. And I have something special. There was shrimp in the market today." They both knew she referred to the illegal black market that thrived in the city. "I will prepare it for our dinner."

"I look forward to it." Hoang's words were preoccupied. His mind elsewhere. A small tremor of disquiet stirred her blood.

"What is it, Hoang? You are concerned with more than the latest round of backbiting and tunnel vision among the ministers."

"You know me too well, Le Thi. I have been ordered to prepare to leave for New York City."

"The United States?" Le Thi felt the room begin to spin in slow, dizzying spirals before her eyes. She took a deep breath and pressed her hand against her heart, which was suddenly jumping in her chest like a small bird caught in a net. *Dear Lord, gentle Buddha, have you answered my mother's prayer at last?*

"I am to join our delegation at the United Nations before the turn of their new year. We shall be among the Yankee dogs for that most conspicuous of their festivals, Christmas." He said the word with a bitter twist of his lips. Hoang was not a Christian, or a Buddhist, or a Communist in his belief, only in the lip service he was required to pay to the party. He cared only for Vietnam and he suffered because his countrymen did. "Will you accompany me to America, Le Thi, and lighten my exile?"

New York. Le Thi had no idea how far that city was in distance from Chicago, Illinois, where Annie Simpson lived. She knew only that she would get there, no matter the difficulty involved. "I will go with you, Hoang." She could barely force the words past the great lump in her throat.

"Thank you, my love." He didn't seem to notice her strange behavior, preoccupied as he was with his own problems. "I think I'd like that tea now, if you will make it for me."

Le Thi's head was spinning with excitement as she left the room to do as he asked. She longed to tell Hoang of her dreams of finding her daughter, but superstitious dread and her worry for his well-being kept her silent. She had prayed over and over again to find a way of going to America, but she had believed her prayers were in vain.

Now in only a matter of a few short weeks she would be able to locate the child she'd lost so long ago. And if the gods smiled on her, soon, very soon, she would have her daughter with her again.

CHAPTER NINE

IT WAS SNOWING HEAVILY as Annie walked down the steps of St. Timothy's. There was almost an inch of fine, powdery snow on the sidewalk that hadn't been there when they arrived for midnight mass just a little over an hour before. Annie looked up at the dark gray sky that seemed to hover only a few feet above the church steeple. Starry flakes stuck to her eyelashes and tickled her nose. The weatherman had predicted a white Christmas, but a major snowfall, as this one was evidently going to be, was more than anyone had bargained for.

Behind her, light spilled through the stained-glass windows beside the carved wooden doors, coloring the falling snow in shades of red and blue, purple and gold. Annie smiled. There ought to be snow for Christmas no matter how inconvenient it made getting around. She pulled on her gloves and adjusted the fur-trimmed hood of her bright red, calf-length coat. The wind was sharp and cold, burning her lungs and making her eyes sting with crystal tears. But the night air felt good after the warmth of the overcrowded church, and Annie took a long, deep breath, then started walking briskly down the street in the direction of home.

She had slipped out of the service before the benediction so that she could be there when the others arrived. She wasn't Catholic, but going to midnight mass Christmas Eve was a family tradition. Chad and Doug had been baptized into the faith by Father Pieter at the orphanage. Mike and she had honored that commitment when they adopted the boys. Leah and the twins had followed in their footsteps at the parish school but were Methodists, nominally, as Annie was herself.

Usually Leah or the twins walked with her after the service, but tonight she was alone. Doug had wheedled the use of the VW out of his brother and driven himself to church. Chad would see to it that the others, including Rachel and her parents, made it back to the house for hot chocolate and cookies. As for herself, Annie didn't mind the cold snow, the three-block walk through Christmas Eve quiet streets. The peace and solitude were good for her soul.

In reality there had been very little solitude in the Simpson household the past two days. Annie smiled again, pushing her hands deep into her pockets to ward off the cold. Her surprise invitation to Rachel's parents to join them for the holidays had been a risky undertaking and she knew it, but so far everything was going well. The elder McKendricks were staying at a nearby motel, doing their best to give Rachel all the time and all the space she needed to accept their love. Yesterday they'd gone shopping, not joining the multitudes of last-minute bargain hunters at the mall, but in the block of antique shops and boutiques that had been restored along Front Street. The trio stopped for lunch near Annie's main clinic and she joined them. Rachel had been relaxed and smiling, her parents talkative and fun to be with as they recounted their adventurous roundabout flight from Florida to O'Hare, which had included stops in New Orleans and St. Louis and, almost, an unscheduled detour to Denver. If Harold and Frances McKendrick were disappointed that neither of their sons was with them for the holidays, their obvious joy at being able to spend Christmas with Rachel eased the pain of separation.

Still, Annie knew in their hearts they were saddened. Her expression tightened into a frown as she lowered her head against the snow-laden wind. This same winter storm that was rapidly giving her neighborhood a Norman Rockwell Christmas card look had also kept Micah away. At least a foot of snow was predicted for Michigan's Upper Peninsula. She recalled for a moment Micah's rough-hewn features, his sad, blue-gray eyes so like Rachel's and his silent, withdrawn manner and wondered if he would have come even if he could.

"We're used to being alone on the holidays," Frances had said with no self-pity in her tone. Micah's home was so isolated, she went on to explain to both Annie and Rachel, that he was sometimes snowed in for days at a time. And Simon? Well, their guess was as good as hers where Simon might be. But having Rachel home safe and sound, being able to celebrate the holiday with their daughter, almost made up for the boys' absence. Her husband had nodded his agreement, but for a quick moment their eyes met across the small restaurant table and conveyed more eloquently than any spoken words that their disappointment, however well they tried to hide it, was great indeed.

It said something about the times they were living in. Families grew apart or were separated often these days. Annie missed her sisters and her parents when they spent holidays in California, but they spoke often on the phone and somehow that made it easier. Mike had been raised in foster homes; his lonely childhood had made her more conscious than ever of her own good fortune in having a loving and stable family background. Still, that didn't always guarantee a happy future, it seemed. Harold and

Frances McKendrick would qualify as good parents in anyone's book. Yet their children were emotionally distanced, alienated by circumstances over which they had no control, the traumas of a war long past, but still very much a part of their present and their future.

Annie turned the corner, her thoughts still centered on the McKendricks. She looked up the street to see a man's dark figure silhouetted against the lamplight from her living-room window shining onto the porch. She stopped walking, as much puzzled as alarmed. It was after midnight. Most of the houses along the block were already dark, their occupants fast asleep, anticipating an early rising to get turkeys in the oven and to watch small children squeal in delight at the presents under the tree. Even on Christmas Eve no one came visiting at such an hour. Uncertain what to do next, Annie stepped into the shadow of a big maple and watched the man for several seconds, trying to make up her mind.

He rang the doorbell and waited. Annie let out a sigh of relief. At least he wasn't a thief. But who could he be? She noticed a car parked in front of the little park across the street from her house. A rainbow optic sticker from a well-known rental agency sparkled in the reflection of a nearby streetlight. She narrowed her eyes and looked at the tall, dark figure a second time. Could it be Micah McKendrick after all? Had she misjudged him? Had he managed, somehow, to drive hundreds of miles over icy roads to spend this time with his parents and sister? But why would he be driving a rental car? Surely he possessed a vehicle of his own. No, Annie decided, the man on her porch wasn't Micah.

The man turned and started down the steps, obviously convinced no one was home. A familiar square-jawed profile was momentarily outlined against the colored bulbs strung along the porch rail and through the shrubs below. Annie's heart skittered upward to beat high and quick in her throat. She began to walk, quickly, her feet almost flying along the snowy sidewalk. The man wasn't Micah. It was Simon. His name sang through her brain like an angels' chorus straight from heaven.

"Simon." His back was to her. He kept on walking. The wind sighing through the pines in the small park snatched her call and sent it winging away. "Simon!" she cried more loudly. He was going to leave. She started to run as he crossed to his car and unlocked the door. She ran to catch him. Snow crunched under her boots, her breath streamed behind her in tattered clouds. "Simon, wait. Don't go."

He turned at the sound of her voice. He wasn't wearing gloves or a hat and his charcoal-gray jacket didn't seem heavy enough for Chicago in December. He'd turned up his collar to ward off the frigid wind and his hair was full of snow. A two days' growth of beard darkened his jawline. He looked cold and tired and so very, very dear.

"Annie?" He didn't hold out his hands, sweep her into his arms, kiss her until she was breathless and giddy with desire. He just stood there, hands shoved into his pockets. Annie skidded to a halt two steps in front of him. She wasn't certain how best to describe the set look on his face...distant and self-contained...unapproachable...the way Rachel sometimes looked. A look that said, *Don't get too close, I don't want to deal with your emotions.* Annie's heart slipped out of her throat and tumbled into the pit of her stomach. This wasn't the man who'd saved her life in a Saigon hotel room. This wasn't the fantasy lover who'd filled her dreams with fire and passion, awakening her to toss and turn, unfulfilled, through the long December nights. This wasn't the man who'd held her and kissed her and promised her... what?

He'd promised her nothing, really, only that they'd meet again. Simon McKendrick had kept his word in that respect. Here he stood, tall and dark, solid and rock hard. The man she was looking at now wasn't the roguish soldier of fortune who'd stolen her heart with his terrible Bogart imitation and his marvelous smile. This was the mysterious stranger who'd appeared at her door that rainy September night, aloof, controlled and dangerous.

Whatever had passed between them later, half a world away, was evidently forgotten, wiped clean from his memory as if it had never been. Or so it seemed from the harsh, uncompromising look on his face. Annie felt like crying. Instead, she spoke the first words that came into her head and hoped her voice wouldn't tremble too badly when she said them.

"ARE YOU LOOKING FOR YOUR parents?"

"Yes, I am." A kind of painful spasm jerked along his spine. *God, just the sound of her voice was enough to make him forget the promise he'd made himself to keep his distance from this woman.* Simon scowled down at Annie's upturned face. Her nose was red with cold, and snow-frosted red curls peeked out from beneath the fur-trimmed hood of her coat. Her slender, arched brows were pulled together into a perplexed frown. It was too dark to read the expression in her brown eyes, but he knew his rudeness was causing her pain.

"They are here, you know," she started talking quickly and a little breathlessly. "They're at mass with Rachel and my children. They'll be along soon. We're having hot chocolate and cookies before they go back to the motel."

It was his turn. He had to say something; he just couldn't stand in the snow staring at her. "I tried to get in touch with them in Florida. When I couldn't reach them I called Micah. He told me they'd come here for Christmas." He hadn't expected his physical reaction to her to be so acute. It was all he could do not to drag Annie into his arms and hold her close, kiss her, caress her, love her the way he'd dreamed of doing through so many sleepless tropical nights. He'd intended to be over her by now. Up until five minutes ago, he'd convinced himself that he couldn't really be in love with her, but obviously he was wrong. The woman who stood before him, the Annie Simpson of flesh and blood, warmth and passion, was just as desirable, just as necessary to his happiness as she'd been when she'd kissed him goodbye on the runway in Bangkok.

"I thought your parents should be with Rachel," she said so softly he could barely hear her above the sound of the wind slipping through the branches of the big maples that lined the quiet residential street. "Christmas is for families, for being together." Her voice trailed off into silence. She clasped her hands in front of her and looked down at the toes of her boots. When she lifted her head once more, the starry brightness of tears swam in her eyes. "Merry Christmas, Simon. I'm glad you're home for the holidays. I'm so happy to see you again." She smiled then, so hesitantly, so sweetly, that all Simon's hard-won resolve blew away on the snowy night wind.

"Annie." He couldn't seem to find the right words, any words really, and he didn't like the helpless feeling that gave him. Yet the need within him to hold her, just to touch her hair, the softness of her skin, was so great it made him ache. He kept staring at her, not realizing how intimidating his expression must appear.

"Simon, are you angry with me? Your parents assumed you wouldn't be back from... from your assignment... in time for Christmas. Rachel didn't want to be alone. I mean, be with strangers...." Annie gave up momentarily on her garbled explanation, took a deep breath and rushed on. "Not that the kids and I are strangers. We love having her with us. And your parents, too. But Rachel needs her family around her even if she isn't ready to admit it. Harold and Frances were lonely in Florida. I could tell when I spoke with them on the phone."

Simon halted the avalanche of words with a finger across her lips. "And Micah?"

"He's snowed in. This storm is a blizzard up north," Annie explained.

"I know." He jerked his head toward the rental car. He ought to tell her Micah wouldn't have come anyway but decided to keep the thought to himself. "My plane got detoured to Indianapolis. I got just about the last rental the airport had."

"The roads must be terrible. It's a hundred miles to Indianapolis. You shouldn't have tried to make it all this way tonight."

"Yes, I did have to try." He reached out to brush a snowflake from her cheek. Her skin was cold to the touch but as soft as velvet. "You did your best to get all the McKendricks together for Christmas, didn't you, Annie?"

"Yes. I'm only sorry it didn't happen."

"I'm sorry, too. But four out of five of us are here now, thanks to you." Simon leaned forward, just to brush a kiss across her lips, he told himself, a small thank-you for what she'd done for his family, nothing more. Their lips met briefly. Hers were warmer than her cheek but just as soft. She turned her head a fraction of an inch. It was as if the tiny movement realigned the universe, set off a chain reaction inside both of them over which they had no control.

"Simon?" His name on her lips was lost in the darkness as he pulled her into his arms, crushed her against him, held her close. She tasted of peppermint. Her hair smelled of incense and snow and flowers in the sunlight. Her soft, rounded curves were hidden beneath the heavy folds of her coat, but his body remembered the delicate weight of her breasts against his chest and the way the flare of her hips fit so perfectly within the cradle of his thighs. She was his match, his mate, and no matter how often his reason attempted to override his emotions, he knew within his heart it was an exercise doomed to defeat.

Simon leaned against the frame of the car so that he could hold her more closely against him. She came into his embrace willingly, eagerly, and he was aware that the passion that flared within him was matched by her own. "I've missed you, Annie. Missed you like hell." His voice sounded strange, hoarse and rough with needs and desires that seemed, now that he'd let them out of the small, dark corner of himself where they'd been caged for so many years, as if they would never be tamed again.

"I thought you'd forgotten me." She framed his face with her hands. Her gloves were thin and supple and he felt the warmth of her fingers against his cold skin. Simon lifted his hands to cover hers. She wasn't wearing her wedding band anymore and he was glad. "One phone call in almost two months. Were you trying to forget me? Was it so easy to put me out of your mind so completely?" She looked him straight in the eye, and despite the near darkness he saw pride and fear mingling in her brown eyes. There was nothing coy or girlish in her question. They were mature adults. They'd both been hurt by love and by life. She was probably as uncertain about her feelings as he was. Sex games were for the young and foolish. He would tell her the truth.

"Yes." Simon settled her more tightly against him. "I did try to forget you." He spread his legs to bring their bodies together as intimately as possible. "I tried like the very devil to forget you. For both our sakes I should still be trying but I can't. Not when you're this close. Not when I can see you and touch you...." The need to feel her lips on his again was so strong it wouldn't be denied. He kissed her once more and as their mouths met and fused he knew a fierce exultant pride at the fire and passion in her response, the wild beat of the pulse in her throat as he slid his hand beneath the collar of her coat. She was his. They belonged together and she knew it.

"I tried, too, but I couldn't get you out of my mind," Annie said when she could speak again. She rested her head against his cheek. "Simon, I'm so glad you came."

"For Rachel's sake?" He tipped her head back to better read her expression in the near darkness.

Annie closed her eyes a moment as if gathering her courage. She spoke very softly. "For my own."

"Help me, Annie. I think I'm..." Simon never finished the declaration of love, which is what it would have been, despite the clamor of warning sirens going off in his brain. A car turned the corner at the end of the block. Headlights pinned them squarely in the glare.

"My kids," Annie said, stepping backward out of his embrace before he could stop her. Her eyes widened, losing the sexy, heavy-lidded look she'd worn just heartbeats before. "Do you think they saw us?" Her hands flew to tuck straying red curls back inside the fur-trimmed hood.

"Whoever's driving probably did." Simon pushed his hand through his hair in frustration. The spell was broken; the moment for speaking of love had passed.

"Oh, Lord, Chad. What will he say?" The cold had brought color into Annie's cheeks, but Simon suspected she was blushing as well. Obviously, having her children catch her necking with a strange man in the middle of the street wasn't something that happened every day in the Simpson household. For that matter, his parents and sister finding him holding a woman in his arms in the middle of a midnight-quiet, snow-covered street wasn't something that happened to him every day, either. "How will I explain?"

"How do you want to explain me?" Simon reached out and captured her hand as she turned to walk away. The station wagon was turning into the driveway.

Annie glanced across the street but made no move to break away from his light hold on her wrist. "I don't know," she said honestly. "I need some time."

Hearing Annie voice her reservations aloud caused a surprisingly sharp pain in his heart. "Then all you have to say is nothing at all." Simon started to cross the street, putting distance between them when he saw his mother and father get out of the station wagon. "The return of one of the prodigal McKendrick sons will cause enough excitement for tonight. You won't have to explain to anyone." He couldn't remember the last time he'd done anything quite so adolescent. Walking away from what was between them wasn't going to solve anything. The unfortunate and unlooked-for reality of falling in love at forty-one is that the condition seemed to produce the emotional reactions of a sixteen-year-old. He'd never felt so off balance in his life.

Annie didn't move from where she was standing beside his car, forcing him to stop and turn toward her when she spoke. "I know I don't have to explain my actions to anyone. But if I choose to do so, I'll say I was welcoming a friend…." She walked toward him and held out her hand. "A very special friend."

"MOM? ARE YOU ASLEEP?"

Annie looked at the clock on her beside table. It was almost ten. She wasn't asleep, not really. But she had been dreaming. Dreaming of the things all women dream of when they're falling in love. Even the dry-as-dust article on record-keeping and charting procedures she'd been reading in the nursing journal lying open across her stomach hadn't been boring enough to put her peacefully to sleep, only allowed her fantasies to run rampant as they had so often these past days. "I'm just reading, Leah honey," she said untruthfully. "Come on in."

Her bedroom door opened and her daughter peeked inside. "We'd like to talk to you for a minute."

"Of course, sweetheart. What's on your mind?" Annie sat up against the pillows, laying the nursing journal and her reading glasses on the bedside table. She crossed her slippered feet at the ankles and smoothed the skirt of the dark blue velvet robe that had been Chad's Christmas gift two days earlier across her knees.

"Chad's with me," Leah said, coming the rest of the way into the room. Her long black hair was loose on her shoulders. She gave a practiced flip and it settled down her back in a shining ebony fall. Chad followed her inside and closed the door. Leah dropped down beside Annie on the big bed. Chad pulled the spindly-legged chair away from her dressing table and turned it around, straddling it and resting his hand on the high, chintz-covered back.

"Ummm, is this just a friendly chat or are you two some kind of official delegation?" Annie kept a smile on her lips but in truth she was a little nervous to see her children looking so purposeful and grown-up.

Leah glanced at her elder brother. "I guess you could say we're here in an official capacity. Doug's downstairs getting the twins set up with that new computer game Rachel and her mom and dad got them for Christmas. We don't want them barging in on us."

"Oh dear, if you're decoying your brothers away from this room, it must be something serious you want to discuss." Annie kept her tone light but she felt strangely off balance. She sat up straighter and folded her hands in her lap. "What's on your minds?"

"It's about Mr. McKendrick. Simon." Leah looked down at her hands. "You've been seeing an awful lot of him the past couple of days."

"He's a guest in our home," Annie said a bit more sharply than she'd intended. Simon had taken a room at the motel where his parents were staying, but most of the time all the McKendricks could be found in Annie's living room or kitchen. This evening, however, Annie and her children were alone. Simon, Rachel and their parents were taking an evening tour of the Loop and Lake Shore Drive.

Annie's tone of voice didn't pass unnoticed. Leah looked at her, frowning slightly, tilting her head so that her hair fell over one shoulder. She pushed it back impatiently with a flick of her wrist.

"Mom," Chad said, after Leah glanced hesitantly in his direction. "We aren't babies like Mike and Jon. We can see there's something special between you and Simon."

"You try too hard to look like just friends," Leah said, leaning forward to pat Annie's hand. "It happens all the time at school when two kids really like each other." She sat back, nodding wisely. Annie looked at Chad from the corner of her eye, but he was watching his sister. Annie kept her expression carefully neutral.

"Don't you like him?" The question popped out, surprising her. Suddenly it seemed very important that her children did like Simon.

"He's okay," Chad admitted.

"He's gorgeous for a man his age," Leah said in the confidential mother-to-daughter tone she'd adopted, which was beginning to make Annie feel very much like a teenager being quizzed by her mother on the suitability of her latest boyfriend.

"He's forty-one," Annie said in Simon's defense. "Only a year and a half older than I am."

"Exactly." Leah smiled, indicating that she also considered her mother well preserved.

"It's just that...well, you aren't used to going out with men anymore, Mom." Chad cocked his head and looked at her from narrowed eyes. It was one of Mike's habitual expressions and Annie swallowed against a sudden tightening in her throat.

"I'm not 'going out' with Simon McKendrick," she pointed out reasonably. But only because he'd never asked her, Annie admitted to herself. She caught herself daydreaming at the oddest moments of what it would be like to be alone with him again, as they'd been that night in her hotel room in Saigon. More and more often her fantasy moments tended to dwell on how wonderful it would be to make love to Simon...every night for the rest of their lives.

"We don't know much about him, really," Leah reminded her, getting to the root of the matter. Annie's heart skipped a beat. Her daughter was right. She really didn't know much about him. But dear Lord, she wanted the opportunity to learn.

"You seemed to be getting along pretty well Christmas Eve." Chad dropped his chin onto his hands and stared at her over the back of the chair. Annie cleared her throat and pulled at the sleeves of her robe. So, he had seen her kissing Simon in the middle of the street. No wonder her children were concerned about her behavior. They'd never seen her kiss any man but Mike.

"We met..." Suddenly she realized she was in danger of getting tangled up in the untold details of her trip to Vietnam. She'd never been good at improvising, and was even worse at outright lies. She was going to have to go slowly or she'd get tripped up by her own evasions. "We met in Bangkok," she said finally. "The government notified him of Rachel and Micah's return from Vietnam. He came there to meet them. We spent some time together. He's divorced. He has no children. He works for the Census Bureau," she finished lamely.

"The Census Bureau." Everyone looked in the direction of the now open door. Doug stood in the doorway, his shoulder propped against the frame. "That's a good one. Guys from the Census Bureau run around with clipboards and geek haircuts and ask you if you've got indoor plumbing and how many television sets you own." He finished the sentence with a snort and folded his arms across his chest. "He's no census taker." Annie had the feeling none of the trio was going to leave her bedroom until they were satisfied they'd learned all there was to know about Simon McKendrick.

"There are plenty of other jobs at the Census Bureau...." Annie looked at the three pairs of skeptical eyes turned in her direction.

"Where are the brats?" Chad asked, cutting in on her not very convincing explanation.

"They're okay." Doug flicked his thumb in the direction of the stairs. "They're trying to save the universe by blowing each other into space dust."

"We want you to be happy, Mama," Leah said, looking so earnest that Annie couldn't help but catch her up in her arms for a hug. "We think Simon... leads a double life. It's just like in the movies and on television." The unintentional drama in her voice was almost too much for Annie. She stifled the impulse to smile.

"He speaks Vietnamese as well as Rachel," Leah continued. "I've heard them talking together." Her voice was little more than a whisper.

"Spanish, too," Chad said. "The brats told me he translated every song on the Spanish-language radio station they're always listening to."

"He's been everywhere in the world," Leah said with more than a touch of awe. "Everywhere."

"And your assessment?" Annie glanced at her eldest son, maintaining a straight face with some difficulty. She'd always been pleased that her children were so imaginative and inquisitive, but she wondered if Simon would appreciate how closely their uninformed conclusions came to reality.

"He's into martial arts. Black belt or I miss my guess," Chad said. He'd been taking karate lessons since he was eight and spoke with authority. "Not your average civil servant."

"Probably CIA." Doug frowned harder than ever.

"No." Annie couldn't let their loving interrogation get completely out of hand. "He's not CIA. Look, kids, I appreciate your worrying about me like this but..."

"We don't want you to get hurt." Chad stood up and walked to the foot of the bed. He stuck his hands into the pockets of his jeans and stared at the bedspread. "We talked it over and decided a guy like Simon McKendrick just doesn't seem the type to settle down in a hick town like this and take a job at City Hall." He swallowed hard, revealing the true extent of his nervousness.

"Hick town?" Annie raised an eyebrow. "We're only fifteen miles from the center of Chicago!"

"It's a state of mind," Chad replied.

"That goes double for me." Doug unfolded his arms. "Simon looks like the love 'em and leave 'em type from where I stand." He balled his hands into fists at his sides, trying to look tough and composed but only managing to look surly. Annie often thought Mike's death had hit him hardest of all. At the moment, she was sure of it. Yet she couldn't let her children's lingering grief over their father's death turn them against Simon. Suddenly Annie was as serious as they. "I'll think about what you've said. I promise. But get this straight, all of you. Simon McKendrick is a decent and honorable man. I do like him very much, but no matter what comes of that friendship it will be our decision, not yours. Do you understand? All of you?"

"We're worried about you," Leah said, stuttering a little in her haste to explain.

Annie's anger melted away as quickly as it had come. "I know that, honey. And I know it must be difficult for you to realize there might be someone else coming into my life." Annie looked past them for a moment into the past. "I loved your father very much. But he's gone. I miss him. I always will, but that doesn't mean there isn't room in my heart to love someone else."

"Is that man Simon?" Leah asked so softly Annie almost missed the words.

She shrugged but couldn't stop the smile that curved her lips. "Maybe." She pulled Leah more tightly into her arms. She looked at her sons, tall and somber-looking, almost men, yet still only boys when it came to understanding matters of the heart. "It's a funny thing about love. No matter how often you tell yourself to use your head as well as your heart when you're looking for that special someone, it doesn't always work that way. You can walk into an orphanage and find two runny-nosed little boys with big eyes and sad smiles and know you belong together. Or a baby girl is thrust into your arms on the corner of a busy street and becomes yours forever." She didn't hear the faraway, dreamy happiness in her voice, or the sadness that was layered beneath. "Or a marine guard grinning down at you from the top of a barbed-wire fence saying, 'What's a nice girl like you doing in a place like this?' Those times are rare and precious because you know beyond a shadow of a doubt that you're going to love those people for all your life. Other times love is slower and grows from day to day. And sometimes," Annie admitted with a small sigh, "sometimes you just can't help who it is you love."

CHAPTER TEN

"DON'T GET YOUR BOOTS TOO near the fire, you'll melt the soles." Simon kicked at the end of a burning log with the toe of his borrowed skates. Rachel was sitting as close to the small blaze as safety permitted. Her nose and cheeks were red with cold. Her slight figure was enveloped by the bulk of an electric blue snowsuit that Chad had outgrown. Beyond them, laughter and squeals of excitement carried clearly across the ice of the windbreak-sheltered farm pond whose far shore was already fading into the shadows of the late December twilight.

"Singeing my boot soles might be the only way I ever thaw out my toes," Rachel complained with a breathless laugh. "Lord, I'd forgotten how cold snow can be. Why did I ever let myself get talked into ice-skating at my age?" Simon listened for the telltale sharpening of her voice that he'd come to associate with the recurrence of painful memories from her past. It wasn't there. Rachel went on, "I haven't been this cold since my senior year in nurses' training. My boyfriend and a couple of other guys came up from Penn State and took us sledding out in the hills. His car broke down on the way home and we had to walk two miles in zero weather." She shivered and pulled off her mittens to warm her hands by the fire. "I swore off winter sports then and there. I'm just sorry I didn't remember that episode this afternoon when Annie invited us to this skating party."

"What are you complaining about?" Simon rubbed his backside and grimaced, drawing a giggle from his sister. Rachel could talk easily about their childhood, even her short marriage to Kyle Phillips, but she still avoided any mention of her years in captivity, and he did not press. "All you had to say was that Annie's old skates were too big for you to wear so you could sit here drinking hot chocolate and looking smug. While I, on the other hand, have made a fool of myself and may never walk fully upright again."

"You looked pretty good out there and you know it, so quit fishing for compliments." Rachel's tone was light and Simon matched it.

"Since you mention it, I agree."

"Until you tried that spin."

"I wiped out," Simon admitted. He sat down very gingerly on the low log bench beside Rachel. He hadn't skated in years and his muscles were protesting the unfamiliar exercise. Landing on his backside once or twice had been a good excuse to leave the ice. He didn't like watching Rachel sitting alone on the bank. It brought out a host of protective feelings he knew she'd neither asked for, nor would welcome. There was a distance between them that Simon couldn't seem to bridge, no matter how hard he'd tried these past few days. His time with Rachel was growing short. He wished she would talk to him about the nightmares that still haunted her before he had to leave for Washington. It seemed she was determined not to do so.

"You could have turned down the offer to use Annie's husband's skates." Rachel wasn't going to talk about herself, but it seemed his problems of the heart were fair game. She pushed a lock of straying hair back underneath the bright yellow stocking cap on her head and smiled knowingly.

"I don't think I could have refused," he said in all honesty.

"You never did like to pass up a challenge."

"Especially when we were young and I was..." Simon stopped talking when he realized what he'd been about to say, but it was too late. Rachel finished the sentence for him.

"When we were young and you were trying to impress a girl?"

Her unwavering gaze left little room for prevarication. He'd meant the remark to be flippant, but his sister refused to take the hint.

"Yes." Simon kicked at the bonfire again, sending a shower of sparks shimmering upward into the cold evening sky. He could hear the twins screaming with delight as Chad and Leah whirled them around in circles on the ice, letting go unexpectedly, so that the little boys went streaking off across the pond in a flurry of whirling arms and legs. Annie skated backward, watching the fun, cautioning the two teens to be careful with the twins, her ears protected by furry white earmuffs, her glorious red hair aglow in the fading light of the sunset. Annie and the kids were a happy, animated group. Only Doug was missing, off, as usual on his own. Simon watched their antics a few more moments in silence, then took up the conversation where he'd left off.

"I couldn't turn down the offer to use Mike's skates. It's almost like the kids are testing me." He stopped, unsure of how to phrase his words. He hadn't intended to admit his feelings for Annie to Rachel, or anyone else for that matter, until he was certain, himself, of where the relationship was heading. "I don't want to fail to measure up in their eyes."

Rachel picked up a thermos from the picnic hamper sitting on a momentarily unused sled behind the low log bench and poured him a cup of cocoa. "It's that serious, is it?" Simon accepted the plastic cup, rested his forearms on his spread knees and stared down at the hot liquid.

"Damn it, yes. It's that serious." More than serious—hopeless. These past days of being near Annie, of never being alone with her, of never having the privacy to take her in his arms and make love to her, even kiss her, had been hell.

"I thought it might be when I saw you two kissing in the middle of the street on Christmas Eve." Rachel made a clicking noise with her teeth. Annie's dog, a big golden Lab–Heinz 57 mix trotted over, tongue lolling to thrust her head in Rachel's lap and have her ears scratched.

"Did Mom and Dad see us, too?" They'd put their parents on a plane back to Florida that morning.

"I don't think so. At least they never mentioned it to me."

"That kiss came exactly five minutes after I'd convinced myself we had nothing in common and that the best thing in the world for both of us was for me to never lay a hand on her again."

"Simon, you're a fool if you believe that." Rachel's voice was sharp, then softened. "Are you thinking of your marriage?"

Simon nodded. "Jenna tried. She just couldn't live with what it takes to be the wife of...someone in my line of work."

"I've always heard the Census Bureau was a real combat zone."

"Rachel, don't start asking for details." Simon grinned, a humorless twist of the lips, nothing more. "In the end, she couldn't take the pressure and I don't blame her."

"I never met your ex-wife, but I'll bet everything I've got she wasn't cut from the same bolt of cloth as Annie Simpson."

Rachel looked triumphant, as though she'd scored the winning point in their debate. And she was right. Annie Simpson was like no other woman he'd ever met. Perhaps she could accept the danger, the separations, at least until he could carve out a new career for himself in a less hazardous line of work.

"I can't argue with you there."

"I think I should warn you—Chad saw the Christmas Eve kiss, too." Rachel altered the direction of the conversation.

"No wonder he's been watching me like a hawk." Simon lowered his head and stared at the curls of steam spiraling up from his cocoa. The dog looked at him expectantly. Simon patted her head.

"Chad loves his mother. He's worried about her happiness, that's all." Simon twisted on the bench to catch a glimpse of his sister's face, but she was putting her mittens on again and her expression was lost in shadow. "Simon, you have big shoes to fill when it comes to replacing Mike Simpson in their lives."

"Yeah, I know." Funny how much that truth hurt. The ironic thing was that he didn't want to replace or erase Mike's memory for any of them. He wanted Annie's children to love him for himself. Simon shrugged, pulling the fabric of his coat tight across his shoulders. The hooded parka, like the skates and the boots he'd been wearing all week, had belonged to Mike. The coat was a size too small, but the boots and skates fit pretty well so Simon guessed they'd been about the same size and weight.

At least while Annie's husband had been alive. Dead, Mike was assuming giant proportions in his mind, and that was another matter altogether.

"Maybe I'm not up to it."

"Not up to what?" Rachel was playing psychologist, but he went along with her because he needed to talk.

"I might not be cut out to be a father."

"Why do you say that?" Rachel poked the fire with a stick but Simon could feel her eyes on him.

"It's pretty hard to compete with a ghost." As a father and a lover.

"You can't replace the kids' father no matter how hard you try."

"Hell, don't you think I know that?" He tossed the untasted cocoa into the fire with an angry flip of his wrist. The flames sputtered and hissed as if equally angry with his gesture.

"I said you can't replace him." Rachel's tone was sharp but she reached out to rest her hand briefly, comfortingly, on his arm. "I didn't say you couldn't find your own place in their lives and in their hearts."

"How the devil do I accomplish that?" He scowled down at the empty cup, then handed it to his sister.

"I'd say with equal parts loving and worrying, discipline and indulgence. You'll get the hang of it quickly enough."

"You make it sound like a piece of cake."

"No." Rachel shook her head slowly, thoughtfully. "I'd say it was about a lifetime's piece of work." Her next question caught him off guard. "Does Mike's shadow come between you and Annie, too? Is that why you're so uncertain about committing to her?"

Simon took a deep breath and let it out slowly, a steady stream of icy vapor in the cold, dark air. It was a question he'd asked himself many times when he'd wakened in the middle of a dark, tropical night. Now he asked himself again, searching his heart, and surprisingly found no doubt there. "No," he said, and meant it. "Annie is a remarkable woman but I haven't got the right to ask her to give up her memories of a good man and a good marriage just to help me deal with my own insecurities." He looked into the distance, watching Venus twinkle into life in the night sky. "I love her too much to expect that kind of unselfish devotion. But I'm also not a complete fool. Annie won't marry me if the kids don't approve."

"Don't be too sure of that." Rachel sounded far more sure of herself than Simon could be.

"I can't offer her the kind of marriage she had, that she deserves. A nine-to-five husband who's home every night for dinner, who takes out the garbage and fixes leaky faucets. I can't think of retiring for eight or ten years. I'll probably end up doing consulting work for State or Defense when I do call it quits, and that's going to mean damn near as much time out of the country as I spend now."

"Are you trying to convince me or yourself that this affair is going nowhere?"

Simon turned his head to face Rachel head-on. She was sitting with her knees drawn up, her arms curled around her legs, watching him thoughtfully.

"Maybe I want my arguments blown out of the water. Maybe I want you to tell me I'm making mountains out of molehills."

"I can't do that." Rachel shook her head. "I do think you're making mountains out of some pretty low foothills, though." She smiled. "And if we're going to lower this conversation to the level of well-worn clichés, how about 'love conquers all' or 'home is where the heart is' or..."

"Or maybe I should just wish on a star and wait for some kind of sign from heaven to make my decisions for me." Simon couldn't keep the skepticism out of his voice. He suspected he hadn't succeeded in keeping the heartache hidden either.

"It couldn't hurt." Rachel's tone was cryptic. She was looking out across the ice. Simon followed the direction of her gaze. The twins stood just beyond the light of the fire, Chad and Leah behind them, Annie bringing up the rear.

"We want to play crack the whip," Mike said, wobbling a little on his skates.

"We need more people to get going really fast," Jon added, grabbing his brother by the collar of his coat to hold him up.

"We need an anchor," Leah added in explanation.

"I don't weigh enough to do a good job." Chad looked at Leah. "If you're not too tired we thought you might help us out."

Simon studied their faces. The twins were expectant and impatient, as always. Leah smiled shyly, enchantingly, while Chad looked uncertain but determined to be friendly for his mother's sake. "I'll give it a try." From the corner of his eye Simon saw Annie press her gloved hand to her lips, as if to still their trembling. He stood up and pulled the guards from his skate blades.

Chad held out his hand for Simon to grasp as he stepped off the low bank onto the ice. "I have to warn you," he said, looking Simon straight in the eye. "This was my dad's job and he was the best there was at this game."

"You won't get any argument from me about that." Simon started off for the middle of the pond. Chad skated backward a few strides ahead of him. Simon wasn't sure how he should react but settled for giving the younger man back stare for stare. "Your dad was a great guy. I think we understand each other on that point."

"He was the best." Chad smiled reluctantly. "I saw you kissing my mom the other night."

"I know you did."

"Do you love her?" Simon braked to a halt, anchoring himself against the pull of five spinning bodies. "Yes, I do."

"Are you going to ask her to marry you?" The others were coming up behind them.

"I don't know." Simon wasn't about to lie to the boy.

"We've decided, the three of us older ones, that it's okay if you do." Chad took off his glove and held out his hand. "Maybe having a stepfather won't be such a drag after all."

RACHEL CLOSED HER EYES, hearing echoes of her childhood in the sound of happy voices and barking dog out on the ice. Behind her eyelids the fire danced, ebony flames against a crimson background. It was good to be with people of her own kind again. It was good to have Simon and her parents with her for the holidays. It was good to feel like part of a family again. But she couldn't stay wrapped in this protective cocoon much longer. She was back in the world she'd left so many years before and it was time to start building some kind of life of her own.

"Enough! Enough!" Annie dropped onto the log bench beside Rachel, her breath coming in quick gasps that silvered the night air like smoke from the fire. "I can't skate another step, I tell you." Her laughing pronouncement cut into Rachel's train of thought.

"But, Mom." There was a distinct whine in Mike's voice. It was growing late and the boys were cold and tired. "Just one more time, please."

"No." Annie started taking off her skates. "I'm pooped. And I have to work tomorrow."

Work. The word was beginning to take on the magical qualities of a talisman for Rachel. The stronger she grew physically, the more heavily time weighed on her hands, the easier it was for the past to intrude on her thoughts.

"Go back out onto the ice and pester Leah and your brother," Rachel ordered, taking charge of the situation while Annie caught her breath. "Here, take the sled." She sent the lightweight wooden sled skimming across the snow to the bank. "Better yet, get Simon to take you for a ride. He used to be pretty good at it."

"Rad," Mike said, perking up. "He can probably get us going as fast as crack the whip."

"Faster," Jon agreed. The twins dragged the sled onto the ice and took off into the darkness beyond the glow of the fire, arguing loudly over who would ride first.

"Poor Simon, they'll wear him out." Annie located her boots and set them close to the fire to warm them.

"He can take it." Rachel poured Annie a cup of chocolate.

"They like him. I think everything will be just fine."

"I'm certain it will." Rachel waited for Annie to say more about her relationship with Simon. Instead, she changed the subject.

"I'm going to be stiff and sore in places I don't even want to think about tomorrow, but I'm glad we came out here anyway."

"It's been very nice." Rachel took a sip of her cocoa. Her teeth were chattering and she hoped Annie wouldn't notice, forgetting for a moment how perceptive Annie Simpson was.

"Are you cold? We can go sit in the car and turn on the heater if you are."

"No." Rachel spoke too quickly, then softened the negative with a smile. Being outside in the fresh, cold air might help her fall asleep that night without resorting to the sleeping pills the doctors had prescribed. Staying outside until she was exhausted might make her tired enough to sleep without dreams. "I'm enjoying myself. I've been away from winter for a long time."

"Remember how we used to talk about nights like this at the orphanage?" Annie asked, leaning back to look up into the velvet dark sky, now studded with a blaze of diamond-bright pricks of light. "We tried so hard to explain to the children about snowmen and icicles. It must have seemed like another world to them. The closest we could come to finding snow for them was the frost in the freezer of the orphanage refrigerator."

There was a long-ago and faraway quality to Annie's voice. For her, Saigon and the war were truly over and done, memories of the distant past. For Rachel, that time and the unspeakably more terrible experiences that followed were always no further away than her next dream.

For years she had successfully repressed those dreams, but now that her health was improving, now that she no longer struggled just to survive another day, they had returned. She had too much time to think, too few tasks to occupy her mind, and so the past gained in strength and importance.

"Annie?" Rachel's reluctance to delve into her memories overcame her uncertainty about dealing with the present. "I'm thinking of getting an apartment of my own."

"Oh dear, what have the twins done now?" It was a typical mother's response, and when Annie realized what she'd said she giggled. Rachel giggled, too, and a little of the tense, achy feeling inside her eased away.

"I can't impose on you indefinitely," Rachel pointed out, serious once more. She swallowed the last of her cocoa before it cooled.

"We love having you." It wasn't just a meaningless platitude. Rachel sensed the affection and sincerity underlying Annie's words.

"I know that. I'm not walking out first thing in the morning. But I am going to start looking for a small apartment close by. I like your town. I have to start my life again somewhere and it might as well be here."

"What about Sarasota? Wouldn't you rather be near your parents?"

"No. They have their own lives. I don't want them fussing and worrying over me."

"Pennsylvania?"

"There's nothing there for me, either. No one knows me here. I can start over, start a new life." Here, among the hardworking blue-collar neighbors, she wouldn't be recognized as the freak she sometimes felt herself to be. If Annie had reservations about the less-than-enthusiastic tone of Rachel's announcement, she kept them to herself. "And it's time I started looking for a job. I know Micah and Simon pooled every cent they could get their hands on to get me out of Vietnam. My parents have very little extra money. I can't go on being a burden to the people I love."

"None of us feels that way, Rachel." Annie busied herself putting the thermos and empty plastic cups into the hamper.

"I know that, too. But it doesn't make it any easier to go on imposing on your hospitality."

"What does Simon say about this plan?" Annie was unlacing her skates. She rubbed her ankles and reached for her warm boots before the piercing cold could seep through her heavy wool socks. She carefully avoided looking Rachel in the eye.

"I... I haven't told him yet." She couldn't talk to Simon about herself. All the questions, the sense of betrayal she tried so hard not to feel, were only inches beneath the surface. He had never offered an explanation of why he'd failed to send word to her to get out of Saigon. She didn't have the courage to ask, to lose the last anchor she had—her belief in Simon's honor and caring.

"I see." Annie's tone said clearly that she didn't see at all. "What kind of job are you going to look for?" She rested her chin on her upraised knee, wrapping her arm around her legs, her gaze fixed intently on Rachel's now averted face.

"I'm not sure." Rachel tried for lightness and missed. "I understand they're hiring at the Pizza Joint. I worked my way through nurses' training as a waitress."

"Why don't you come to work for me?"

"I'm not a nurse anymore, Annie. I haven't been one for a long, long time."

"That doesn't mean you can't be one again. A damn good one."

"It's been so long." Rachel pushed down the small bubble of hope that insisted on floating upward toward her heart. *Could she return to her profession? Could she catch up with almost two decades of new techniques, new procedures?*

"You'll never know if you don't try." Annie made a cup of her hands and hollered out over the ice. "Michael, Jonathon. It's getting late and I have to be up at six tomorrow. It's time to leave." Obviously, she wasn't going to beg Rachel to accept her offer.

"I don't want charity," Rachel heard herself say perversely.

"I'm not offering charity." Annie ignored the pleas of "just a little longer" and "five more minutes, please" that hurtled back at her from out of the night. She met Rachel's anxious expression with a level, head-on stare. "I'm offering you a job as a nursing assistant. If you don't feel you have the qualifications, say so."

Rachel was backed against the wall. She'd just voiced her intention of becoming independent again. She simply hadn't expected everything to move so fast. Could she do it? Her chin came up. "I . . . I think . . . I can handle that," she amended with more conviction. She wasn't a quitter. She never had been, but her heart beat faster, her palms grew moist at the thought of going back into the world, back into medicine.

"I can't pay you much more than you could make at the Pizza Joint." Annie's tone was brisk, businesslike, allowing Rachel to keep her treacherous tears of gratitude and self-doubt at bay. "The benefits are only adequate and the hours are terrible."

"I can handle it." No hesitation this time. Rachel managed a smile that didn't tremble too much.

"And one more thing."

"What's that?" Rachel tilted her head. The sternness was gone from Annie's expression. Her brown eyes were bright with warmth and caring and more than a hint of deviltry.

"I'd think twice before saying 'yes' if I were you. I hear the tips at the Pizza Joint are pretty good."

CHAPTER ELEVEN

"OKAY. WE CAN WATCH Dick Clark hosting *Rockin' New Year's Eve* on channel nine. Or yet another rerun of *It's a Wonderful Life* with Jimmy Stewart and Donna Reed on channel five. Or a three-hour retrospective of Lawrence Welk's greatest shows on PBS. Quite a selection." Simon tossed the *TV Guide* onto the coffee table with a snort. He pushed his hand through his thick black hair and tugged impatiently at the knot of his tie.

Annie stopped at the doorway and watched him pace the length of the living room. He was wearing a dark gray suit and subdued striped tie, but he still reminded her of some big jungle cat caged in a zoo. It was always with him, that aura of danger and intrigue, of restless energy ruthlessly harnessed and held in control. How would he feel living here in a small suburban town, a married man, stepfather to a whole brood of kids, with ordinary, everyday problems and responsibilities? It was very possible he wouldn't want such a life. The realization made Annie's heart ache with sadness.

"I'm sorry I had to change our plans at the last minute this way." She remained at the foot of the stairs, a tray of dry toast and glasses of 7-Up in her hands, a nondescript cotton apron over the copper-spangled, full-skirted party dress she'd spent hours shopping for just the day before. It was a very special dress that was to have given her the courage to take matters into her own hands, to be a woman again, to give of herself to Simon wholly and completely so that he would take the gamble of loving her and forging a future with her, no matter what the odds against them.

"Don't apologize for my bad temper." His voice was harsh, calling her thoughts back from their inward path. He was angry at himself, not at her, but understanding his mood didn't make the nervous flutter in her stomach go away. If only she could have glided down the stairs in the dress of cinnamon-colored silk, flattering and feminine, to dazzle him with her beauty and charm; it would have made all the difference in the world to her peace of mind. Instead, she'd greeted him at the front door with a garbled explanation of the twins' sudden illness and a dash up the stairs to deal with yet another bout of vomiting.

"I should have called you and canceled our date, but everything here was in such an uproar." Her words faded into silence as Simon crossed the room in two swift strides. He reached out to touch her cheek, an achingly gentle caress that was over much too quickly.

"I said, no more apologies. I'm the one acting like a jackass here, not you."

"Perhaps we can reschedule dinner for tomorrow night...or the night after." Annie stumbled into silence. She wished he would touch her again. She smiled but it was frazzled around the edges. Simon didn't comment on her suggestion but asked a question of his own.

"How are they?"

"I think the worst is over." Annie hurried into speech to cover the sting of his perceived rejection. "The boys have been cranky and out of sorts all day, Leah said. They both just picked at their dinner but I assumed that was due to the excitement of being invited to their first real New Year's Eve party. And then, while I was getting dressed . . ." She glanced down at the dowdy apron covering her lovely dress and sighed.

"Let me guess. All hell broke loose?" Simon was smiling now and suddenly everything seemed just a little brighter. "What can I do to help?"

"Nothing really. It's one of those intestinal viruses that just seem to strike without warning. It just has to run its course. I think I've got things under control." Everything, that was, but her heartbeat. Somehow she couldn't seem to slow it down to a normal pace anytime Simon McKendrick was nearby.

"Always in control, aren't you, Annie love?" His voice was low and rough around the edges, dark and dangerous-sounding, as it had been that night in her hotel room in Saigon. The night he'd kissed her, held her in his arms, fought to protect her and keep her safe. Annie shivered, but the dancing spark of sensation racing up and down her spine was far more pleasure than pain. Her pulse accelerated several more counts.

"With five kids you learn to be resourceful." The words came out breathless and squeaky. Simon was looking down at her as if she were anything but a soon-to-be forty-year-old mother of five. He was looking at her as if she were the only woman in the world, in his world, the most desirable creature alive. It was a frightening, exhilarating, sensual experience and she longed for more, much more.

"I wish I could heal with a touch." Simon's tone dropped even lower. "I'd give the boys anything their hearts desire, transport them anywhere in the world they wanted to go so that in turn, I could fulfill a wish of my own."

"A wish?" Annie couldn't stop herself from asking what he wanted.

"My wish is to be alone with their mother..."

"For the next three hours?" Annie was rapidly being swept beyond her depth.

"...for the rest of time." Simon dropped a kiss on the tip of her nose. "Let me carry this tray upstairs for you." Annie came up for air in a huff. She felt as if she'd taken a step and found a six-foot drop beneath her feet. The spell was broken, as Simon obviously intended it should be.

"Are you sure you want to go up there?" Annie made a comical face as she fought to regain her poise. "It's pretty bad. Those two do not suffer in silence." The universe had settled back into place around her and she felt a little safer, enough in control to tease him a little. Until Simon's hand accidentally brushed over hers on the tray.

"No, I don't want to go up there." He stared at the invalid food on the tray a long moment, then lifted his gold-flecked hazel eyes to hers. "I've never been much good in a sickroom, but I do want to be with you. I don't plan to spend the evening sulking in front of your TV while you watch over the twins by yourself." He took a deep breath and let it out slowly. "Where is everyone anyway?"

"Simon," Annie reminded him gently, secretly pleased by his actions, "it's New Year's Eve. Doug and Chad are at parties with friends. Chad will stay over at the Frat House if it gets too wild. And Doug is at the home of a boy whose parents have promised to make sure there is no liquor and no drugs and that everyone will be safely home by 2:00 a.m."

"Sounds like a pretty laid-back evening for Doug."

Annie sighed. "I thought so, too, but Chad says he's got a terrific crush on this boy's younger sister." Annie realized she was frowning and smiled to hide the little dart of worry that always accompanied any discussion of her second son.

"That explains it." Simon nodded sagely. "Girls can work wonders on even the most hardened character."

"Oh, Simon, do you really. . . you're teasing me."

"Yes, I'm teasing you but I'm surprised you noticed."

"I do worry about him."

"He's a good kid, Annie. He'll find his way." His hand moved to cover hers on the wooden tray. This time there was nothing accidental in his touch. Simon's thumb traced tantalizing circles on the inside of her wrist. He smiled down at her and the floor tilted under her feet. "That leaves only Leah and my sister to be accounted for."

"Rachel and Leah went to the movies and then out for pizza. Leah's boyfriend dumped her just two days ago to take another girl to the class party. She's devastated. Swears she can never show her face at school again."

"Being a teenager is one major crisis of the heart after another."

"Do you speak from experience?" Annie had the satisfaction of seeing him wince in embarrassment.

"Yes."

"Breaking hearts? Or having yours broken?"

"Both. And you?" Simon narrowed his eyes, one dark brow rising slightly as he waited for her answer.

"Both," she admitted. "I just wish when I was fourteen I'd had Rachel's prescription for mending a broken heart."

"Which is?" His fingers still held hers captive on the tray. Annie could barely keep her thoughts in order.

"She recommended a Mel Gibson movie and a large deluxe pizza with extra cheese."

Simon laughed out loud. "I think my sister is starting to find her way back into the swim of things."

"I think she is, too. Did she tell you she's coming to work for me at the Lyman Street clinic on Monday?" Annie hoped that if she kept talking he would keep making those caressing little circles on her skin with his thumb.

Simon wasn't laughing anymore. He looked very serious all of a sudden, very serious and a little sad. There were so many things unsettled between Rachel and Simon, and Micah, for that matter. Annie wanted so badly to give the McKendricks, all of them, peace and happiness, but she wasn't certain how to begin. "Yes, she did tell me. I've said this before. I'll say it again. You are a remarkable woman, Annie Simpson. Rachel has come further in the two weeks she's been with you and your family than in all the weeks before."

"She's a strong woman. She'll find her way." Annie attempted to keep her concentration focused on Rachel but her mind kept skittering away on paths of its own; traitorous, erotic paths that weakened her knees and sent her heart skipping into her throat.

Simon was so close she could feel the warmth of his skin, smell the faint spicy scent of his after-shave and the heady underlying male scent that was Simon himself. She could feel her own body softening, straining in its response, drawing closer to his strength, and to the vulnerability hidden deep beneath that great strength.

Annie found herself wondering where this night might have ended for them if the twins hadn't become ill.

Would she have found herself alone somewhere with Simon? Somewhere they could be together to explore their feelings, to speak of love? Someplace magical and private where she could feel like a woman whole and complete again, after so many lonely, passionless months?

"Mom!" Mike's voice came drifting down the stairs, weak and plaintive, filled with urgency. "Mom, Jon's barfing again. Come quick! Mom? Do you hear me?"

Annie opened her eyes, uncertain when she'd closed them, to find Simon only inches away, staring back at her over the tray that separated them, a funny, puzzled look on his face. The magic sparkle of sexual tension in the air dissipated like champagne bubbles in a glass. For Annie the disappointment was almost a physical pain.

"Damn." Simon stepped backward, taking the tray from her numb fingers.

"Oh dear, here we go again." Annie bit her bottom lip. What was between her and this man was so new, so untested. Would this ordinary domestic crisis, and the radical difference in their life-styles that it so glaringly exposed, kill their fragile new love?

"Poor kids." Simon's voice was gruff with some emotion that Annie was unable to decipher.

"Simon, I'm..." Her mind and heart remembered the addictive taste of his kisses. Her body felt betrayed to have been so close to that ecstasy again after days of denial, yet her mother's heart was torn.

"Don't worry. Go." He pressed his finger against her lips. "I'll be right behind you and tonight I'll be here for as long as you want me to stay."

AN HOUR AND A HALF LATER Simon was still wondering what had made him say those words aloud. Another near declaration of love, another last-second denial. Why couldn't he tell Annie straight out that he loved her with all his heart and soul? He'd admitted as much to Rachel, and Chad. Why not Annie herself? The answer was as obvious as the question. He was still not sure he could give Annie and her family everything they needed from a husband and a stepfather.

He stepped past the lighted Christmas tree, pulled aside the curtain in the living room and looked outside. Cars were parked up and down the street. Neighbors on both sides were having parties. If he leaned forward he could see the brick bungalow two houses down where the twins were to have spent the evening. Light spilled out onto snowy lawns. Guests in party finery came and went. Simon glanced at his watch. It was a few minutes past eleven.

In less than an hour it would be a new year, a season of new beginnings. For the first time in more years than he cared to remember, Simon wanted to look at the future optimistically. He wanted to spend all his tomorrows with Annie Simpson and her brood of five. Despite misgivings about his abilities as a husband and father, he'd been pondering the whys and wherefores of marriage since his talk with Rachel at the pond.

Was it possible to mix the kind of life, settled and secure, that Annie deserved, with the reality of his clandestine existence? He was almost certain it couldn't be done, but if there was a woman anywhere on the face of the earth who could help meld two such different lifestyles into a seamless whole, it was Annie. Three months ago he hadn't even allowed himself to contemplate such a future. Tonight, he realized with sudden insight, he was living it.

Simon grinned. The decision had made itself. He'd handled the fretful twins fairly well. The worst was over.

Jon's bout of retching had indeed been the last. It hadn't been easy to stick it out in the sickroom, but he had. Both boys had been coaxed into taking a few sips of 7-Up, and Mike had even managed a couple of bites of dry toast. They'd both fallen asleep quickly after that but not before Simon had promised to bring noisemakers and funny hats up to their room at midnight for a celebration.

Annie had shooed him away then, telling him not to pay any attention, saying the boys would be asleep in ten minutes, which of course they were, but he'd taken his promise seriously. Grabbing his coat, he'd slipped out to the corner convenience store just as it was closing its door, to pick up the last package of party favors they had in stock. He'd added a bottle of indifferent sparkling wine and some cheese and crackers to his purchase as well.

On reflection he found he was damned hungry himself, so he ate a few while arranging the snacks on a plate he found in Annie's cupboard. The wine was already chilled. He liberated two wineglasses from the dining-room china cupboard and carried everything back into the firelit living room. If the opportunity of a few stolen moments with Annie presented itself, he was more than ready to make the most of it.

"Simon?" She was standing at the foot of the stairs. Simon had been so caught up in his thoughts and schemes that he hadn't heard Annie approach until she spoke. In other circumstances the lapse might have cost him his life. Tonight he was in a different world, safe and secure, where the sound of her voice, her nearness, was the only thing that mattered.

"In here." He moved out of the shadows near the big window and held out his hands. She'd taken off the dowdy, overall apron. As she glided into the room, the firelight was caught and held prisoner in the copper spangles on the bodice of her dress. The material alternately clung and swirled around her in a mesmerizing sensual dance. Simon made himself take a breath, hold it, let it out on command. His blood surged through his veins, pounded in his ears. He wanted Annie in a fiercely primitive way, yet at the same time he found himself longing to treat her as though she were a delicate crystal blossom that might shatter at the merest touch. The dichotomy of feeling must have shown on his face, in the taut lines of his body. Annie veered out of his path, avoiding his gaze. She moved to the stereo, turned on the radio, fiddled with buttons until she found an FM station that suited her.

Phil Collins was singing "A Groovy Kind of Love." She hummed a few lines under her breath, then started to sing, a low, melodious alto. "The twins always get a kick out of my knowing the words to 'their' songs." Simon came up behind her, took her in his arms.

"May I have this dance?" Annie nodded, still not looking directly at him. She slipped her arms around his waist. He'd discarded his suit jacket and tie long ago. Her breasts pressed against his chest. He could feel her heartbeat beneath the thin, gauzy fabric of her dress. Her hair was as brilliant as flame against the white of his shirt. They moved slowly, almost imperceptibly, to the beat of the music. If events had gone as he'd planned he would have wined and dined this woman on the best food in Chicago. He would have taken her to a downtown hotel and they would have been able, for the first time, to steal an hour or two of lovemaking. Annie wasn't a woman for backstairs rendezvous, heaven knew, but in view of their circumstances Simon had seen no other way for them to be alone together. Now that fantasy, stronger than ever in his mind, was no longer even remotely possible.

At least not in the foreseeable future. He was leaving tomorrow, on an early plane. Special hearings were being called in Washington. A few key senators and congressmen needed to be briefed. All the information he'd brought back with him from Nicaragua now had to be relayed before the new legislative session opened in January. So little time alone with Annie. Could he afford to let this opportunity slip away?

"Would you like a glass of wine?" he asked, stalling, as he searched his brain for just the right words, the right phrases to tell her of his love, and hopes, and fears.

"No wine, thanks." She spoke so quietly he could barely hear her over the pounding of his heart. Her body fit against his so perfectly. She would fit with him perfectly in other, even more intimate, more delightful ways. "Wine makes me sleepy and it's been a long, long day. I wish it was midnight so that I could curl up and go to sleep." Simon stiffened, so caught up in his own imaginings of Annie's sleeping body, naked and soft against him, that the statement caught him unaware. He felt her tense as she became aware of his reaction to her words. Annie pulled away, but only an inch or two, because he'd let her go no farther. "I . . . I didn't mean . . ."

"I know what you meant." He wished he didn't. He wanted to believe she was thinking of being in his arms, in his bed, loving him as he'd been doing just heartbeats ago. "I don't have to tell you what I was thinking about." He pulled her tightly against him once more and let her feel the extent of his desire, let her see the passion that tightened his jaw and tensed the muscles of his neck and shoulders.

Annie leaned back in his arms, their lower bodies still touching. She wasn't avoiding his eyes any longer. She was looking at him directly. "Do you truly believe you can read what's in my heart, Simon McKendrick?" she asked softly.

Sadly, he could not. He shook his head. "No, Annie. But I'd give a great deal to be able to do just that, to anticipate your thoughts, provide you with everything you've ever wanted, will ever want in the future. The hard, cold reality is that I can't do anything like that."

"Then I'll have to show you what it is I want right now, at this very moment." She stood on tiptoe. Her arms wrapped around his neck, warm, strong, supple and demandingly feminine. "I want you, Simon. All of you. I want you near me, with me—" she took a deep breath, her lashes fluttered closed, her voice faded to a whisper "—inside me." Her pent-up breath slipped out in a sigh. Suddenly she was looking at him once again and there was no coyness, no teasing glint in her brown eyes. "I love you. I think I've loved you since that night you saved my life in Saigon."

"You're confusing love with gratitude." Simon wasn't sure why he felt compelled to be his own devil's advocate.

Annie didn't flinch but the luminous sweetness of her expression slipped into sadness. "Simon, I'm not a child, or a young girl caught up in a bout of hero worship. I will be forty years old in just a few months. I've been in love before. I thought I'd never love again but I was wrong, wondrously so."

All he had to do was release her from the prison of his arms and she would go. That would be the best thing for both of them. He willed his arms to open. He willed his body to step away but he couldn't move. She looked uncertain now. If he pressed his advantage she would turn and walk away. "Annie."

"I love you. If you can't love me in return I'll try to understand, try to live with it." She was also trying to look noble and composed, but there were tears in her eyes and her fingers at the back of his neck trembled.

"I love you." He spoke before common sense, self-preservation, cowardice, could rise up and demand that he be cautious, that he be silent. He spoke while the powerful talisman of her warm brown eyes gave him courage. "I love you. It's been so long I'd almost forgotten what it was like." He let the wonder he felt be heard in his tone. "Perhaps I never really knew." He couldn't imagine, suddenly, letting Annie walk out of his life with barely a backward glance the way Jenna had done. Not in a lifetime, not in a thousand lifetimes.

"Simon?" She tilted her head, looking at him unguardedly, her love shining like golden flames in the darkness. "I didn't tell you this to pressure you into a declaration. I've never told any man but Michael that I love him, that I wanted him to make love to me. I...know it's not the way these things are usually done." She stopped talking and a blush rose to her cheeks.

"Annie." Simon could barely force her name past the sudden constriction in his throat. What had he done to deserve this woman's love? "I care for you above all things. That doesn't change the fact that I don't have much to offer. Financially nearly everything I had went into acquiring the pearls to ransom Rachel."

"I see." Annie continued to look up at him, her gaze reflective. "Go on." Obviously, she wasn't going to let money become an issue.

"Most of the time I won't even be able to offer you myself. I'm in no position to change my life, Annie. I'm not sure I want to."

She tightened her arms around his neck, pressing closer. "I understand. I'll do my best to accept what I can't change." She smiled then and her lips beckoned with all the delights of a woman in love. "All I ask for now is that you kiss me, Simon McKendrick. I've been waiting since Christmas, since Bangkok, and I can't wait any longer."

Simon needed no more encouragement. He lowered his head, tasted her lips, the satin of her cheeks, her eyelids. He attempted to push all the questions that clamored for immediate answers to the back of his mind. How could he make a long-distance marriage work? Did he have it in him to succeed with Annie, and her five children, where he'd failed so miserably when it was only Jenna and himself? Reason demanded answers. His lonely heart demanded love. "God, Annie. I want you. I need you. I can't see the future without you in it." He couldn't tell her he was scared to death of giving in to love again. He couldn't ask her to marry him until he was sure of himself.

"Don't try to look so far ahead, Simon." She laid her cheek against his. "It scares me, too," she confessed, her breath soft against his neck. "But since Mike died, I've learned to live in the present without making my dreams hostage to the future. Just be with me now, tonight, for as long as you can." She turned her head, seeking his lips once again. Simon tightened his hold, pulling her softly rounded hips into the cradle of his thighs.

"I'll stay with you tonight, Annie love. But that's all. Tomorrow I have to leave for Washington. There's no way to get out of going."

"I'll be waiting when you get back." Their kiss grew deeper, spiraling out toward the edges of thought and being, taking them with it, demanding a joining more intimate, more complete. Yet Simon knew that physical fulfillment was an impossible dream for the moment. The twins could wake up and come downstairs searching for Annie at any second. Love in the impersonal privacy of a hotel room was a possibility, however lacking in romance; making love in Annie's living room wasn't to be considered.

That restraint acted as the last tie holding inclination hostage to reason. He wanted nothing more than to sweep Annie off her feet and carry her into the heated velvet oblivion of shared passion. She wanted nothing more than to go. But they could not. Simon had never regretted his innate sense of balance and judgment, the inborn caution that had kept him alive and successful in a dangerous and demanding way of life, as much as he did at that moment. He wanted to throw caution to the wind and ask Annie to be his wife. But he could not. Simon McKendrick, husband and father, was a dream not yet ready to become reality.

BELOW HER, THE ICY SILENCE of Manhattan at midnight spread off in every direction as far as the eye could see. Le Thi turned away from the window of the hotel suite where she'd spent the past ten days. New Year's Eve here was very different from the February celebrations of Tet, the lunar new year, in her homeland.

She had never felt so lonely and alone. She wished Hoang were with her, that she could confide her great joy and even greater fears to him. But he was attending a party given by one of the UN delegations and she needed time to be alone. Her health, always a concern to her husband, had provided an excuse. She had never lied to Hoang before, and the look of concern and worry on his face when he left her alone in their suite had nearly succeeded in making her physically ill. Yet the results of her evening's work had been worth the risk and the heartache of deceiving the man she loved.

In a small coffee shop some distance from the hotel she'd completed negotiations with a countryman, a member of the delegation's security team, a man open to bribery, as were so many officials, a man with few scruples and little honor. Still, she had no choice but to deal with him. She had promised him everything of value she owned, the gold and emerald earrings and ring that her father had given her mother as a betrothal gift. It was the last link to her old life, but she didn't regret the loss. If she had known about the jewelry before her mother's last illness they could have sent for it from the security of its Hong Kong bank vault and used it to buy their way out of the beleaguered city. But fate had not been kind. Her mother regained consciousness only hours before her death and it was too late to flee.

Now she would have the man she'd hired locate her daughter in Chicago. Then she would fly to that city and take charge of the child herself. They would go away together somewhere warm and bright, away from these eternally cold and gray cities. In time, her daughter would forget her American way of life. She would forget her adopted family. She would be Le Thi's child again.

She had been practicing her English. She was growing very proficient. After a few days alone with her daughter she would let Hoang know where they were. He would come for them and they would return to Vietnam, a family at last. Le Thi smiled into the darkness of her quiet room, humming a lullaby in a singsong voice of great sweetness. Her plan would work. She would not even let herself consider that it might not.

As for Annie Simpson, she would have to understand, accept the inevitable. Le Thi's right to the child took precedence over her own.

"Soon, my darling baby girl," she crooned aloud to herself, her arms folded over her breast as though she held a newborn child close to her heart. "Soon we will be together again. And this time it will be forever."

CHAPTER TWELVE

"MRS. LEWANDOSKI, YOU shouldn't be out on a day like this." Rachel's voice carried clearly from beyond the partition that separated Annie's closetlike office from the waiting room of the Lyman Street clinic. Annie glanced out the small glassed-in opening of the oversized delivery door that served as her office window, a reminder of past days when the clinic had been a mom-and-pop grocery store. It was still snowing, seemed as if it had been snowing forever, with no end in sight.

"It's Wednesday," responded a quarrelsome old voice with the faintest trace of Middle European accent. "I always come on Wednesday for my blood pressure check. Why let a little thing like eight inches of snow stop me? Here—" the raspy tone mellowed just a little "—I brought you some valentine cookies. I baked them myself." Annie conjured an image of the grandmotherly widow in her mind's eye.

"Mrs. L," Rachel said with a touch of exasperation. "You shouldn't have. You know I have to start watching my weight." Annie heard the heavy footsteps of the old lady move off down the hall as Rachel led her into an exam cubicle.

"Don't be ridiculous." The martial quality of the old lady's speech returned. "You're too skinny for your own good."

"Mrs. L, I've had to buy clothes two sizes larger just since I came to work at the clinic." Rachel's protest fell on deaf ears.

"You still look like skin and bones. And it's Valentine's Day. Splurge. I could have brought you chocolates but these days they're full of chemicals and preservatives. Nasty stuff." Annie smiled as she shamelessly eavesdropped on the pair. "These cookies I baked myself. All natural. Wholesome. Eat. Enjoy." It was an order, not a request. "Good," Mrs. Lewandoski said, satisfied, as Rachel evidently accepted the plate of cookies. "Where's Annie? I want she should have some, too, even if she doesn't need the extra weight like you do. A fine figure of a woman, that one. It's a shame she should be alone."

Annie looked up from the report she was working on and smiled ruefully. Eavesdroppers never heard good of themselves, wasn't that the old saying? It was certainly true in this case. And here, she'd just been congratulating herself for losing three pounds since the first of the year. She tried to ignore Mrs. L's last remark, but couldn't. *Alone. Perhaps she wouldn't be alone much longer.* Simon had promised to come, as soon as he could get away from Washington, possibly as early as tomorrow. They had talked often on the telephone in the weeks just past, not about his work—the congressional briefings were classified—but about Rachel, her children, themselves . . . and the future.

Rachel said something too softly for Annie to catch, but Mrs. Lewandoski's reply came plainly through the wall.

"Why shouldn't my blood pressure be up a little?" Annie frowned. She didn't like to hear that and made a mental note to check with Dr. Montoya if the readings were more than slightly elevated. "Terrible things going on in this neighborhood. Three people mugged since Christmas and one of them that nice Mr. Johnson who fixes the plumbing in my apartment building. It was never like this when my Ferd and me were raising our family on this street. It was a nice, neighborly place. Why, I used to do all my grocery shopping right on this block. In this very building. But no more. Now it's a giant supermarket, everything in plastic, and most of it tastes like it's made of plastic, too."

"Well, these cookies certainly don't taste like plastic," Rachel said with a pleasurable sigh. "They are absolutely delicious."

Mrs. Lewandoski gave the compliment a dismissive snort, but Annie didn't need to see her to know there was a pleased smile on the wrinkled, timeworn face. "I told Mr. Johnson myself at Christmas not to carry his Social Security around with him anymore, that it wasn't safe, but he didn't listen and now look. He's in the hospital with a broken arm and a concussion. Punks. That's who runs this street now. Punks and worse. Drug dealers."

"You don't carry your Social Security check around with you, do you, Mrs. L?" Rachel's tone was concerned.

"What do you think, I'm *meshuga*? Of course not. I have Uncle Sam deposit it directly to the bank. I write checks for everything. All the money I carry around is bus fare. If those punks want that they can have it, my blessing."

"Mrs. L, you are one very smart lady. Now tell me, how's your daughter and the new grandbaby? Do you have any pictures with you?"

No matter how busy they were, Rachel always seemed to find time to ask each patient, especially the elderly ones, about their families, their grandchildren, or their pets. She had adjusted to the sometimes frenzied, always hectic pace of clinic routine far more quickly than Annie had expected. She preferred the Lyman Street storefront to the two larger clinic locations, and for the past two weeks had worked there exclusively.

Six weeks into the new year. Sometimes Annie found it hard to believe how fast the time had gone since Simon left her in the dark hour before dawn New Year's Day. At other times she felt as if every minute since they'd parted had stretched itself out a hundred times its normal length. She missed him so badly. She could feel it in the newly awakened sting of desire in her bones, taste it in the bittersweet memory of his kisses, suffer it in the aching emptiness of her arms when she awakened, alone, in the middle of the night.

"Annie? Annie, are you busy?" Mrs. Lewandoski stood in the doorway, plastic rain hat on her head, black rubber boots on her feet, her serviceable black cloth coat with its lamb collar tightly buttoned against the cold. "I want you should have some of my cookies. I left them with Mrs. Phillips for you. Such a nice woman."

"Thank you very much, Mrs. L. Take it easy getting on the bus now. We don't want you to slip and fall in the snow."

Mrs. Lewandoski laughed. "Don't you should worry about that. There's enough padding on this *toches* that I'll bounce right up again like one of those little roly-polys my grandchildren play with."

Annie looked mischievous. "You're a fine figure of a woman, Mrs. L."

"You heard me, did you?" The old lady wasn't a bit disconcerted. "It's true you've got more meat on your bones than Rachel, but not enough that you should let my cookies go to waste."

"Don't worry. They won't go to waste. They'll just end up *around* my waist." Mrs. Lewandoski laughed, and Annie joined her, if a bit ruefully.

"Waste and waist. I like that."

"Goodbye, Mrs. L."

"God bless."

"Goodbye." Rachel appeared in the doorway in the old lady's place. "Her BP is up ten points," she said, turning her attention to Annie.

"It might be her anxiety over Mr. Johnson's mugging and the exertion of being out and around on a day like this. Let's make a notation on her chart and if it's still elevated next week we'll call in Maria."

"I'll see to it."

Annie noted with pleasure each small step forward Rachel made in regaining her confidence to practice nursing. Several days earlier she'd talked about looking into auditing some classes at the university in order to take the state board exams, if that should be necessary to have her license reinstated. Returning from the dead after so many years was proving to be a complicated process. So much of Rachel's life was still in limbo, so many gray areas still existed. Annie's heart cried out for her friend, but she gave her help and advice only when it was asked of her. For the most part Rachel was handling things very well for herself.

There were still rough days when she seemed to hold on to her fragile new confidence with great difficulty. Nights, Annie suspected, when old demons and new fears haunted her sleep. But aside from the annoying attentions of two so-called "celebrity agents" from California, and a tenacious New York publisher who had managed to learn her whereabouts and was determined to obtain the rights to her life story, so far her privacy had remained intact. Rachel's greatest setback was a bout of malaria, her second since returning from Vietnam, that kept her confined to her bed for several days. The fever had subsided almost as quickly as it flared up so that Maria Montoya and the expert on tropical diseases she consulted were both cautiously optimistic that the disease may have run its course.

Rachel was almost settled into her new apartment, a cozy one-bedroom flat on the second floor of a big Victorian house about three blocks from Annie's house that Leah had helped her find. It needed work, but Chad had volunteered a weekend to help paint and recaulk bathroom tile, and Leah was always ready for shopping expeditions to buy lamps, and sheets and towels. Surprisingly, even Doug had offered his services when Rachel was ready to buy a car. After a couple of sessions behind the wheel of Annie's station wagon, she'd declared herself ready for a driver's license. Ten days later she'd passed the exam with flying colors and was now the proud owner of a four-year old Toyota.

"Mrs. Simpson, Mrs. Phillips." Gabby Marins, the receptionist, stood in the open doorway of Annie's office, her good-natured, black face wreathed in a smile. She beckoned to Rachel, who had walked on down the hall to finish charting Mrs. Lewandoski's visit. "These just came for you ladies." In her arms she held two long, slender florist boxes.

"Goodness. Roses," Rachel said, opening her box to find half a dozen long-stemmed white ones. "The card says: 'Happy Valentine's Day, Simon.'"

"What about yours, Mrs. Simpson?" Gabby looked very interested in the contents of Annie's box, and it made Annie self-conscious. She opened it with hands almost as clumsy as blocks of wood. Nestled inside in green tissue and white baby's breath were six pink roses and a card that said, simply: "Soon."

Annie sensed Rachel reading the message over her shoulder. "Hmmm." She looked around the tiny utilitarian room for a vase. "Mrs. Simpson's roses are from my brother, also," Rachel explained for Gabby's benefit.

"Wasn't that nice of him to remember you both this way?" Gabby looked smug.

"Yes, it was. Very nice," Annie agreed quickly, too quickly, she decided when she caught the tail end of Gabby's knowing smile. "Thank you for bringing them in, Gabby. Will you send the next patient back, please?"

"Aren't you going to put your roses in a vase?"

"I'll find something, Gabby. You go on back out front."

"Yes, Mrs. Phillips."

"Thanks." Annie smiled. "No one around here has ever seen a man send me flowers. I appreciate your jumping in so I didn't have to explain. Gabby's a great receptionist, but she's also the world's foremost gossip."

"You're just lucky Mrs. Lewandoski left before these things arrived." Rachel picked up one of her white roses and sniffed appreciatively.

"Lord, yes." Annie shook her head, imagining Mrs. Lewandoski's probable response.

"Simon's note wasn't exactly an impassioned declaration of love," Rachel remarked. Annie felt Rachel watching her very closely. "Or maybe it was?"

Color rushed into Annie's cheeks. For her that one word did hold a wealth of meaning. *Soon.* To see Simon again, to feel his touch and taste his kisses. To be alone, together, soon. It also left her prey to doubts.

"Nothing's settled between us yet." Annie heard the unease in her words and wished she could banish the niggling worry from her heart and her thoughts, but she could not. She had fallen in love with a man in a secretive and dangerous line of work, a man whose first marriage had failed because of it. Was she stronger than Simon's first wife? Could she give him her love and keep her fear to herself?

"I think I'm going to have a long talk with my little brother when he comes to town." Rachel was looking thoughtful in her turn, her expression mirroring the uncertainty in Annie's.

"Rachel...I..." The next patient came galloping down the hall at that moment and Annie never finished her sentence. It was young Elbert Woods, followed more sedately by his mother.

"I'm here to get my stitch out," he announced importantly when he saw Annie and Rachel in her office. "I promise not to cry."

"Good." Elbert had made a diving tackle of his next elder brother in an impromptu living-room game of touch football. It was a great tackle, Elbert insisted, as Annie had patched him up. It was just that the coffee table had got in the way of his chin. The incident had occurred a week before. The stitch was ready to come out.

"Why don't you let me take care of it, El?" Rachel suggested, holding out her hand. "Annie's real busy today with some reports that have to be filled out before she goes home."

The little boy looked up at Rachel, not so very much taller than himself, and nodded. "Okay." He called over his shoulder to his mother, "Annie's got homework so Rachel is going to take out my stitch."

"If you'll just step into the next cubicle, please, Mrs. Woods." Rachel smiled. "I'll be with you in a moment."

"Hurry up," Elbert directed as he walked away. "I want to be home in time to watch *Teenage Mutant Ninja Turtles* on TV."

"What did he say?"

"Never mind." Annie hid a giggle by pretending to sniff one of her roses. "I'll explain later."

"Did he say Ninja Turtles?" Rachel shook her head in bewilderment. "Leah and I are going to the mall later this evening. Would you tell her I'll pick her up at a quarter to seven?"

"Of course. I have an Amerasian Children's League meeting at seven-thirty, but we'll make connections before I leave."

"How are things going?"

"Slow. Very slow. But Jake Paderwiski called me the other evening and said he has a pretty good progress report on the seven youngsters and their families who came out with us."

"I'm glad to hear that. Perhaps..." Rachel hesitated, looked down at her box of roses still sitting on Annie's desk and touched one of the velvety blooms with the tip of her finger. "Perhaps I could join you at one of the meetings... soon."

"You'll be most welcome any time, Rachel, you know that."

She smiled, just a faint upturn of the corners of her mouth. "Yes, I do know that."

"What are you and Leah shopping for tonight?" Annie asked before the subject of the conversation could upset Rachel further.

"I've been told I'm in dire need of hot rollers and a different curling iron if I'm going to keep this hairdo under control." Rachel seemed relieved to talk about something else. What painful recollections had been stirred to life in her memory this time, Annie wondered.

Rachel touched her fingers to the sleek, face-framing cut that flattered her small, delicate features and gave her something of the look of an elfin queen. "Leah goes in search of drawing materials for her new class."

Annie groaned. "Still lifes this session. The house is beginning to resemble the Farmer's Market. Last night, for a snack, the twins ate the models for her latest composition. It was a memorable evening to say the least." Annie giggled. She couldn't help it, recalling the stricken look on Leah's face, the twins' protestations of innocence, of not knowing the bowl of bananas and apples and kiwi fruit had been anything but a bedtime snack, Leah's indignation when she found out the dog ate the expensive kiwi, and the hurried late-evening trip to the supermarket to replace the lost provisions. It had all made for a lively evening.

Rachel laughed with Annie, the cloud of sadness that always lurked behind the blue-gray of her eyes disappearing for a moment or two. "I'll probably hear Leah's side of the story this evening." She turned to walk out the door, still smiling, her hands deep in the pockets of her white lab coat. "I'll come with you to one of the ACL meetings, Annie. Sometime soon."

"Whenever you're ready."

After Rachel left, Annie tried to return to her report, but the scent of roses filled the air, filled her senses, and

Rachel's last words kept repeating in her head. But for Annie the meaning it held was for her alone, private, special. Soon... soon... soon.

"I THINK I HAVE EVERYTHING I need." Leah frowned down at the handful of charcoal pencils in her hand, her finely chiseled features set in an expression of deep concentration. Along with the pencils she carried a tablet of heavy canvaslike drawing paper and a small box of pastel-colored chalks. "I probably shouldn't buy these pastels," she said, giving Rachel a rueful smile. "If I do it'll take the rest of my allowance and it's only Wednesday."

"We can always come back and get them some other day." Rachel smiled back at her young friend. Some things hadn't changed all that much since she was fourteen. Her allowance had never lasted for an entire week, either. She wondered if any teenager's did?

"You're right, I can wait to buy these next trip." Leah put the box of chalks back on the shelf and flipped her long black hair. Her expression remained wistful. "I don't think I've forgotten anything." She looked at her purchases once more. Satisfied, she headed for the checkout.

Rachel walked on to the front of the small art supply shop. The mall was emptying fast. She glanced at her watch to check the time. It was one of the little things that others took for granted but that she could not. It was still a luxury, however small and commonplace, to be able to know the exact time of day at a glance. For years she'd had no idea of time; hours and days ran together in the work camp. And later, after the terror, in the village she rose with the dawn and went to sleep with the coming of darkness as did everyone else. Once, not long after they arrived in the Hlông village, Father Pieter had tried to fashion a sundial, but during the long rainy season the sun seldom broke through the heavy cloud cover, so for the most part it was ineffective.

Father Pieter. She still thought of him often, although not quite so often since she'd returned to the States. She knew the government had notified the Vatican, who, in turn, had informed his order and his family in the Netherlands of his death. A week ago Rachel had received a letter from his two elderly sisters, in stilted, formally correct English, asking for news of their brother and what his life had been like in his last years. As yet she hadn't been able to write the reply. She was afraid she might never be able to send the two old ladies in Holland anything more than a few pages of meaningless platitudes and harmless anecdotes, the assurance that their brother had died at peace with God.

How could she tell them of what he—the two of them—had actually endured? Why should two loving old women suffer in turn for something that was long over and past? Rachel sighed, aware as always that for herself the past wasn't yet over and done.

"Rachel? Are you all right?" Leah was plucking at the sleeve of her coat, her gray eyes clouded with concern. "I asked you for the time, but you've just been staring off into space."

"What?" Rachel blinked and looked into Leah's anxious, tilted eyes. Sidestepping Leah's observation on her lapse of concentration, Rachel glanced at her watch again.

"It's time for us to go. The mall closes in fifteen minutes."

It had been a long, busy day and Rachel felt fatigue beginning to build up pressure behind her eyes. They turned left out of the art shop and headed for the main entrance of the mall.

"Are you sure you're okay?" Leah continued to look worried. Rachel hurried to reassure her.

"I'm fine, really. Just a little tired, that's all."

But she wasn't fine, not really. Nothing in her life was what it appeared to be. She pretended for Annie's sake, for her parents and Simon and Micah, but deep inside she was still afraid of everything new and unfamiliar. Sometimes it was so hard to keep up the pretense. And now, tonight, or perhaps tomorrow at the latest, Simon would be back. He would be staying in her new apartment, sleeping on the secondhand sofa bed in the living room. They would be alone together. He would hear her if she cried out in her dreams in the middle of the night. He might even come to her room to ask her what was wrong.

And there, in the dark vulnerable time between midnight and dawn, could she have the strength, the courage, to keep her questions to herself? Or would she blurt it all out? Ask him point-blank why he hadn't come for her as he'd promised that long ago April? Why hadn't he at least sent her word that the end was so near?

She didn't ask, because, God help her, she dreaded his answer more than anything she could imagine. What if he had no excuse? What if he confessed he'd forgotten her? What if all those lost years, the terror and heartache, the pain and misery had been in vain?

"Rachel? Rachel, the car is this way, remember?" Leah was standing about ten feet away. They were outside the mall, on the sidewalk. The parking lot, which had been half full of cars when they arrived, was almost empty. Her Toyota was out of sight, down a slope that led to the street, in the opposite direction from the way she'd been walking.

"This place is kind of creepy with all the cars gone," Leah said, her giggle more nervous than amused. "I never realized it was so big." Running footfalls sounded behind them. Leah glanced around. "Or so spooky."

"We're almost there." Rachel kept her voice steady. The weather had turned warm the past couple of days and melted some of the snow. At night, as soon as the sun went down, all the melted snow turned to ice. She wasn't all that confident driving on slippery city streets. She was in a hurry to get home.

"There's someone behind us." Leah's whisper was urgent.

"Probably just somebody walking this direction to get to their car." She felt very exposed suddenly, alone, vulnerable in the middle of the big empty lot. Maybe Mrs. Lewandoski's accounts of the muggings on Lyman Street had affected her more than she'd like to admit. The running footsteps behind them grew closer. Leah turned to look over her shoulder again.

"Those two men. They're following us. There aren't any other cars in this row." They had topped the rise of the lot. Rachel's Toyota was sitting all alone under one of the big arching lampposts that dotted the lot—sitting in shadow because the light above was burned out.

Rachel looked behind her. The two men were only a few dozen yards away. They were small, slight men, with the swinging stride of athletes. Rachel shifted the heavy plastic bag with her new hot rollers and curling iron to her left hand while she dug into the outside pocket of her shoulder bag for the car keys. She wasn't scared, she told herself, she wasn't going to panic. It was just better to be prepared to get into the car in a hurry.

She lengthened her steps. The car was only twenty feet away. Rachel glanced back over her shoulder as Leah hurried along at her side. The two men were still behind them, their bodies backlighted by the neon of a K Mart sign. The overhead lights of the parking lot cast their faces into bold relief. Asian faces. Hard, emotionless, cruel. Rachel's breath caught in her throat. She stumbled and almost fell on a patch of ice. *Vietnamese faces.* The men were Vietnamese and they were coming after her. They had found her and they were going to take her back to prison, to death in life, and she couldn't let them. For a moment panic blanked her mind. Then she looked up and saw Leah's face, wide-eyed and frightened, and felt her hand on her arm. "Rachel, hurry. I'm scared."

"It's okay." The words came out all choked and whispery. "Don't go around to the other side of the car." She couldn't allow Leah to move that far from her side. For some reason she couldn't explain or analyze, she knew she must keep Annie's daughter close to her side. "Stay with me. As soon as I unlock the door, slide across to the passenger seat. We'll be okay. They won't hurt us." As she spoke Rachel slid the key into the lock. She missed in the near darkness and had to try again. The men were running hard now, almost on top of them. The door opened. Leah threw her bag of art supplies into the car just as the first of the two men made a grab for her arm. He said something short and sharp. Leah screamed. Rachel didn't waste her time or strength in screaming.

She pushed Leah away from the man as hard as she could with her right hand. With her left she swung the heavy sack of small appliances directly into his face. He let go of Leah's coat sleeve with a grunt of pain and stepped back, knocking his partner off balance as he attempted to move around behind Rachel and shove her out of the way. Leah had scrambled across the seat of the car. Rachel threw herself into the driver's seat, slammed the door and slapped the lock home before the second man could jerk it open again. She pushed the key into the ignition with hands that were as steady as a rock. Leah was sobbing as she stared out of the window at the two angry men beyond the glass.

"Hurry, Rachel, let's go! They may have guns!" The little car started at once and Rachel said a silent prayer of gratitude for the tune-up Doug had given the engine just the weekend before. They tore out of the parking lot, dodging small mountains of piled-up snow. Rachel never looked back as their two assailants raced off on foot.

"They tried to rob us," Leah said, pushing her hair out of her face, hiccupping as she tried hard to stop crying. "We should report this to the police."

"No." The steely calm that had enveloped her during the confrontation with the two men was wearing off. Rachel could feel the trembling start deep inside, and with it the roiling fear of old terrors reawakened and all the stronger for their sleep. She could see the men's faces, transposed to another time and place, far from the cold, wintery shores of Lake Michigan. In her mind's eye they were no longer wearing dark leather jackets and stocking caps on their heads. They were wearing combat fatigues and the gold star on red background of Vietnamese army regulars on their hats and collars. Sights and sounds and smells she'd kept buried for years were fighting their way to the surface of her consciousness, and Rachel was too tired and too drained to hold them at bay. Yet she knew that if she gave in, let those memories come, the pain would follow right behind.

"I've never been robbed before," Leah said, clutching her purse as if she would never let go. "I would have given them my money. I only have two dollars left anyway." She took a deep breath, licked dry lips. "They didn't have guns or knives, did they?"

"I didn't see any weapons." Rachel thought her voice sounded like small splinters of ice breaking free of her throat. It was what she had heard that frightened her now, as much as what she'd seen. A few words only, spoken in Vietnamese with a curious overlay of flat midwestern drawl. One sentence, a command really, nothing more, yet she couldn't forget it, even though she couldn't begin to fathom the meaning behind it.

"Get the girl!" she'd heard the first man say. "Don't worry about the other one, just get the girl!"

CHAPTER THIRTEEN

"HELLO, RACHEL." Simon unfolded his length from his sister's sofa and turned to face the open door. "Your landlady let me in out of the cold when I came up with enough identification to satisfy her that I was your brother not some..." He stopped talking abruptly. Rachel stood just inside the room, the key to her door still in her hand, a hand that was shaking hard. Leah was just behind her, her gray eyes wide, her face as white as a sheet.

"Simon?" Rachel's voice was as dazed as her expression. Simon felt his chest tighten, his muscles contract in answer to an unseen enemy. Fear had walked into the room with the two women. Danger, possibly, lurked somewhere nearby. Simon accepted that fact without thought or analysis, purely on instinct honed to a razor's edge. The flippant remark he'd been about to utter about being Rachel's Valentine's Day surprise died in the back of his throat.

"What happened?" He realized how harsh the two words sounded almost as quickly as he said them. He softened his tone. "Has there been an accident?" He walked quickly to the door, looked out into the closet-sized vestibule at the top of the outside stairs and shut the door, sealing them inside Rachel's small, cozy living room.

"No." Rachel walked to the couch and sat down without taking off her coat. She wasn't wearing a hat. Her hair was different, Simon noted peripherally. The shoulder-length curls she'd been wearing at Christmas were gone. Her style now was more sophisticated, more mature. The soft, swingy cut framed her face and made her eyes look enormous. His sister was a very attractive woman—when she didn't look half scared to death.

"Two guys tried to mug us," Leah stammered, her voice breathless with excitement. "One of them tried to grab me, and get my purse, I guess." She shrugged slim shoulders, unwilling to conjecture further. "Rachel hit him with a bag of her stuff." She halted, her hand to her mouth. "Oh, Rachel, your things. Where are they?"

"I...I must have dropped them in the parking lot. I...I have my bag, though." She lifted a small shoulder bag out in front of her and looked at it as if she'd never seen it before. Simon was afraid she was going into shock.

"Your hot rollers and new curling iron were in that sack. They cost a lot of money." Leah looked at Simon. "We should call the police."

"No!" Rachel clutched her handbag as though it were a lifeline. "No police." She glanced imploringly at her brother.

"How did you get back here?" Simon directed his question to Leah, his troubled hazel eyes still on Rachel. He sensed her fear, and the tight rein she held on her emotions.

"Rachel drove us," Leah explained. "I thought she was all right. I didn't know if anyone was home at my house, so we came here. But now...should I call my mother?" She glanced worriedly at Rachel, who was still wearing her coat, staring at the closed door of the apartment with haunted eyes.

"Yes." Simon nodded his agreement. His own need to see Annie again was surpassed only by his helplessness in the face of Rachel's distress.

Leah hurried to the phone on the kitchen wall. She punched out the numbers and waited. "It's busy," she explained over her shoulder. "I bet the twins forgot to put the upstairs phone back on the hook the last time they picked it up. Chad lets them get away with anything when he sits. Damn." She colored prettily and looked at Simon. "I'm sorry."

"That's okay. I feel like swearing, myself."

"I'll run home and get Mom. She should be back from her meeting by now—it's after ten," Leah said, brightening a little. "It's just three blocks. We'll be back in fifteen minutes."

"No." Rachel took a step toward the girl. "Stay here. I'm fine, really."

Leah walked over to Rachel and patted her hand. "Don't worry. Those men are long gone by now. They probably picked up your bag of stuff and took off in the other direction."

"I...I don't think you should go out."

"Why, Rachel?" Simon spoke as gently as he could manage. "Do you think the two men followed you back here?"

"No," Leah responded with great emphasis. "I watched out the back window for a long time. No other cars even came out of the mall entrance for as long as I could see it."

"Leah." Rachel looked as if she wanted to say more, but only made a helpless little gesture with her hands instead.

"I'll be all right, Rachel, truly. This is a nice neighborhood. I know Mom's home by now. It's past the twins' bedtime. Don't worry, please."

"Go on, Leah," Simon urged quietly. "Rachel, let me take your coat."

"I'm cold." She sounded more like a frightened child than the elder sister who had bullied him, watched over him, laughed with him and at him, for the first eighteen years of his life. Rachel let him take her coat despite her protests and hang it on the oak hall tree in the corner behind the door. Leah gave Rachel one last worried glance and scurried out into the night. Simon walked to the window overlooking the street and watched until Leah was out of sight. When he turned back into the softly lighted room, Rachel was still standing by the couch, her shoulders stiff, her face taut with strain.

"What happened, Rachel?"

"Two men followed us into the parking lot. They were Vietnamese," she responded flatly.

"Are you certain?" There was a fairly large Southeast Asian refugee population in the area. Most were hardworking, family-oriented, good citizens and neighbors, but there were always a few bad apples in the barrel. He couldn't dismiss Rachel's words out of hand.

"I heard them speaking Vietnamese," she said in the same emotionless tone.

"Damn, what rotten luck," Simon muttered under his breath. He pushed his hand through his hair in frustration, dragging a dark lock down over his forehead. He wondered what the odds of his sister getting mugged by two Vietnamese purse snatchers would be. In the thousands, or tens of thousands, probably. "It was just damn bad luck, that's all."

"I don't know." Rachel shook her head, bewildered. Simon walked toward her slowly, held out his hand, touched her sleeve gently.

"It was coincidence, nothing more."

She blinked, then focused her tear-bright eyes on his face.

"Why did you leave me there, Simon?"

"I don't understand...." He was unprepared for her abrupt change of subject.

"Did you forget your promise?" Her voice was only a whisper, a mere thread of sound in the quiet room. He could smell the faint perfume of the roses he'd sent her wafting up from their vase on the coffee table behind them. "Did you forget me?"

"We never forgot you. None of us. Mom and Dad always had faith. Hope. Micah and I did what we could." The past was strong tonight. He could feel it pulling at him as strongly as Rachel could.

"You said you'd come for me. You sent word to the orphanage. You said the end was coming but not to worry, that you'd get me out of Saigon. That you'd let me know when to leave and take the children with me." She was looking at him, but Simon knew she saw nothing of him, or of the room around her. Her eyes were focused on a time and a place half a world away, and half a lifetime ago.

"I waited, Simon. I waited for you to come but you never did." Tears slipped down her cheeks. "You left me there. Alone." She crumpled into a little ball on the couch, her arms folded tightly around herself, holding her fear, her misery inside.

Each word she said hit Simon like a hammer blow. *Dear God, all these years had she thought he'd deserted her? Or worse, that he'd forgotten her?* It was clear suddenly, the distance he'd felt between them, the holding back that couldn't all be accounted for by Rachel's experiences, her reluctance to open herself to loving again. She'd held herself back because she thought he'd failed her in her greatest hour of need.

"God, Rachel." Simon pulled her into his arms. Her body refused to relax against him, although hard, dry sobs racked her with shudders. "I tried every way I knew how to get through to you." He didn't know if she believed him. He wasn't even certain if she'd heard him or not. She rocked back and forth in his arms. He could feel her pain, the terror of her memories, and it matched his own.

"You were in Bangkok. The people at the embassy must have known what was going on. I know you don't work for the Census Bureau. I think even then I knew you weren't some low-level liaison for the Thai agricultural project as you claimed." Sobs still racked her too-slender shoulders, but there were no tears on her cheeks, only in her eyes. "You had to have known what was happening. And you left me there. I had to make sure Annie made it to the embassy. It was too risky for her to stay any longer. Father Pieter and I got the nuns and the kids out, or at least we always hoped so." Her voice broke. "But when they came...when the North Vietnamese soldiers ransacked the orphanage...I was alone." She shuddered and went still in his arms. "Why didn't you come?" Her quest was a cry from the heart.

"I tried, Rachel." Simon's voice was rough with unshed tears of his own. "God help me, I tried." He found himself looking backward at memories, emotions he'd suppressed so successfully for so long it was as if they'd happened to another man. Perhaps that was why he'd never thought to bring the subject out into the open himself before tonight. He'd wiped the aborted efforts to rescue Rachel from his mind so completely he'd never thought to set her mind at rest.

She turned her head, her face ravaged by grief, and looked into his eyes. "Did you try, Simon?"

"Yes." He felt the corners of his mouth twist into a mirthless grin. "I couldn't get back to Saigon to warn you. I wasn't in Bangkok. I was in Can Tho."

"Can Tho?" Rachel's voice held a question. Can Tho had been a busy trading center eighty miles south of Saigon and the site of a large American consulate. "A friend of mine was in Bangkok for a couple of days of R & R. He shanghaied me into going back with him when he got word things were going sour. That was just after I got through to you the last time by phone."

"A week after Annie arrived." He felt her relax against him ever so slightly. The horrible racking sobs had ceased but her breathing was still ragged and uneven.

"Nobody knew how bad the situation really was. The Vietnamese were holding their own in the delta. They stayed by their positions until they were ordered to surrender. Jack was responsible for evacuating American citizens and Vietnamese dependents. When he found out he was sending people up to Saigon, into a gridlock that got them nowhere, he nearly went berserk. I couldn't leave him to cope alone. On the twenty-ninth we got a phone call. They said 'get out' and the line went dead. Then the CIA began to pull out, leaving most of their civilian dependents behind. That's when we realized things in Saigon must be desperate. Jack comandeered a couple of landing craft and started rounding up civilians." Simon stopped talking and took a deep breath. He couldn't tell Rachel that he still had nightmares of that last day, of driving through crowded streets looking for people he knew only from Jack's description of them, trying to convince them to leave with him immediately, with only what they could carry, or be left behind to face almost certain death.

"How many people did you get out?"

"Almost four hundred, mostly women and children. One of the people the CIA left behind was their radioman. He had a portable set with him, but Saigon never bothered to furnish us with the classified evacuation frequencies, so for two days we floated downriver, dodging enemy shells and deserting South Vietnamese regulars. We had no food at all and very little water. The Vietnamese were seasick and most of us Americans were amateur sailors at best." He shook his head, remembering. "We reached the mouth of the river in the dead of night, in a driving rainstorm that damned near swamped both craft, and just kept drifting out to sea. On the second day we spotted an old Liberty ship evacuating refugees. They took us in tow. By the time I could hitch a flight back in country, the city had fallen and you were gone."

"No one in authority bothered to warn us at the orphanage, not until it was too late," Rachel said. "Annie said everything at the embassy was in chaos. When she and the boys were separated from the rest of us, it was the first chance we'd had to get anyone out at all. Oh, Simon. So much waste of life, so much suffering and misery."

"I tried to get to you, Rachel, but there was no way back."

"And Micah?"

"The air force grounded his squadron. He had no idea you were trapped. He nearly got court-martialed for going back into Laos to evacuate the native pilots and their families. Some of them here Hlông tribesmen." He didn't tell her about the bad years that had followed for Micah, that still haunted his present, as much as their memories did theirs. "It was his old Raven contacts who finally got word about you out to us last spring."

"And you? What did you do after Saigon fell?"

"You can't court-martial an agricultural liaison, but they damned near tried." He realized how curt and choppy his words had become. There was no other way he could get them out without giving in to emotions he'd thought dead, or at least dealt with, years ago.

"Did you stay in country?"

"Thailand mostly, off and on during the next few years." This time it was Rachel who reached out to comfort him. She held his hands between her own. Her fingers were icy cold. He suspected his were, too.

"You were looking for me." She smiled then, tentatively, as though a great weight had been lifted from her heart.

"I was doing my job." At the time that was what he truly believed. Now, looking deeper into his soul he knew, like his parents, he'd never wanted to give up hope. He'd just buried it so deep it couldn't surface again. "I was always on the lookout for information. There just wasn't any for a long, long time. Tracking down missing civilians was even harder than getting information on missing servicemen, and that was damned near impossible." When his base of operations was shifted to Latin America a few years later, the task became harder still.

"But you never gave up trying to find me? Any of you?" Rachel's voice took on a wondering tone. "Maybe that's why I could never give up, give in, and let my sanity..." her voice was barely more than a whisper, she held on to him as a lifeline "...and my life slip away."

"Mom would say that was faith." Rachel didn't hear the door, which hadn't been locked after Leah left, open. Simon did. He looked over the top of Rachel's head to see Annie silhouetted in the doorway. She was wearing an ivory suit and a cobalt-blue blouse that intensified the glorious red of her hair. One of his pink roses was pinned to her lapel. She looked as if she'd been hurrying through the cold. Her expression was calm but concerned, her eyes were full of love and tears.

"Faith?" Rachel shook her head. "I don't know. That's what Father Pieter called it, too. All I know is that I had to go on...through everything that happened... everything I lost." She leaned her head against his shoulder. Simon felt himself captured by the power and glory of Annie's eyes. "It wasn't all for nothing. Annie found Mike, and made the children her own. Father Pieter and I did get the rest of the children to safety. You saved hundreds of other lives, and so did Micah, from what you tell me. Knowing all that makes it easier." She sighed, almost a yawn, and Simon hoped she would be able to rest, to sleep, after this emotionally trying confrontation. "I should have asked you these questions weeks ago instead of keeping the hurt and uncertainty all bottled up inside."

She wasn't telling him everything, but Simon was unwilling to press his sister for further revelations. She was too fragile, still. "We love you, Rachel. We always have. We always will."

Rachel straightened in his arms; she reached out to touch his beard-roughened cheek, a fleeting butterfly caress. "I know. I've always known. And someday, soon, I think I won't be afraid to love you, all of you, again."

SIMON WAS LOOKING OUT THE window onto the dark, quiet street below. Annie closed the door of Rachel's bedroom very quietly behind her. He heard and asked without turning away from the window. "Is she asleep?"

"Yes. I gave her a sleeping pill. Evidently the doctors in Washington prescribed them. She didn't want to take it, but I persuaded her that tonight it was best that she did. She needs a good night's sleep. She's stretched very thin, Simon." Annie smoothed the folds of a brightly colored afghan over the back of the couch. Rachel had done wonders in just the two weeks she'd lived in her apartment. It was already beginning to look like a home.

"It's a miracle she manages as well as she does. Most women in her position would be basket cases. Hell, so would most men." He continued to stare out into the night.

Annie's brow creased in a worried frown. "She told me the men in the parking lot were Vietnamese. She seems to think they wanted Leah." She stopped talking, wanting him to deny the statement.

Simon turned away from the window in one swift, controlled movement. "She told you that?"

"Yes." Annie moved to his side. "I'm afraid she was just so scared she imagined it. Leah was frightened, of course, when she got home, and a little bit excited." Annie looked down at her clasped hands, trying to remember Leah's breathless garbled explanation precisely. "She did describe the men as Asian, but she couldn't be certain they were Vietnamese. She didn't tell me that she heard them say anything at all. I'll question her more closely when I get home."

"If anyone has the right to be paranoid about what happened tonight, it's Rachel." There was a wealth of self-loathing evident in his low, dark voice. Simon turned back to the window. He stretched his arm out over his head, leaning his weight against the window frame. "Fourteen years of living in one hellhole after another, at the mercy of men who were no better than hardened criminals. Even after she made it to the Hlông village, it would be like living in the Stone Age." His hand balled into a fist of impotent rage. "All that time she thought we'd abandoned her. Forgotten her, left her to her fate. I should have realized from the very beginning that she'd question...."

Annie had seen strong men caught up in guilt for situations not of their own making before. She didn't intend to let it happen to Simon. She laid her hand on his arm. The muscles were locked, as hard as steel beneath her fingertips. "You did everything you could. Micah risked his life by going into Laos to rescue your sister. So did you by going back to Vietnam to bring them out." She didn't mention the sacrifices obtaining the pearls had cost him in monetary terms. She knew he had forfeited the money willingly. That he would have raised twice, three times, that amount if necessary and never regretted the loss.

Simon smacked his open palm against the wooden frame in frustration. The movement loosened Annie's touch on his arm. Her hand dropped to her side. "I coerced you into smuggling those pearls into Southeast Asia. I put your safety in jeopardy and then I meekly followed you across the border hanging on to your apron strings." His mouth snapped shut on the last words.

"I don't even own an apron with strings." Annie's feeble attempt at humor fell on deaf ears. She tugged at his arm with determination, making him turn away from the window, from his introspection. His eyes were bleak, shadowed. He seemed to stare through her and his detachment made her blood run cold. "How could you have smuggled those pearls into Vietnam on your own? How could you have gotten in and out of there without blowing your cover if the League...and...I hadn't been on our way there in the first place?"

His laugh was bitter. "You are an innocent, Annie Simpson. I would have found a way. Using you was the best course of action, the most expedient way." He refused to meet her eyes. He stared at a point somewhere beyond her left ear. Annie felt desperation tug at her heart. She had to make him see reason. This emotionally charged confrontation with a haunted stranger was not how she'd fantasized their reunion. And heaven help her, she had fantasized all through the long, dreary February day, all through the meeting of the Amerasian Children's League, where she was ashamed to say she could barely keep her mind on the subject at hand, because she'd been thinking of Simon...and herself... alone...together.

"Do you think I'm going to hate you because it was less risky to use me as a courier?" She lifted her chin, squared her shoulders to do battle. "Do you think I'll condemn you now because you used me, someone you sensed you could trust, to carry those pearls into Vietnam?"

"I didn't give you a choice." He wasn't budging an inch. Annie felt righteous anger burning away at the edges of her desperation. She smiled a little, a woman's knowing smile, and only to herself. He was a strong man, like her father, like Mike, upright, loyal, full of principles and integrity. And as stubborn as a mule. He wasn't James Bond. He was a man doing a dangerous job because it must be done. What she had heard him tell Rachel of his experience in Vietnam made her see things more clearly. He was a gatherer of information, and perhaps, just perhaps, some of that information would help save lives, help free innocent people like Rachel from captivity. If he wanted to continue to do those things she wouldn't stand in his way, but not at the expense of his happiness or her own.

"Don't kid yourself." Annie let her anger burn a little brighter. Simon did look at her then, warily, as though she had suddenly grown horns and fangs and might attack without warning. "I carried...smuggled...those pearls into Saigon. I stood up to Ky and his threats because I wanted to help Rachel and Micah. That's all. I didn't do it for you. I did it for my own peace of mind. Don't try to take the blame for everything on yourself, Simon McKendrick. I won't stand for it." Outwardly she was calm and in control. Inwardly she cried for his solitude. What a burden it must be to be always strong, always silent, and alone.

"I nearly got you killed in that hotel room." His voice was harsh, his jaw rigid, but his eyes were no longer green-gold ice.

"You saved my life," Annie corrected. If she wanted to spend the rest of her life with this man, she was going to have to prove to him that she was strong enough to live with the burden of knowing the danger of his chosen profession. "I..."

Simon moved so swiftly she couldn't step away. He took her by the shoulders, shook her, not roughly but hard enough to make her shut her mouth. "Don't you think I see where you're going with this? I love you, God help us both. But I can't ask you to marry me."

Annie took a deep breath. "All right. I'll ask you."

"What?" He stared at her, dumbfounded. Small, blazing fires kindled in the gold flecks of his eyes. Annie felt her heart jump into her throat. Rising hope beat through her with each quickening beat.

"Will you marry me, Simon McKendrick?"

"Damn it, Annie." She smiled at his confusion, slid her arms around his waist, pressed herself closer until there could be no doubt that she desired him as much as his arousal proved he wanted her. "You don't have any idea...." She lifted her hand, pressed her finger against his lips to silence his words.

"On the contrary, I have a very good idea. And furthermore, I think I have what it takes to be the wife of a...an employee of the Census Bureau." She moved against him, slowly, provocatively, love making her bold. She framed his face with her hands, urging his mouth down to hers. She kissed him, her lips soft and pliant, coaxing him to taste the addictive honey of her mouth, the promise of fulfillment in her willing body.

"You make me want to believe in dreams again, Annie. That's dangerous for a man in my line of work." Simon kissed her as if he couldn't help himself, as if her taste and touch and scent were a narcotic stronger than any opiate known to mankind. His hands moved to hold her closer, mold her hips to the hardness of his thighs. His hands skimmed over her waist to settle possessively just below the generous swell of her breasts.

"It isn't believing in dreams that's dangerous, Simon. It's the lack of dreams, the darkness of not believing, that causes us heartache and grief."

"I do need you, Annie, your warmth and your light. I need you and I want you even more."

"Are you accepting my proposal?" His thumbs were moving in circles over her breasts, his breath tickled her ear as he nuzzled her temple. She could barely think straight; the woodsy tang of his cologne, the heady scent of his skin made her head spin with desire.

"Yes, I'll marry you, Annie Norton Simpson, for better or worse."

"Soon," Annie murmured, wanting more than anything to be swept into his arms and carried away to his bed so that they could seal their pledge in the oldest and most pleasurable of ways.

"Very soon." Simon ceased the magic of his caressing fingers. He lifted his mouth from hers, resting his forehead against the top of her head. His breath was ragged; his heart thundered against the wall of his chest. "I should have made love to you that night in Saigon."

"I wish you had." Annie sighed. She knew what he meant. They wouldn't make love tonight. She stepped away, a small distance only, because Simon wouldn't let her go. "There's no place for us to be alone, is there?" She hadn't meant to sound so forlorn but she couldn't help it. Physical frustration at very nearly forty was every bit as painful as it had been at seventeen.

The heavy frown between Simon's dark brows vanished. A reluctant smile curved his mouth. "We seem destined to celibacy. I can't leave Rachel, not tonight."

"I have to get back home." Annie tried a smile of her own. It came out crooked and shaky. "Leah was adamant that I come to make sure Rachel was all right, but she was scared. Chad was there to watch over her and the twins, thank goodness. But now that the excitement's worn off I should be with her. Simon?" She looked at him, searching his hazel eyes for any sign of second thoughts. "You're going to have to make adjustments, too, you know. My children..."

"Will be as important to me as they are to you. Now go." He turned her around, his hands warm and strong on her shoulders. "Go, before I change my mind and ravish you here and now on my sister's living-room rug."

"I wouldn't put up much of a struggle," Annie said wistfully.

"Then I'll be strong for both of us."

"No." Annie was completely serious again. "We'll be strong together." She touched her finger to his lips in a quick caress and walked out of the room.

CHAPTER FOURTEEN

LE THI SHIVERED AND TURNED away from the depressing view of the fire escape and the dirty brick wall of another building only a few feet away. Her hotel room was as confining to the spirit as the view outside. And it was only marginally warmer. She pulled her sweater close around her. Outside it was snowing and a wind so cold it must have come all the way from the North Pole sent more snow swirling between the buildings.

From what she had seen of Chicago, Illinois, it was colder and dirtier and grayer, even, than New York City. She longed for the smell of flowers, the clamor of street traffic and the singsong music of shop vendors bickering outside shuttered windows, the bright sunlight and steamy warmth of her homeland. Here she had only her dreams to keep her warm.

Beyond the thin wall she heard the phone ring in Nguyen Duc's room. Le Thi's heart beat more quickly. She sat down on the edge of her bed, her legs refusing to hold her upright. The phone call had to be from the men Nguyen had told her he'd hired to locate her daughter. Men he knew who had left Vietnam but who still retained ties to their homeland. It had to be them. No one else knew of their whereabouts. Even Hoang. Especially Hoang.

Le Thi hugged her arms to her breasts to avoid thinking about her husband. It had been a long, tiring day but she was too keyed up to rest. They had stolen away to the airport early this morning, as soon as Hoang left for an emergency meeting at the UN that would last all the rest of this day and far into the night.

It was as if the spirits had chosen to smile on her at last. Only yesterday she had been sitting in her hotel room in New York staring at a day-old, heart-shaped basket of fruit the management had presented her for Valentine's Day, saddened to be alone yet again, when Nguyen had knocked on the door. "I have located the child," he said bluntly, his face a mask that effectively hid whatever emotions he possessed. "If you wish to go to her it must be now."

Le Thi had been frightened to leave New York, to leave her husband, but she had had no choice. She had come too great a distance to miss the chance to be reunited with her daughter. And, thank Buddha, so far her fears of discovery had been groundless. She could only marvel at the ease with which Americans moved around their huge country.

She had paid cash for the airline tickets and no one had even questioned her right to board the plane. They had taken a cab to this shabby suburban hotel, and the cabby, an immigrant from Pakistan himself, assumed they were Japanese. Le Thi had said nothing to make him think otherwise. Later, after they checked into the hotel, the two men Nguyen Duc had hired provided them with a car of their own.

Le Thi did not know how to drive a car, but that was only a minor stumbling block after the great difficulties she had already overcome. It would be easy to take her daughter anywhere she wished in the vast country. They would travel someplace warm and sunny and wait for Hoang to make arrangements for all three of them to go home. The sooner she could be reunited with her daughter, the sooner she could return to the man she loved. She would have to get away from Nguyen Duc somehow, but she could manage that. There were enough dollars left from her jewelry to pay for his silence. She hoped. Le Thi neither liked nor trusted the man, but so far he had been essential to her plans.

The slightly uneasy frown that marred her fine-boned Eurasian features faded away, replaced by a soft and private little smile. Her English had improved a great deal. She could cope with the difficulties of traveling with an infant in a foreign land.

Infant. A shiver danced across her skin, but it came from within her, not from the cold. She must not think that way. Her daughter was no longer an infant. She was almost grown, a young woman. Many years had passed since that terrible day of separation. Years that could not be returned to her no matter how much she wished they could. She must remember that. She wrapped her arms around her to hold in the grudging warmth of the soulless room and waited for Nguyen Duc to take her to her child. She began to hum a lullaby.

"OKAY. MOM'S TALKING ON the phone to one of the nurses about some report or other that she needs," Mike said, creeping back into the dining room with exaggerated stealth. He looked over his shoulder to make sure Annie was out of earshot. "What are we going to do for her birthday? It's only a few weeks away."

"The big four-oh." Jon nodded his head judiciously.

"She'll throw a fit if we do anything stupid." Doug leaned back in his chair and folded his arms across his chest, but for once his negative comments sounded as if they'd been voiced in order to contribute to the discussion.

Doug was an unknown factor in Simon's future with Annie. The boy hadn't said anything since Simon and Annie had told the five children and Rachel, earlier in the evening, of their plans to be married sometime in the spring.

"A party," Leah said. "A big one so that we can be in practice for the wedding reception in June." Simon hid a chuckle behind his napkin. They hadn't gotten as far as picking a wedding date as yet. But obviously Leah had.

It was funny how quickly he'd gotten to know these kids. Leah's slightly exotic looks hid the heart and soul of a typical American teenage girl. Parties, weddings, romance; she loved them all. The twins, on the other hand, couldn't care less for weddings and their accompanying pageantry. They were more interested in their stomachs. Chad would be next to comment, cautioning fiscal responsibility and common sense in the midst of runaway enthusiasm.

"Don't get carried away, you guys," he said as if on cue. "I happen to know you're three weeks ahead on your allowances already and it's still February."

"Children can't be expected to manage money." Leah tossed her head. The smile she bestowed on her small brothers was sweetly condescending.

"Aren't you the one that just hit me up for a five-buck loan?" Doug asked, crumbling a chocolate-chip cookie into pieces on his plate. Simon was grateful Doug had stayed to share the impromptu celebration dinner of lasagna and salad, fruit, cookies and ice cream. For a few minutes after he and Annie had made their announcement, he'd thought the boy was going to bolt.

"I have expenses. Art supplies are very costly." Simon caught a glimpse of Rachel's face from the corner of his eye. She was smiling at the rapid-fire give and take around Annie's dining-room table, but there were fine new lines around her eyes and a tightness in her shoulders that spoke of inner stress.

"I can chip in for a gift, but I'm pretty short on funds myself if it comes to staging a big blowout," Chad confessed with a frown that reminded Simon of Annie's.

"We have to do something." Leah made a steeple of her hands and rested them on her chin. Her expression was thoughtful. "Something simple but elegant. The way I want Mom and Simon's wedding to be." She sighed and waved her hand in an airy, dramatic gesture.

"No way!" Mike exclaimed. "That means gaggy little fish eggs on soggy crackers like Brian Feeney's sister, Mary Margaret, had at her wedding reception. Remember when we had to be ring bearers and dress up like sissies and walk down the aisle holding hands with Ashley DeMarco and her stupid cousin. And Jon barfed." He gave his brother a smoldering look. "As usual."

"Did not."

"Did too." Mike sat up straighter in his chair, ready to do battle. "I want pizza from the Pizza Joint."

"And some of the great shrimp dip that Rachel and Simon's mom gave us the recipe for at Christmas time," Jon added for good measure.

"Pizza is not elegant," Leah hissed across the table. "But I did like your mother's shrimp dip." She smiled at Simon, on her left, and then at Rachel who was sitting across the big cherry table from her.

"Fortieth birthdays are getting to be pretty popular events these days." Rachel focused the subject more firmly on Annie's birthday and away from the as yet nebulous wedding plans. Simon gave his sister a grateful smile. "Remember when we were Chad and Doug's age, Simon? We wouldn't listen to a word anyone over thirty had to say, let alone celebrate the fact that they were so incredibly ancient."

Rachel was putting up a good front, but Simon was aware she hadn't slept the two nights since the attack in the mall parking lot. The strain was beginning to show. Her dreams were filled with nightmares, and her happy laughter was only a thin veneer covering her unease. She'd shrugged off Annie's suggestion that she make an appointment to see a therapist, or a counselor at the veterans' center. "Now forty is rad," she said, giving Mike a saucy wink.

"Yeah, but it's still old," Mike insisted.

"There's this really cute little gift shop a couple of streets over from the clinic on Lyman." Leah directed her comment to Rachel, ignoring her brother. "They have all kinds of decorations and favors. Funny banners and black balloons and little hats, things like that. Maybe we could go over there and check out some prices. You know, get an idea of what it would cost to give Mom a really great party."

"That does sound like a good idea." Rachel stirred her coffee, looking down at the cup as she spoke.

"We could go this evening. They're open until nine."

"I...I don't know." Rachel's hand jerked, slopping coffee into the saucer. Simon was aware his sister hadn't driven her car after dark since the attempted mugging.

"You see, if we go now, then we can know how much of our allowances we'll have to save to have enough for Mom's party," Leah went on, unaware of Rachel's reaction to the suggestion.

"I...see your point." His sister gave in with good grace. Being around Annie's kids was good for Rachel, Simon realized. It kept her from retreating into herself.

Rachel continued, "And I think since Simon is going to be part of your family soon, he'll want to contribute to the party expenses so that you five can get just the perfect birthday present for your mother." Rachel shot him a challenging glance.

"Would you, Simon?" Leah clasped her hands in front of her.

"I'd be honored." Simon bowed his head in a courtly gesture. Chad grinned and stood up from the table, the matter being settled to his satisfaction. "Time to get the dishes taken care of."

"It's Mike and Jon's turn to load the dishwasher," Leah said, coming down off her romantic high in a hurry.

"Is not!" both twins cried in unison.

"I'm afraid it is, guys." Chad's tone brooked no argument. "Finish your ice cream, Mike. You're not going to get out of loading the dishwasher by dawdling in here." He fixed his brother with a gimlet stare. "And hurry up, I have to get back to the dorm and study for a psych test." Mike struck his spoon into his ice cream, still grumbling under his breath.

"What did you do to celebrate your fortieth birthday, Simon?" Leah asked, turning slightly in her seat to face him more directly.

"I was out of the country." Simon found himself trying to recall just where in Central America he'd been at the time.

"Spying," Jon said succinctly, swirling his ice cream into intricate patterns with his spoon.

"Jon."

"Well, what else do you call it?" Mike asked agreeably.

Annie had warned him that her children had more or less guessed what he did for a living, so he'd been able to take their comments in stride. He wondered what his bosses at the State Department would do if they knew how quickly Annie's brood had blown his cover. He'd decided they'd either lock them up somewhere and throw away the keys, or more probably, put them all on the payroll.

"I was inspecting a resettlement camp in Costa Verde," he said, remembering.

"Where's Costa Verde?" Mike frowned at him over a spoonful of double chocolate chip.

"It's one of those little countries that's always having a revolution." The answer, surprisingly, came from Doug.

Simon nodded. "I'm afraid that about sums up the situation down there. We needed to see how many people should be allowed to come to the United States." And weed out any subversives, or death-squad hit men posing as refugees, trying to make their way to the States. He'd almost forgotten his birthday, but not the trip itself. It was outside his usual sphere of operation, a simple fact-finding mission to the huge refugee camp on the border of the small, politically unstable dictatorship. It had involved no elaborate cover story, no secret identity, no subterfuge. Only talking and listening, and learning. Something about the war-weary men, the hungry women and sad-eyed children had stayed with him. His quiet, classified report to his superiors, while cautioning vigilance and continued screening of refugees, had also recommended an increase in Costa Verde's resettlement quota. This year congress had acted to do just that. Two thousand more souls, not enough by any means, but a beginning.

"What about your birthday, Rachel?" Mike had ice cream on his chin. He swiped at it with the back of his hand. Simon felt his nerves tighten. Chad and Doug were silent. Leah looked stricken.

Rachel was silent, too, for a long moment. "The Hlông don't celebrate birthdays the way we do. But let's see." She looked into the past. "It was the year the village drilled a new well. We were all very excited. It meant we women and children only had to carry the water half as far." She smiled but her eyes remained haunted. It was also, Simon calculated, the springtime that Father Pieter had died.

"Bogus," Mike said, making a face. He put an end to the conversation with his next observation. "Shhh, here comes Mom."

IT WAS VERY QUIET IN THE dining room, too quiet. Something was going on. Annie walked around the table and sat down next to Simon. Her ice cream melted into a puddle in the bowl.

"Do you want more ice cream, Mom?" Leah asked.

"No thanks, honey. What's been going on in here?"

"Nothing."

"I see." She took a cookie from the plate Doug handed her. "Just small talk?" A smile curved the corners of Simon's mouth. She loved to see him smile. He seemed to be enjoying himself and Annie felt a small knot of tension uncoil deep within her. She wanted everything to be perfect. And tonight it nearly was. The family was all together for dinner, an increasingly rare occurrence in a household containing two teenagers and a college student. Her children had accepted the fact that she and Simon were going to be married. In time she knew they would learn to love him as she did. For the present, acceptance and affection were a good beginning.

"You don't have to go back to the clinic tonight, do you, Mom?" Jon asked. Phone calls in the evening usually meant extra work for Annie, and they all knew it.

"I have to pick up a report at Lyman Street. That was Gabby Marins, the receptionist. She forgot to remind me to bring it home."

"Rachel and I can pick it up if you give her a key," Leah offered. "We... we have an errand to run not far from there."

"Not far from Lyman Street?" Annie looked puzzled. A small shiver of worry tickled at the back of her neck. She'd been almost as nervous and jumpy as Rachel since the mugging. She didn't like the idea of the two of them being out at night on Lyman Street.

"Ummm... yes. There's something at the Oak Street Plaza I need for art class. You know, it's only three blocks over from Lyman." Three blocks that were the difference between a thriving business district and a decaying neighborhood.

"Are you sure it's not an inconvenience?" Annie directed the last question to Rachel. She couldn't let her bout of nerves affect the others. Fear was contagious. Still, she couldn't shake the feeling that someone was looking over her shoulder at the oddest times. She took a second look at every strange car on the street outside the house; a wrong number made her imagine all kinds of sinister results. Only Leah seemed to have recovered completely from the incident.

"It's no problem." Rachel smiled. Her voice was firm and confident.

"I would appreciate it, then." Annie firmly banished her doubts to the back of her mind. "I have a ton of other paperwork to do this evening."

"That doesn't sound very romantic for a woman who just got engaged. I think you and Simon should go shopping yourselves. For a ring." Leah left the table with a twinkling glance at her mother and Simon.

Jon pushed his chair back and stood up, also. "Homework?" Annie asked automatically, hoping Leah's parting shot hadn't brought a blush to her cheeks. An engagement ring? She hadn't even had time to think about it.

"Finished."

"Mike?" Annie brought her attention back to the subject at hand, although she knew the answer to this question before she asked.

"Almost finished." Mike refused to meet her eyes. "I'll do the rest after *Star Trek*."

"You'll do it now."

"Mom, it's English." Mike looked disgusted. "We have to write a whole page on some article we find in the newspaper. I don't know what to do it on." He looked down at his empty ice cream bowl for inspiration. "I hate English."

"Mike." Simon cleared his throat as if it had suddenly gone dry. "I haven't got much to do this evening while your mom's working on her report. Want to take a look at the newspaper together? Maybe we can come up with something you can use in your report before your program comes on the TV." Only Annie, and perhaps Rachel, noticed the wariness in Simon's tone, the tautness in the set of his shoulders. It was the first time he'd had an opportunity to interact as parent with one of the twins. Annie held her breath. What if Mike, the easiest to approach of her children, turned him down?

The little boy looked at Simon for a long moment as if gauging the sincerity of his offer. "Okay," he said finally. "Jon already picked the good stuff, about politics and junk like that. Sister eats that stuff up." He shot his brother a poisonous glare.

Jon stuck out his tongue, then left the dining room before Mike could retaliate.

"There have been some pretty bad floods in Kentucky and Tennessee," Simon ventured.

"Floods?" Mike looked interested in spite of himself. Annie bit her lip to keep from smiling. Disaster and destruction were two of Mike's favorite subjects. "Did anyone drown?"

"I'm afraid so." Simon's tone was appropriately solemn, but his lips twitched as he fought to hold back his own smile.

"That doesn't sound too boring." He thought it over. "Okay," he said after a moment or two. "I'll do it." He looked over at Annie, his face innocent of guile. "It'll take a while to get it written. I don't think I have enough time to help with the dishes."

"Hey, that's not fair," Jon yelled, coming back into the dining room to see why no help in the kitchen was forthcoming. "He can't get out of doing dishes because he didn't get his homework done before we ate."

"Mom just surprised me too much by telling us she was going to marry Simon." Mike smiled at Annie and she wondered what wayward branch of her family tree was responsible for his gift of blarney.

She stood up. "Good try, Michael, but it's no go." Annie caught Rachel's amused expression and she smiled just a little in return.

"Your mother's right, Mike. We'll all pitch in and it won't take long to get the kitchen cleaned up." Annie rested her palms on the tablecloth and let Simon handle the twins' latest altercation. He was going to be a good father whether he was aware of the fact as yet, himself, or not.

"You sound just like Dad used to," Mike grumbled, but he stood up and headed for the kitchen with his bowl and spoon.

"Not like Dad," Doug growled, pushing away from the table so quickly his chair nearly tumbled over. "Not my dad. Just a stepfather." He turned and stalked out of the room before Annie could stop him and make him apologize for his rudeness.

Simon was standing, also. She looked at him, not knowing what to say, what to do. "Don't force the boy, Annie," he said, his voice low and soothing to her aching heart. "We've got all the time in the world to be a family."

"I THINK IT'S A GOOD THING that Mom and Simon have found each other," Leah said, sounding very grown-up and worldly-wise as she settled herself in the front seat of Rachel's car. "Older people shouldn't be alone." She caught her breath and stuttered out an apology. Rachel could see the blush that stained her cheeks as they passed a streetlight. "I... mean..."

"I know what you mean. I'm very happy for both of them, too." She'd been a bit surprised by the couple's announcement this evening, but she wasn't worried about the future of their union. If anyone could handle being thrust willy-nilly into Annie's energetic and sometimes chaotic family, Simon could. And if any woman could learn to cope with the pressures, and inevitable separations caused by Simon's way of life, it was Annie.

"Why don't we stop at Lyman Street first and pick up Mom's report," Leah suggested, squinting down at her watch when they stopped for a red light. "That way we can spend all the time we like at the party shop."

"Okay," Rachel agreed, swinging right at the next corner. She would just as soon be away from the Lyman Street neighborhood before it got much later, herself.

"I don't want to have to stop there later in the night." Leah echoed her thoughts. "It's pretty creepy at night. So many old people live there, it always looks deserted. Except for the winos and weirdos." The teenager was suddenly very quiet and Rachel guessed she was thinking about their ordeal in the mall parking lot. She didn't want her young friend to dwell on the incident, so she changed the subject.

"I saw a great T-shirt we could get your mother as a gag birthday gift. It said It's My Mid-Life and I'll Crisis if I Want To. It's a takeoff on a great old song, 'It's My Party and I'll Cry if I Want To,' that Leslie Gore sang. I think," Rachel qualified the statement. She screwed up her forehead, frowning with the effort to remember exactly which of the famous girl singers of her teenage years had made a hit of the song.

"I like that." Leah giggled and clapped her hands. "We'll need bunches of black balloons. Helium ones, of course, so they'll float above the gifts and the cake." She prattled on unmindful of the loneliness of the dark storefront clinic as they pulled up outside.

Leslie Gore, The Beatles, The Beach Boys. They all seemed so long ago and far away. Before the war, before her life had been so drastically altered. Hadn't there been a sequel to that song? Something about someone crying?

Rachel crying, alone and chained in the dark? Her baby lost forever in the darkness of a jungle grave. She shivered and tried to bring her thoughts back to what Leah was saying.

"Rachel? Did you hear me? I think we need black helium balloons and black crepe paper hanging from the ceiling."

"What?"

"The decorations for Mom's party."

"Of course. Sorry. I was thinking of something else."

"Mom will just freak out."

"'Judy's Turn to Cry,'" Rachel heard herself say aloud.

Now it was Leah who looked blank. "What?"

"'Judy's Turn to Cry.' That's the song I was trying to think of." *The title of a song. That was all. Nothing else. Nothing.*

"That drives me crazy when it happens." Leah nodded her head in sympathy. A nondescript blue Chevy drove past them and turned at the next corner. Otherwise Lyman Street was deserted, even though it was only a little after eight o'clock. "A friend of mine whose mother was forty last year had a cake with little vultures, or buzzards or some kind of ugly bird perched all over it with black frosting and sayings like 'Rest in Peace' and stuff like that." She paused for breath, slamming the car door. Standing on the sidewalk, she shoved her hands in the pockets of her coat as Rachel fished the keys to the clinic's front door out of the pocket of her jeans. "All her friends dressed up like they did in high school. You should have seen their hair. I mean teased out to here." She made a spreading gesture with her hands, the wide sleeves of her short coat looking like bat wings in the gloomy half light. "It was so bad it was almost radical."

"I had really long hair in high school," Rachel said, smiling at Leah's description of hairstyles that had been the height of fashion for the Class of '62. "My cousin and I used to iron ours every night."

"Iron it? You mean you had curling irons back then?" Leah stood in the darkened doorway of the clinic while Rachel inserted the key in the lock. The older woman laughed. "No, I mean we used my mother's steam iron and ironing board to iron our hair straight as a string." She'd almost talked herself out of worrying about the deteriorating neighborhood, or what had happened to them two nights earlier. She didn't notice the midsized sedan glide back into view and park at the end of the block, or that two men got out of the car and began walking quickly in their direction.

"Iron your hair? And Mom complains about my using too much mousse. I wonder if she ever did anything like that?"

"Why don't you ask her when we get back?" The door swung open and Rachel motioned Leah inside the darkened reception area at the front of the building. One overhead fluorescent bulb, above the partitioned walls separating the exam cubicles, was the only light available. She turned to close and lock the door and found herself standing face-to-face with the men who had accosted them at the mall. Both were wearing stocking caps and dark leather jackets as they had before. Only this time they spoke English. And one of them carried a gun.

"Get inside. Move," the taller one, holding the gun, ordered, pushing Rachel farther inside the building. "Now! Do as I say."

"Rachel?" Leah sounded scared. She was clutching Rachel's hand so hard her nails cut into the skin. "What's happening?" Rachel focused all her attention, all her strength on the feel of Leah's shaking fingers curled tightly around her wrist. Her responsibility to the girl was the only thing that kept her anchored in reality. The past was pulling very strongly, the fear and pain, the degradation of all those lost years. She could feel herself retreating into some warm, dark corner of her soul as she'd done so often during those brutal times. But she could not let go, sink into oblivion, for Leah's sake.

"What do you want with us?" This was no chance purse snatching as she'd almost convinced herself their first encounter had been. The odds against them being victimized twice by the same two thugs had to be astronomical. "Why have you followed us here?"

"Silence!" The man with the gun waved it in Leah's face.

"Go into the office. Both of you." Rachel weighed her options and found there were none. She turned to do as their captor bid.

"Vang."

The second man stepped forward. He was younger than the leader, his face broader, his features less well-defined. "Notify them. I do not wish to stay here any longer than necessary. Remind Nguyen Duc to bring our money. All of it."

Vang asked a question that Rachel didn't catch as she walked, shepherding a silent, terrified Leah ahead of her toward Annie's office.

"Use the car phone." The men spoke in Vietnamese. They had no reason to believe that Rachel could understand them. "I do not want to take any chances that the call might be traced to this location later on." Vang nodded his understanding of the orders and left the room, closing the front door carefully so that the lock didn't catch and shut him out.

"Sit down!" The first man switched to English once again and motioned Rachel and Leah inside the small office, pointing to two rickety folding chairs along the far wall. The old delivery door that opened out onto the alley was bolted at night as a precaution against theft. It would take far too long to open to be useful as an escape route. The only other way out of the room was past the man now standing at his ease in the doorway.

"What is this all about?" Rachel asked, fighting to keep her voice steady. Leah still held tightly to her hand. Rachel squeezed her fingers reassuringly but didn't look her way. "There are no drugs on the premises."

"Or any money," Leah piped up, her voice faint but defiant. "The nurse in charge takes the cash drawer home with her when she locks up every night. I know because my mom owns this building." She stared down her nose at the man in the doorway. "You'd better let us go right now."

"Be quiet, girl, or I will gag you."

Leah subsided in a huff. The man crossed his arms and leaned against the doorway, obviously prepared to wait.

His accomplice returned. "They come," he said in Vietnamese. The two men looked enough alike to be brothers. Rachel did her best to remember details of their features so that she could give a description to the police. If she ever got the chance.

Several minutes passed in silence, the seconds dragging by one after another. Rachel felt terror creeping over her like an icy shroud. How many times had she waited like this, in the dark, on the whims of one or more of her captors? It was the waiting that was the worst, that wore down your soul and sapped your strength of will.

The phone rang once, and the answering machine clicked on with a whir of tape. Leah jumped and Rachel felt her own heart leap into her throat, pounding so hard it nearly choked her. The recorded message played through. The Vietnamese seemed as shocked by the sudden interruption of their silent vigil as Leah and Rachel. Annie's voice came on the machine. Leah tensed, but Rachel squeezed her hand so hard she grunted in pain. The two men were beginning to look nervous. She didn't want Leah doing something rash, causing them to act irrationally in return.

"Rachel? Leah, are you there?" Annie paused. "I forgot to tell you to bring the master patient index file along with the report. It's in my top desk drawer. The report's right on top of it." Another pause. "Ladies, are you there yet?" There was laughter in her voice. "They must still be at the Oak Street Plaza." Her words were fainter now, as if she'd turned away from the phone. "I'll..." The line went dead. Leah seemed to collapse in on herself as her mother's voice faded away. She leaned against Rachel's shoulder and began to cry.

"Quiet her." A note of exasperation had crept into the leader's voice. "And silence that machine." Vang moved to the desk, fiddled with the buttons on the answering machine and finally, with an angry growl, ripped loose its cord. Leah began to cry harder.

Rachel put her arms around her and stroked her hair. "It's all right, honey. They can't keep us here forever."

Leah raised a tear-streaked face. "What do they want with us at all?"

Rachel stood up, her arms still protectively around Leah's shoulders. She faced the two men with all the courage she could muster. Her knees were rubbery with fear, her breath came in short painful gasps, but she would not cower at their feet, not now, not ever again. "I want to know why you're holding us here and I want to know now."

"You are in no position to demand answers." Vang, still standing by the desk, spoke directly to her for the first time. He raised his hand as if to strike her. Rachel flinched. Leah cried out in fear. A woman's voice, sweet and light, rose above the noise and movement in the small, poorly lighted room.

"Stop!" Rachel raised her arm to ward off a blow that never fell. She blinked, focusing on the small feminine figure, wrapped in a heavy capelike black coat, standing in the doorway. "Nguyen Duc," the woman said, "send these men away."

Behind her a taller, heavier Vietnamese man growled a command to their captors. Vang stepped away from Leah and Rachel, his threatening stance dropped. The other man's gun disappeared into a shoulder holster hidden under his leather coat. A short, sharp nod sent them out of the office. The woman stayed behind, clutching her coat tightly around her, as if she could never be warm again. Her eyes never left Leah's face.

New uneasiness stirred in Rachel. *What was this all about?* She was certain now the attack in the mall parking lot was no mere purse snatching. She had heard the men correctly. They had wanted Leah then. They wanted Leah now. Or, more accurately, this unknown woman did. Rachel strained her eyes to see, but the light from the single overhead fixture was far too dim to allow her to make out details of the woman's features with any accuracy.

The woman's companion returned. "Are they gone for good, Nguyen Duc?" she asked in Vietnamese.

"I have given them what they were promised. They will not return."

"Good. We need light." She looked behind her for a light switch.

"No." The man's voice was gruff. "It is not wise to draw attention to this building at this hour of the night."

The woman ignored him. "I must see her."

"Very well." With calm efficiency the man took a newspaper from the wastebasket by the desk and tape from the dispenser on top of the filing cabinet and blacked out the small window in the delivery door. The doorway behind the woman had no door. He frowned but flicked on the desk lamp anyway.

Leah blinked at the light. The woman stared at the girl as though she were seeing a ghost. Rachel wondered if she was, too. The curve of the other woman's cheekbones, the classically elegant line of her nose and chin proclaimed her European heritage, just as it did Leah's.

"What is your name?" she asked in a sweet, soft voice, a faint but discernible hint of French in her accent.

Leah sniffed and rubbed her hand across her cheek to wipe away the tears. "Leah Jessica Simpson. I was named after my grandmother," she added for good measure.

"Le-ah." The woman repeated the name wonderingly. "That is very pretty." She spoke carefully and precisely, as though weighing each English word against its Vietnamese counterpart.

"Who are you?" Leah asked bluntly, far too upset to worry about her manners.

"My name is Le Thi," the woman said, bowing in ceremonial greeting. "I have searched for you for many years."

"Do you know my family in Vietnam?" Leah asked, still staying within the comforting circle of Rachel's arms.

"Yes. I have come to take you back to them." Le Thi walked forward, brushing her hand, as gently as a feather, down the shining ebony fall of Leah's hair. "You see," she said, her smile as sad and beautiful as a temple maiden carved from finest jade, "I am your mother."

CHAPTER FIFTEEN

"I'LL . . ." ANNIE HUNG UP the phone, rested her elbows on the desk and dropped her chin onto her palm. "I feel like such a fool talking to an answering machine," she confessed to Simon with a shrug. "I can never think of what to say. Most of the time I can't manage a complete sentence."

"They affect some people that way." Simon was lounging in the doorway to her first-floor study. She let her gaze wander over his strong profile, and drop further, to the width of his chest and the lean, hard length of his thighs. Lounging was probably not the best word she could find to apply to the coiled strength only partially concealed by the nonchalant stance of the man across the room, but it would suffice.

"The thing of it is that if I don't manage to contact Leah and Rachel, or if Rachel doesn't notice the master file under the report, their whole trip will have been for nothing. I'm going to have to go to Lyman Street myself. I have to mail this report to the State Nursing Board before midnight tomorrow and that's all there is to it."

Simon crossed the small expanse of hardwood floor that separated them. He rested his palms on the edge of her cluttered, dusty oak desk, the same one she'd had in her blue and white bedroom all during high school, and leaned forward, bringing their bodies closer together, setting off sparks of awareness in the depths of Annie's soul. "Asking me to marry you has thrown your whole routine out of sync, hasn't it?" There was just the faintest hint of teasing in his gold-flecked hazel eyes. His left brow rose a fraction of an inch.

Annie placed her palms on the desk, also, using them as leverage to stretch upward so that her lips were only inches from his. "Yes, it has. And very pleasantly so, I might add." Simon bent his head. Their lips touched, parted, then met again. Annie's mouth opened softly, accepting the heated exploration of Simon's tongue. He tasted of chocolate and coffee; his after-shave reminded her of woodlands and spice. The movement of his mouth over hers mimicked a joining far more intimate, more complete, and she longed for that completion with all her heart. She let her thoughts wander further into dreams of love, of knowing the hard, strong length of his body next to hers, of learning the taste and touch and scent of him, of falling asleep in his arms, awakening by his side.

His mouth left hers. "Soon, love."

Annie's eyes flew open. "How did you know what I was thinking?" she asked with a smile, her lips warm and tingling from their kiss.

"Because I'm thinking the same thing." Simon straightened to his full height. "I came in here to tell you Mike and I found two articles to base his report on. He's made a good stab at an opening paragraph. Tell me something. Do these homework crises occur with any regularity?"

"Like clockwork." Annie stood up and walked around the desk. "Just be thankful you missed science projects. It was a madhouse, I can tell you."

"I'll take your word for it." Simon fitted his palms to the curve of her hips, pulling her close, letting her feel the evidence of his desire against the softness of her stomach.

"Are you having second thoughts about marrying me, Simon McKendrick?" She slipped her arms around his neck. "Because if you are..." Annie let her voice trail off into ominous silence.

"A gentleman never goes back on his word." Simon pulled her tighter against him. "My mother was very strict about such things when I was growing up." He lowered his head to nuzzle her ear.

"Remind me to thank you for being such a stickler for good manners." Annie's voice was soft, breathless, filled with longing and unfulfilled desire. "You will marry me soon, won't you?" She looked at him, letting him see all the love she felt for him reflected in her eyes.

"Simon! How do you spell 'torrential'? Are there two *r*s or just one?" Mike's voice carried clearly from the living room. Simon stepped back and a swirl of cool air passed between them. Annie felt suddenly bereft. His lips were still only inches from hers but the heat of his body no longer stirred her blood.

"You'd better answer him or he'll be in here looking for you in about ten seconds." She glanced down, below his waist, and grinned mischievously.

Simon grinned back, although a little sheepishly. "I ought to make you go help him. It's your fault I'm in this state. What if he notices?"

"Then you can have a talk about the birds and the bees with him and save me the trouble." Annie reached up and traced the line of his jaw with the tip of her finger. "I'm glad you want me, Simon. I want you, too, so badly I can't think about anything else when we're together. And I want us to go on feeling like this not only now, but tomorrow, and for the rest of our lives. Now go to Mike."

She sighed and stepped out of his embrace reluctantly. "I'm going to try to intercept Rachel and Leah at the clinic once more. If I can't reach them by phone I'll have to drive over there myself."

"I'll drive you. Doug can stay with the twins."

"Is he still in the house?" Annie glanced at the clock. It was almost nine. She'd been working steadily on her paperwork since dinner, and time had gotten away from her.

"He's in his room."

"Ask him to get the twins started off to bed, will you? I'll make the call." She turned back to the phone on her desk.

"At least in the car I'll have you to myself." Simon's last words drifted back over his shoulder as he walked out of the room.

TWENTY MINUTES LATER THEY turned onto Lyman Street. The heater in Simon's rented car purred warmth, holding at bay the frigid February night outside the car. "I can't imagine what went wrong with the answering machine," Annie said for at least the third time since they'd pulled out of her driveway. "It was just dead. The whole line was dead. I should have called the phone company before we left."

"Annie, answering machines go on the blink all the time. If it isn't something you can fix on the spot, like a loose connection, we'll call the phone company as soon as we get back. They won't send anyone until tomorrow anyway."

"I know." She settled back against the seat. She looked more like a little girl than a successful nurse practitioner/entrepreneur with an ax to grind with the phone company. A riot of red curls was peeking out from under a cream-colored toque. She was wearing the red-hooded coat she'd had on when he kissed her Christmas Eve and her jeans were rolled up in cuffs around her ankles. He thought she was the sexiest woman he'd ever seen. He started to tell her so.

"We're here." Annie leaned forward again as they pulled up in front of the clinic. "There's Rachel's car. They're here. Darn that machine. We could have saved a trip if it had been working properly." She was out of the car before Simon could respond.

The short hairs at the nape of his neck stood on end. Something wasn't as it should be. There was only a faint light inside the clinic, nothing sinister there. The street was deserted except for a dark green sedan parked outside. The car looked out of place on the desolate street. It didn't belong to a pimp or drug dealer—too ordinary and too inexpensive. It certainly didn't belong to any of the elderly women, most of whom were on fixed incomes and didn't drive, who still lived in walk-up flats above boarded-up storefronts. The sedan definitely looked out of place, and in his line of work anything that was out of place was suspect. Maybe that was what was setting off warning signals inside his brain. He turned off the engine and got out of the car. Annie was already at the door.

"That's funny. It's open." She turned around, giving him a puzzled look.

"Annie, wait!" She didn't hear him. She stepped inside, calling Rachel's name, walking into the darkness as she spoke. Simon made it inside the door in three quick strides. Annie was standing in the entrance to a long, narrow hall, leading to what he supposed were offices and examination and treatment rooms; standing quietly, as still as death. Now he knew for certain something was wrong, but there was nothing he could do about it. Hell, he was on vacation, visiting his sister and the woman he loved. No one, even State Department spies, carried guns into Annie's world.

But the man blocking Annie's path didn't know that. The gun in his hand was Chinese, blunt-nosed, large-bore and deadly.

"What are you doing here?" Her voice was shaky but commanding. He should have known Annie's behavior in the Saigon hotel room hadn't been a fluke, that she could hold her own in any demanding situation.

The man didn't answer, but Leah's voice came from within one of the cubicles. "Mom? Mom, is that you?" She sounded as if she'd been crying, was still crying. Annie's shoulders beneath the bright red coat tensed. She was prepared to go through the man standing between her and her daughter if she had to, gun or no gun.

"Annie." Simon stepped forward to hold her back. Immediately the gun swung in a short arc to cover him, just as he'd intended. "What do you want with the girl?" This was no ordinary breaking and entering. Simon didn't waste his breath pretending it was.

"Nguyen Duc, let them pass." A woman appeared in the doorway of one of the offices—a small woman, enveloped in a capelike wool coat, high-heeled leather boots giving a measure of stature to her almost childish figure. "Mrs. Simpson, please." She made a courteous ceremonial bow. Her henchmen stepped aside, reluctantly. He was big for a Vietnamese but under the right circumstances Simon knew he wouldn't have any trouble taking him down. However, at the moment those circumstances didn't exist. He balled his hands into fists at his sides and bided his time.

"Madame Chi?" Annie's tone was full of questions. She didn't move for a long moment. "What is this all about? What are you doing in America?" She walked past the man holding the gun, her posture tense, her tone bewildered. "Why are you here, at my clinic, holding my daughter?" Simon, following her down the narrow hall, felt the weapon aimed at his back.

The office they entered, Annie's he guessed, was small and appeared crowded with people. Rachel and Leah sat huddled together on folding chairs at the back of the room, which wasn't more than eight or ten feet across. Le Thi stood by Annie's desk, her face drawn, her dark eyes haunted and full of confusion. By her left hand the cordless remains of the answering machine gave mute testimony to why Annie couldn't reach Rachel and Leah by phone.

There was a second exit, Simon noted, with a sweeping glance. A heavy steel door, its window obscured with newspaper. Its bolt, securely drawn, was directly in front of where he stood. Unfortunately, it would take too long to open to be feasible for a quick escape. Simon made himself relax. He turned his back to the delivery door, facing Nguyen Duc, and prepared to wait for the man to make a slip, even a small one, anything that would give him the split second he needed to make a try for the gun.

"Mom!" Leah jumped up and rushed into Annie's arms. "I don't know what's happening. This woman says she's my mother. My real mother and she wants to take me away with her."

"Your mother?" The words were barely more than a whisper. Annie turned to Le Thi, her face drained of color so that her freckles stood out across the bridge of her nose in stark relief. "You are her mother," she stated a low, wondering tone. "I can see the resemblance, now.

In Vietnam I never made the connection. Why didn't you say something then?"

"I could not believe it was really you." Le Thi refused to meet Annie's eyes. "I have longed for my child since the day I gave her to you but I thought there was no hope. Then, that night at the dinner party..." She made a helpless gesture with her hands, as small and fragile as hummingbird wings. "It was as if the spirits had answered my prayers." Le Thi spoke slowly, carefully, as if she weighed each unfamiliar English word before it left her tongue.

"How did you come to be in America?" Annie asked in the same bewildered tone, her hand still stroking, soothing Leah's tumbled ebony hair.

"My husband was chosen to be part of our country's delegation to the United Nations. I, too, had never expected to see you again. Any of you." She looked at Simon consideringly. "You are the reporter, Ley-ton," she said, dividing the surname into two words in the Vietnamese fashion. "Or is it not Ley-ton?" She looked at Rachel, her almond-shaped eyes narrowed as she searched their features. "You are very similar." Rachel sat quietly. She didn't say a word, didn't change expression.

"My name is Simon McKendrick. Mrs. Phillips is my sister." He nodded in Rachel's direction, never taking his eyes from Le Thi or the man behind her, blocking the door.

"I recognize her as the woman who was found in the hill village. The one who has been hiding since the war ended. The one my government arranged to be returned to this country." Simon didn't bother to correct her. It was the official line, the story the media had been given, that both Washington and Hanoi had agreed on. "She is your sister? Yes, I see that now.'' She shook her head slightly. ''Who are we to question the whims of the spirits?''

''Mom, she wants to take me away with her.'' Leah burrowed deeper into the comfort of Annie's embrace.

''Yes.'' Le Thi stepped forward eagerly. From the corner of his eye Simon saw Nguyen Duc's finger tighten on the trigger. The man was nervous, long on brawn, short on brains, like a lot of hired bodyguards. It was hard to anticipate the actions of that kind of individual. It made their situation precarious. Simon wondered, briefly, just what the man's function with the Vietnamese UN delegation was supposed to be? And what amount of money had Le Thi scraped together to make a satisfactory bribe to tempt him into this dangerous breech of protocol? ''We will go someplace warm and sunny, Le-ah. We will learn to know each other. We will learn to be mother and daughter.'' Le Thi held out her hand. Her slender fingers trembled noticeably. Leah only shook her head, refusing to look at the woman who claimed to have given her life.

''I can't go away with you. I... I have to go to school tomorrow,'' she said, sniffing back her tears. ''And my...my mother's birthday is in three weeks. We're going to have a big party.'' Her voice trailed off again as her gaze shifted to the silent, armed man in the doorway. ''I can't go with you, don't you understand?''

Simon could see, in her physical reaction, the moment Leah came to the conclusion that Nguyen Duc was capable, willing, to harm Annie, Rachel, himself, all of them. Her face paled. She clung tighter to Annie's waist.

''You will come to love my...our country,'' Le Thi insisted. She looked very close to the edge, as if she might shatter into tiny pieces at any moment. Simon remembered her near collapse the night of the Saigon dinner party. It hadn't been from physical weakness, he now realized, but emotional shock. That must have been when she recognized Annie as the woman she'd given her infant daughter to fourteen years earlier. "Do you know how you came to leave Saigon with...your mother?" She smiled, very faintly, very sadly when she said the word.

Leah nodded, rubbing tears from her cheek with the back of her hand. "You came out of an alley. You couldn't have been much older than me." She recited the facts as though repeating an often told and beloved fairy tale.

"I was only seventeen," Le Thi told her.

"There were people everywhere, panicking, trying to escape. My Mom already had Chad and Doug with her because they got separated from Rachel and the others." Le Thi nodded, her own thoughts visibly retreating to that same harrowing scene. "You saw my mother." Leah met Le Thi's eyes for a brief moment, defiance in her own. "You put me in her arms."

"It was her hair." Le Thi's voice sounded lost, far away. "Only Americans have such hair. It was *rouge*." She lapsed momentarily into French, then shrugged apologetically. "So red."

"Do," Leah said with a very small smile. "Rachel is teaching me Vietnamese."

Le Thi bowed in Rachel's direction. *"Cám on ông,"* she said simply. Rachel made no response. Along with everything else he had to worry about, Simon felt a mounting anxiety for his sister's mental well-being.

"What about Leah's father?" It was Annie who asked the question.

"He left me soon after I told him I was pregnant. He was one of the first Americans to go from the embassy." There was bitterness in the lost, sad voice.

"What is his name?" Simon was aware of the reluctance with which Annie requested that information. For almost fifteen years Leah had been hers alone, with little possibility of being confronted with her natural parents ever again. Now Le Thi stood in front of her, and learning Leah's natural father's name meant that he, too, could be traced, could become a factor in her life.

"Mom! No! I don't care about him." Leah put her hands over her ears and began to sob. "My dad's dead. He was a great guy. He saved all of us. I don't want to know who the man she's talking about was. Ever." She tore away from Annie's arms and dropped down onto the chair beside Rachel, crying bitterly. Rachel moved, stiffly, slowly, to draw Leah into her embrace.

"I will tell her of her father later. When she is ready to hear." Annie stiffened at the words, and the detachment in Le Thi's tone sent a chill racing down Simon's spine as well. Silence stretched out around them, filling the room with its weight.

"I did not think she would have grown so tall...." Le Thi spoke in Vietnamese, as if to herself, or an unseen companion. "I will have to buy her things. American things so that her homeland will not seem so strange to her at first. And Hoang. I must tell him where we will be so that he can make arrangements for us to go...home."

Annie stepped forward, putting herself directly in front of Le Thi, blocking the other woman's view of Rachel and Leah huddled on the folding chairs. Annie didn't understand Vietnamese, but Simon suspected Le Thi's meaning was perfectly clear to her. Her words confirmed this. "You can't take Leah away from me," she said softly but implacably. "I won't allow it."

Le Thi looked equally convinced she was in the right. "She is my daughter."

"Enough talk among women. It is time to go." Nguyen Duc's clipped words dropped into the silence like stones into water. Simon tensed. He didn't know how in hell he could get to Nguyen Duc without endangering the women. It was obvious to him that Le Thi's henchman couldn't afford to leave any witnesses to what amounted to a kidnapping. "Go with your mother," he commanded, gesturing toward Leah with his free hand.

"No!" Annie and Leah spoke as one.

"Le-ah, come, everything will be all right." Le Thi held out her hands. She smiled shyly.

"Everything won't be all right, Madam Chi." Simon spoke slowly, deliberately in Vietnamese.

Le Thi's head, with its sleek chignon of heavy black hair, swung in his direction. "You know my language?"

Simon bowed his head in acknowledgement.

"No more talk!" Nguyen Duc jabbed the gun at Simon's chest. Annie frowned, as if by merely willing it hard enough she could decipher the meaning of the strange words.

Simon ignored the other man's order to be silent. "He will kill all of us after you leave."

Le Thi's eyes widened in horror. She raised one slender hand as if to ward off a blow. "No! No more killing. No one will be harmed." She shook her head as if to physically deny his words.

"He can't afford to let any of us live."

She whirled to face Nguyen Duc. "This is not true. I order you to put the gun away. I want no harm to come to these people."

The Vietnamese stood, as solid as granite, but once more Simon detected the slight, involuntary tensing of his gun hand.

"Take the girl and go to the car," he ordered. "I will deal with these three."

"What he says is true." Le Thi looked stunned, as though her dream so long cherished, was turning to nightmare before her eyes. "You will kill them all? The woman who gave my daughter back her life, to whom I owe everything? No!" Before anyone could move she hurled herself at Nguyen Duc, trying, possibly, to knock the gun from his hand. Instead his arm came up, hitting her above the breasts, sweeping her against the wall to fall to the floor, a crumpled, broken doll.

It took only an instant, a heartbeat of time. No one uttered a sound. For those few precious fragments of a second, Nguyen Duc was off his guard. Simon took silent, deadly advantage of the small opening. He launched himself across the room, smashed his fist into Nguyen Duc's middle, twisted him around, levering his gun hand upward. A shot went off, incredibly loud in the small enclosed space. Leah screamed. The bullet buried itself harmlessly in the ceiling.

Simon began methodically, ruthlessly hammering the other man's hand against the door frame until his fingers loosened and the gun slipped from his grasp. He knelt, scooped up the weapon in one swift movement and trained it on the Vietnamese as the man slid to his knees, cradling his injured wrist. It was all over as quickly as it had begun. Silence returned, except for the sound of a woman's heartbroken sobs.

"Simon, should I call the police?" Annie stepped to his side as he rose from his knees, her voice uncertain. She looked shaken, as she had that night in her Saigon hotel room, but her gaze was level, steady. She smiled at him, tremulously, then with more conviction, and Simon couldn't help grinning back. They'd pulled this off together, against all odds, just as they had in rescuing Micah and Rachel. Annie's smile faded as she shifted her gaze to Nguyen Duc. She, too, was realizing that repercussions from this incident would send shock waves ricocheting around Washington for a long time to come if it came to the attention of the civil authorities and the media. "What are we going to do with them?"

Simon turned his head slightly to see Rachel kneeling by the dazed and weeping Le Thi. "How is she?"

"Just shaken up, I think." Rachel looked at him but Simon felt her gaze go through him as though she didn't really see him at all, as though she'd retreated somewhere deep inside herself. She looked almost as detached and unresponsive as she had on the runway at Tan Son Nhut.

"Rachel, are you all right?"

"I'm fine." She wasn't fine, but he had other things, more urgent, if not more important, to deal with at the moment.

"I think we should send word to New York to Minister Chi. We can put Nguyen Duc, here, on ice until he can take delivery of him. The fewer people who know about this whole affair, the better."

"I agree wholeheartedly with your assessment of the situation, Mr. Leyton, I believe your name is." A tall Vietnamese in a black trench coat stood in the doorway. His dark hair was windblown, his hands shoved into the pockets of his coat. "I heard a scuffle. The door was not locked so I entered the building." He bowed politely; his dark eyes, after one quick assessing glance at his wife, sitting up now supported by Rachel's arm, remained locked with Simon's. Nguyen Duc struggled to his feet, his arms hanging limp at his sides.

"The name's McKendrick, not Leyton," Simon informed him. "It seems your timely arrival has saved us the trouble of trying to track you down in New York."

"It would seem that it has," Hoang agreed. "I have been searching for my wife for two days." His hand came out of the pocket of his black trench coat. It was holding a gun, smaller, more elegant in line and form than the one Simon had taken from Nguyen Duc, but just as deadly. "I think, perhaps, it would be best for you to hand over the weapon, Mr. McKendrick. If not, I am perfectly capable of shooting you now and asking questions later."

Annie gasped and Leah gave a little squeak of fright. Simon weighed his options for the space of two heartbeats and decided he had none. "Well, I'll be damned," he said quietly, reversed the gun and handed it over.

CHAPTER SIXTEEN

"HAS MY WIFE BEEN HARMED, Mrs. Phillips?" Hoang Van Chi asked, his voice harsh with concern for Le Thi.

"She's all right."

Le Thi continued to sob quietly, helplessly, as Rachel supported her with an arm around her shoulder. Rachel couldn't seem to take her eyes off the gun in Hoang's hand even as she spoke. She forced her gaze up, studied his face. He was a hard man, ruthless and determined. A man who had faced many hardships, overcome great obstacles. An honest man, honorable and fair within the framework of his own code of ethics. Rachel tried to recall seeing him or his wife in the crowd of faces on the runway at Tan Son Nhut, but her mind remained a blank. All her memories of that day, indeed of the first few days after her return to America, were faint and insubstantial, clouded with fear and fatigue. She felt much the same way now, frightened but detached. It was not a pleasant sensation, as though reality were slipping away and she were losing touch with those around her. That frightened her even more.

Hoang watched Rachel studying him. He glanced briefly at the gun in his hand, then shifted his night-black gaze to Simon's face. "Nguyen Duc must be returned to New York. I think you will agree with me on that point."

Simon nodded. He had stepped back from the doorway after surrendering his gun to the Vietnamese. Now he propped one hip on the corner of Annie's desk, his hands relaxed in his lap, and faced the newcomer. "The sooner the better."

"Yes." Hoang nodded in agreement. "I have, as you Americans say, covered my tracks as much as possible. However, in the same way that I was able to find Le Thi and trace her to this building, so may others learn of my whereabouts. That could cause considerable embarrassment for both our governments. And I think, Mr. McKendrick, you also understand the precarious position this places Le Thi and me in?"

"I do understand." Rachel's heart contracted with a sudden clutching fear of what he meant by those words. She pushed the old darkness ruthlessly away. Simon continued to sit calmly, one leg swinging free, the worn brown leather of his jacket stretched tight across his shoulders, one lock of night-black hair falling forward onto his forehead.

"Simon, he was going to kill us." Annie had taken Leah into her arms. They were standing a little behind Simon. Rachel's view of them from her kneeling position on the floor was blocked by his body, but the anger in Annie's voice was unmistakable. "Isn't he going to be punished at all?"

"Annie." Simon turned his head. "Hard as it is to believe, the guy's probably got diplomatic immunity. The cops couldn't do a thing to him."

"It isn't right." Annie didn't say anything more. Rachel could hear an occasional hiccupping sob from Leah, then the soft soothing murmur of Annie's reassuring voice.

"It's the way things are." Simon shifted his gaze back to Hoang Van Chi.

"It would be best if he returned to New York at once."

"If not sooner," Simon agreed with a curt nod.

Hoang glanced at the sullen, defeated Nguyen Duc, then back at Simon. The faintest twist of a smile curved his thin lips. "We think alike, Mr. McKendrick." He bowed ever so slightly.

"Take your car and find your way back to New York," he ordered Le Thi's henchman. "If a single word of what has happened here reaches the ears of any of our comrades, you will learn to your great regret that there are far worse things in life than being detained by American police." This time his slight bow was for Annie. "Do I make myself clear, Nguyen Duc?"

"Thau co."

"Then leave my sight."

Nguyen Duc cast one last hate-filled glance in Simon's direction, but did as he was told. Hoang followed him into the corridor and watched him leave the building.

"He will trouble us no more. And I think we can trust each other enough to dispense with this." The gun disappeared into his pocket.

Simon nodded and stood up. He smiled at Annie and Leah. Annie smiled back, a brilliant testimonial to her love and trust in his judgment. Leah smiled, too, hesitantly at first, then more fully, like sunlight breaking out from behind a storm cloud. He walked over and knelt down by Rachel.

"Let me help you get Le Thi on her feet."

"No." Le Thi jerked away. Kneeling still, she wept, her face in her hands. "It is all going wrong. I meant no harm to anyone. All I wanted was to find my child. To have her with me. It is all turning to dust, all my hopes and dreams."

"Le Thi," Hoang spoke softly, his harsh voice muted. He held out his hands and she looked up at him, her coat spread around her in heavy folds, like a nun's habit. Simon stood up, his hand under Rachel's elbow, urging her to her feet. She backed away to leave Hoang and his wife in a small pool of solitude. "Your dreams cannot be, my love. The child is yours no longer."

"You speak as if you know of her, of Le-ah." Her face mirrored her confusion. Rachel glanced in Annie's direction. Even though the couple spoke in Vietnamese she guessed Annie, in her mother's heart, could understand. "How is this possible, Hoang? I have never spoken of her to you."

"Did you not guess that there might be others who felt it was their place, even their duty, to inform me of your having had a child by an American?"

"All these years... you knew?" Two more great tears slipped down her cheeks. "I never meant to deceive you. I thought you were dead...."

"You do not have to explain anything to me." He drew her to her feet. "Nothing at all."

"I have never loved any man but you, Hoang."

"I know." They looked at each other in silence for a long moment.

"It was as if the spirits had answered my prayers when Mrs. Simpson came to our country," Le Thi went on in a dreamy, lost voice. "I recognized her. Later, when you told me we would come to the United States I couldn't help but hope, and plan." Le Thi turned her head slightly to look at Leah. Her voice dropped to a whisper, a tiny thread of sound. She smiled briefly, all her mother's love shining in her eyes. "She is a beautiful child, is she not, Hoang?"

"She is as beautiful as her mother."

"We could be a family," Le Thi continued hopefully. "You can make all the arrangements for Le-ah to return home with us."

"Are you talking about me?" Leah, recognized her name, moved out of the comforting circle of Annie's arms. Her eyes were red-rimmed from crying, her voice cracked with emotion.

"My wife, your mother, wishes to have you live with us in Vietnam," Hoang translated. He studied Leah's face, assuring himself that she was indeed Le Thi's lost child.

"I can't go." Leah looked very earnest. She also looked sad; sad for Le Thi and the sacrifice she had made. "I don't belong in your country. I'm an American."

"I understand. But please do not forget that you are also Vietnamese."

"I'll remember, I promise." Leah smiled shyly.

"She is learning to speak Vietnamese, Hoang," Le Thi said proudly, in English, and Rachel felt the pain of that mother's pride in her very soul.

"Rachel is teaching me," Leah responded in halting Vietnamese. "Did I say that right?" she asked, glancing at Rachel for confirmation of the words. Rachel nodded, forcing a smile to curve her stiff lips.

"Le-ah..."

"Don't ask me to go with you again," Leah said very fast. "I...I'd like to write you if I can. Maybe I can even visit you someday when I can earn enough money with my paintings to afford to go so far away. I...I could send you some of my drawings. I'm...I'm pretty good," she finished up with a blush.

"Hoang, speak to her. Convince her," Le Thi begged.

He shook his head. "No, my love." She whirled toward him, her tormented eyes flashing dark fire. Leah backed away, into the familiar comfort of Annie's arms.

"I cannot give her up," Le Thi said.

"You will give her up because you must." Rachel heard her own words but couldn't believe that she had said them. She felt as if she were somehow detached from the scene, that another woman spoke from her lips, moved with her body. Only her emotions seemed to be her own, responding to something in Le Thi's heartbroken expression that touched her more deeply than anything she could remember in a very long time.

"I cannot bear to do that." Le Thi's eyes narrowed. She hurled the words at Rachel from the hellish depths of her own anguish. She hugged her arms close around her as though she were very cold. "It is easy for you to say that I must turn my back on Le-ah and walk away forever. You have never lost a child."

"Yes, I have," the woman inhabiting her body said aloud. Rachel shrank within herself. She had kept her secret so long, protected herself from its searing pain so carefully. Now the words seemed to echo over and over in the small, crowded room. "I lost a child. A son, an infant only nine days old. He was conceived in a prison camp in the north." Each word tore into her heart with slashing agony. "I have nothing left of him but memories of holding him in my arms for a few short days. You have the knowledge that your daughter is growing into a beautiful and intelligent woman with a wonderful future ahead of her, and a loving, caring family to surround and protect her all her life."

"You conceived a child in the camps?" Le Thi stopped crying. She looked at Rachel closely, as though searching her face for signs of falsehood. Rachel bit her lip, met her eyes and held Le Thi's gaze, forging a tenuous bond. A bond between women, a bond of shared suffering and loss.

"He was the son of the camp commander." Rachel clamped down on those memories with a strength born of her will to survive. "He was born too soon, too small to live." She couldn't say any more. The despair of those months hadn't dimmed with time, she was discovering, now that she'd deliberately broken the icy veneer of forgetfulness she'd erected around them.

"I grieve for you," Le Thi said simply.

"I grieve also, for my son." *And for myself.* Rachel took a deep breath. She wouldn't cry now. She couldn't give in to the beckoning oblivion of paralyzing weakness and the bottomless pit of ceaseless regret.

Whenever she did give in to melancholy it became harder and harder to climb out of the pit again. "You must believe me, Le Thi, when I tell you I understand the pain inside you, the way your heart bleeds for what can never be again. But you must also listen to me when I tell you you can't take Leah. She is no longer your child. She belongs to another and always will."

"I'M NOT SURE WE SHOULD have let her go back to her apartment alone." Annie turned away from the front door, closing it, finally, against the freezing cold of the February night. The red taillights of Rachel's car had disappeared down the street seconds before. Annie had no excuse at all for staring out into the darkness any longer except concern for her friend's peace of mind.

Simon's arms came around her from behind. She could feel the tension in the muscles of his arms beneath the soft old leather of his jacket. Rachel's disclosure that she had borne and lost a child had shaken him badly. "I'll be right behind her," he promised. "I'm almost positive she won't talk to me about it tonight. It may be a long time before she'll feel like talking about it." He rested his forehead against her hair. "Are you sure you'll be all right here alone?"

Annie longed to have him hold her close, to comfort him in turn, but she shook her head "yes." If she kept him with her it would only divide his loyalties, compound his guilt. Rachel needed her brother tonight, even more than Annie needed the man she loved. Simon had always been ready and willing to take responsibility for Micah and Rachel. Now he was adding her to his list. She loved him for it. Except that she could take care of herself, and her children, and him when he needed to be taken care of. The last thought gave her courage and new resolve.

"I want you to stay with me, but not because I'm afraid to be alone." Annie stared straight ahead of her, wondering how and where she'd learned to be so open with her feelings, knowing suddenly that the love she'd shared with Michael had allowed her to mature into the woman who could give that same kind of unselfish love to Simon. "I want to be with you, to love you, to have you love me because I need and want to be with you more than anything else on earth." She turned in his arms. "Not because I need a protector or a knight in shining armor. But because I love you just as you are. And tonight the man you are knows his place is with Rachel." Reaching up on tiptoe, she touched her lips to his in a fleeting kiss that was a promise of things to come.

Simon traced the curve of her lips with the tip of his finger. "Obligations are fearsome things."

"Not when they are owed to those we love."

He groaned, a sound laced with physical frustration. "Someday, Annie Simpson..."

"Don't." She placed her finger on his lips in turn, silencing his fantasy before it could come to life in words. "I'm going to be spending the rest of the night in Leah's room." The golden flames of desire in her brown eyes burned away, leaving only glowing embers.

"She's going to have a lot of questions about what happened tonight." Simon laid his cheek against hers. His beard was heavy so late in the day. The slight roughness felt good against her skin.

"Questions I may not be able to answer." Annie couldn't help wondering where Le Thi and her husband were at this very moment. It was well after midnight. Their plane was probably somewhere over Ohio or Pennsylvania by now. Her heart ached for Le Thi's sorrow, but she could never have given Leah up, no matter what the circumstances. And Le Thi had Hoang to love and comfort her; that helped Annie's guilt. And Le Thi was still young. Annie prayed that she would yet conceive another child of her own.

"When the time comes to answer Leah's questions you'll find all the right answers." Simon's breath tickled her ear in a way that sent shivers racing up and down her spine. Annie sighed and snuggled deeper into the circle of his arms, letting him wrap her in cocooning strands of silk and steel.

"Will I know the right things to say?"

"Yes."

She tilted her head back to read his expression, saw the confidence in his eyes and was reassured. "And you, we, will both find the right answers for Rachel when she comes to us."

"I'm not so sure." Simon's dark brows drew together in a frown. Annie lifted her hand to smooth away the doubt with the tips of her fingers.

"I am. Very sure."

"I love you, Annie Simpson," he said gruffly.

"And I love you, Simon McKendrick." She touched her fingers to his lips when it looked as if he would speak again. "I know what you're going to say next."

"Do you?" His left eyebrow quirked upward a fraction of an inch.

She nodded. "It's the same old argument." She was only half teasing. "I know you'll be gone a lot of the time. I know what you do is dangerous and classified. And that you intend to keep on doing it. I can accept that. What I can't accept is your worrying about me and the kids while you're doing it. Promise me one thing, Simon."

"If I can." He was watching her closely.

"Promise me that you'll remember that as much as I want to be your wife, your partner, your lover, I am also a reasonably intelligent and capable human being who can take care of herself."

"I'm beginning to see that," he said dryly.

"If you end up in some awful...place they put nosy Census Bureau employees...in the jungle...or someplace...and I have to mount a one-woman campaign to get you out of...wherever you are, I don't want to have to deal with knowing you got there because you were worrying about us and it made you preoccupied and careless."

"I'm never careless."

"Simon, I'm serious." She looked up at him in exasperation.

"So am I. This guilt thing works both ways, Annie. I'm very good at what I do. I've been doing it for twenty years. I've always gotten home safe and sound."

"But if something goes wrong . . ."

"Then I will count on you to raise hell from here to Washington and back. They'll have to get me out just to settle the dust you'll kick up."

"I know," Annie said, pleased with herself. It must have shown in her face because Simon bent his head and kissed her then, a long, lingering kiss that left her heart pounding in her throat and her knees weak and rubbery.

"I wish you wouldn't do that," she grumbled, still clinging to him for support.

"Do what?" he asked innocently, but his voice was rough and his heart thundered against his rib cage beneath her hand.

"Kiss me like that, as if you wanted to sweep me up, carry me upstairs and never let me out of your arms again in this lifetime."

"You're projecting your fantasies onto real life again," he warned with a grin that was sexy enough to set off new thrills of pleasure in every square inch of her body.

"No fantasies, just thinking of Rhett and Scarlett in *Gone with the Wind*," she confessed wistfully.

"So was I."

"When?" Annie whispered, stepping back, out of his embrace to mount the stairs, slowly, reluctantly.

"Soon, Annie love," he promised. "Very soon."

CHAPTER SEVENTEEN

SIMON YANKED HIS TIE LOOSE from the collar of his tuxedo and popped two pearl studs into the palm of his hand. The neck of his shirt was half a size too small, testimonial to the amount of time that had passed since he'd last worn it. He hadn't minded the discomfort too much during the wedding ceremony, but now that the toasts, and cake cutting, and his new mother-in-law's insistence on photographing every minute of the festivities for posterity, were over, he figured he'd endured enough.

They'd been married two hours ago in a little Methodist church down the street. Leah had acted as Annie's maid of honor and Micah was his best man. Their immediate families, minus Annie's two sisters, who couldn't make it back to Illinois on such short notice, were the only guests. It had been a very busy week, but he was glad their time of waiting was coming to an end.

He was alone in Annie's debris-strewn living room, his living room, too, now. Rachel and his mother had collected plates, cups and silverware and were loading the dishwasher in the kitchen. Annie was in there, too, overseeing the packaging of leftover wedding cake for the twins to take with them on the honeymoon.

That's what Leah had taken to calling the children's weekend outing to a nearby motel/shopping/recreation complex that Rachel and Micah had presented to Annie and Simon as a wedding gift—two days and nights of solitude in their own home. Simon's parents had supplied them with enough gourmet food and wine to last far longer than two days. Annie's parents had contributed a set of satin sheets and a down comforter for the bedroom. Annie's sisters had sent her a lovely and very revealing peach satin negligee. Simon was beginning to wonder just how many people knew, or had guessed, their celibate state.

Chad was already on his way back to campus to study for midterms scheduled to begin on Monday. Doug would be staying at the motel with the others, using Rachel's Toyota to drive back and forth to work. Even the dog had been banished to the garage. Simon figured that the house should be emptied of people within the next thirty minutes and he would finally be alone with his wife.

Micah walked into the living room, his rented tuxedo straining across the broad expanse of his shoulders. His rugged, windburned face bore a pained expression. "These damned shoes of yours are a size too small," he complained, scowling down at the black oxfords on his feet. "I can't wait to get them off."

"I appreciate your volunteering to help keep track of the kids this weekend," Simon said by way of greeting. What he really meant was that he was glad Micah had agreed to be his best man. It wasn't often that he could be lured away from his wilderness stronghold.

"I wouldn't miss your wedding," he said gruffly. "Annie's a damn fine woman. You're a lucky man, do you know that?" Micah refused to meet Simon's concerned gaze.

"Yes, I know exactly how lucky I am." Simon pressed his advantage. "Does she remind you a little of Elaine?"

Micah's head jerked up. Old ghosts flickered briefly behind his eyes. He shook his head. "Do you mean does she look like Elaine might have if she...were still alive?"

"Yes, I guess I do." Simon was worried about his brother's continued refusal to rejoin the living. Maybe it was because he'd found Annie that he wanted Micah to have such happiness in his life, also.

Micah was silent for a moment. "They both had that same shade of fiery red hair and freckles. But no...Annie's strong and independent, a survivor. Elaine...wasn't."

"Her death was an accident." Simon kept his voice low but emphatic.

"That's what the medical examiner's report said." Micah looked down at his big, callused hands. "We both know different, don't we?"

"Micah, what happened to you after you got back from Nam happened to a lot of other guys, too."

"Sure. We both know thousands of guys came home and went off the deep end, made their wives' lives such a hell they went and swallowed a bottle of sleeping pills."

"Elaine's overdose was an accident." Simon didn't bother to lower his voice this time.

Micah curled his hand into a fist. For a moment Simon thought he might hit him; then with a visible effort his brother relaxed, the anger faded from his eyes. "Sure it was. A damned tragic accident. I've learned to live with it but I'll never get over it. Just like the war." He laughed and the sound sent shivers of unease up and down Simon's spine.

"Micah..."

"Let's change the subject." He did just that. "Looks like a tornado struck in here. How can we get this much debris from just a cake and punch reception?"

"Beats me." Simon bent to pick up a wadded-up piece of wrapping paper and toss it into the fire. "Micah, Annie and I both want you to know how grateful we are...." He had dreams, long, involved, erotic dreams of making love to Annie—his wife—in front of that fireplace.

"That hard to find some time alone, eh?" Micah grinned, refusing to be led back into deeper conversational waters.

"That's putting it mildly."

"In that case, I'll go see if I can hurry the women along." Micah took two steps, then turned and looked back. "How is Rachel doing?"

"Okay, I guess. She still won't talk about it." Micah knew the events of a week ago. Simon had also told him, without Rachel's knowledge, of her disclosure that night. Simon trusted his brother. Micah would never mention Rachel's child and its death unless she broached the subject first, herself. "She promised Annie and me she'd get professional help if things get too tough to handle alone."

"I don't know what else we can do for her right now."

"You can see the twins don't con her out of her last cent this weekend." Simon raised his voice, changing the subject as his mother and Rachel came back into the room.

"Don't worry about me," Rachel called back, overhearing his remark as he'd intended she should. "I'm on to those two. I'll be fine. Is everyone ready to go? I know Micah must be dying to get out of that tux."

"You look very handsome," his mother said proudly.

"Thank you, ma'am." Micah grinned, white teeth flashing through his beard.

"Annie's parents and Dad already left for the motel," Simon said. "Doug and Leah are driving Rachel's car.

That only leaves the three of you and the twins to go in Micah's Jeep."

"I still don't know how I got stuck riding in a Jeep," Frances complained. "Is chivalry dead in this family?"

"If you weren't so busy directing every phase of this wedding you wouldn't be the last to go, Mom," Simon reminded her with a hug and kiss on the cheek that robbed the words of their sting.

"It's a knack," she said, not at all offended. "I'll get my coat." She bustled off.

"Here we are." The twins hurtled down the stairs, each carrying a duffel emblazoned with their school mascot.

"They'll settle down once they get to the motel," Annie promised Micah as she came out of the kitchen. Her wedding dress was apricot lace, with a skirt that swirled in soft pleats just above her ankles. The deep V-neck was covered by gauzy lace that circled her throat.

"If you say so," he answered dubiously. Micah bent to drop a kiss on Annie's cheek. "Welcome to the family, Annie McKendrick. My brother is one lucky guy."

"Thank you, Micah. Thank you for being here." She gave him a quick, hard hug.

"Mom, Rachel. Let's go." He followed the twins out the door.

"We're coming." Frances gave Annie a quick, distracted peck on the cheek. "Have a nice restful weekend, dear," she said without a trace of irony in her voice. "I know how busy you've been getting ready for the wedding."

"I'll try, Frances," Annie said. It was almost dark and there was only the light from the fireplace, but Simon saw the blush that stained Annie's cheeks.

"Goodbye, you two." Rachel gave Simon a hug.

"Thanks, Sis. This is the best wedding present you could give us."

"I know." She smiled, and the shadows that darkened her blue-gray eyes lightened for a moment.

"Thanks, Rachel. Don't hesitate to call if they get to be too much of a handful." Simon hoped Annie only said that because it was what mothers were supposed to say.

"Not on a bet." Rachel squeezed Annie's hand, the left one, where the wide gold wedding band he'd put on her finger just hours ago glowed softly in the firelight. "Don't worry about me, either of you, I'll be fine."

"I know." Annie squeezed back. Rachel closed the door firmly behind her.

"We're alone?" Annie's voice held a wondering tone. "I can't believe it."

"Neither can I. It's been a long week." He'd spent three days in Washington tying up loose ends for the special committee, whosc hcarings were finally coming to a close. The rest of the time was taken up attending to wedding details. He'd barely spoken a word to Annie alone in all that time.

"Would you like another glass of champagne?" Annie's voice shook. She was as nervous as he was, Simon realized. He moved forward, took her in his arms.

"No champagne."

"There's half a bottle. It will lose its sparkle...." She stopped talking, made a small satisfied sound deep in her throat as he silenced her words with a kiss.

"I don't need champagne. I need you." He began to pull the small ivory silk roses and baby's breath combs from her hair. Red curls tumbled onto her shoulders. He pushed a straying tendril gently behind her ear, caressing the curve of her earlobe, the line of her jaw. Her fingers, too, were busy; two more studs popped free of his shirt-front.

"Let's go upstairs," he said, abandoning his plan to make love in front of the fireplace—for the moment.

"Let's do."

Simon turned to scoop Annie into his arms, remembering her fantasy of Rhett and Scarlett, wanting to make it come true. The front door slammed back on its hinges. Jon burst into the living rom like a small blond tornado.

"Hey, Mom, did you sprain your ankle?" he asked, catching sight of his mother in Simon's arms.

"No, she did not sprain her ankle. What are you doing back here?" he growled, realizing he sounded very much like an exasperated father.

"Leah forgot to pack my swimsuit. It's a good thing I checked my bag before we got too far from home. They have a water slide there and everything! Where's my suit, Mom?"

"I . . . I'll get it." Annie wiggled in his arms. Simon let her slide free, reluctantly.

"Wait a minute." He reached into his back pocket and took out his wallet. He pulled out a hundred-dollar bill. Annie gasped and Jon's eyes got as big as saucers. "Take this. Buy yourself a new suit. Buy everyone a new swimsuit. Just don't come back again until Sunday night, okay?"

"Okay!" Jon grabbed the money and bolted back out the door.

"Simon," Annie's voice sounded shocked. "You shouldn't have done that. They'll think you're made of money."

Simon closed and locked the front door. He turned and started back toward Annie. "Be quiet, doll," he growled in his best Bogart voice, which, as Annie had pointed out to him before, wasn't very good at all. "You unplug the phone?"

"Yes, but, Simon..."

He didn't give her a chance to chastise him further. He scooped her into his arms once more and started for the stairs. At the half-landing he looked down, saw the neck of her apricot lace dress gaping open, exposing the round softness of her breast. Distracted, he bent his head, kissing the faintest shadow of one rosy tip through the gauzy lace that covered her creamy skin. He kissed her throat and once again the tantalizing sweetness of her mouth.

Her arms tightened around his neck. Her mouth flowered open at the first brush of his lips on hers. Their kiss grew greedy with need and desire. "Are we going to make love here?" Annie asked, her eyes gleaming molten, golden brown in the dim light at the top of the stairs.

"If you like," Simon said, but started moving slowly, purposefully, toward the bedroom. It was their first time. He wanted it to be perfect. Later, perhaps, they would try the stairs.

"I would like it anywhere," she answered boldly, with unfeigned passion. "Just so we don't have to wait any longer."

"No," Simon agreed, his arms tightening around the woman he loved more than life itself, the woman he was about to make his forever. "I think we've waited long enough."

PASSPORT TO ROMANCE VACATION SWEEPSTAKES

OFFICIAL RULES

SWEEPSTAKES RULES AND REGULATIONS. NO PURCHASE NECESSARY.

HOW TO ENTER:

1. To enter, complete this official entry form and return with your invoice in the envelope provided, or print your name, address, telephone number and age on a plain piece of paper and mail to: Passport to Romance, P.O. Box #1397, Buffalo, N.Y. 14269-1397. No mechanically reproduced entries accepted.
2. All entries must be received by the Contest Closing Date, midnight, December 31, 1990 to be eligible.
3. Prizes: There will be ten (10) Grand Prizes awarded, each consisting of a choice of a trip for two people to: i) London, England (approximate retail value $5,050 U.S.); ii) England, Wales and Scotland (approximate retail value $6,400 U.S.); iii) Caribbean Cruise (approximate retail value $7,300 U.S.); iv) Hawaii (approximate retail value $ 9,550 U.S.); v) Greek Island Cruise in the Mediterranean (approximate retail value $12,250 U.S.); vi) France (approximate retail value $7,300 U.S.).
4. Any winner may choose to receive any trip or a cash alternative prize of $5,000.00 U.S. in lieu of the trip.
5. Odds of winning depend on number of entries received.
6. A random draw will be made by Nielsen Promotion Services, an independent judging organization on January 29, 1991, in Buffalo, N.Y., at 11:30 a.m. from all eligible entries received on or before the Contest Closing Date. Any Canadian entrants who are selected must correctly answer a time-limited, mathematical skill-testing question in order to win. Quebec residents may submit any litigation respecting the conduct and awarding of a prize in this contest to the Régie des loteries et courses du Quebec.
7. Full contest rules may be obtained by sending a stamped, self-addressed envelope to: "Passport to Romance Rules Request", P.O. Box 9998, Saint John, New Brunswick, E2L 4N4.
8. Payment of taxes other than air and hotel taxes is the sole responsibility of the winner.
9. Void where prohibited by law.

PASSPORT TO ROMANCE VACATION SWEEPSTAKES

OFFICIAL RULES

SWEEPSTAKES RULES AND REGULATIONS. NO PURCHASE NECESSARY.

HOW TO ENTER:

1. To enter, complete this official entry form and return with your invoice in the envelope provided, or print your name, address, telephone number and age on a plain piece of paper and mail to: Passport to Romance, P.O. Box #1397, Buffalo, N.Y. 14269-1397. No mechanically reproduced entries accepted.
2. All entries must be received by the Contest Closing Date, midnight, December 31, 1990 to be eligible.
3. Prizes: There will be ten (10) Grand Prizes awarded, each consisting of a choice of a trip for two people to: i) London, England (approximate retail value $5,050 U.S.); ii) England, Wales and Scotland (approximate retail value $6,400 U.S.); iii) Caribbean Cruise (approximate retail value $7,300 U.S.); iv) Hawaii (approximate retail value $ 9,550 U.S.); v) Greek Island Cruise in the Mediterranean (approximate retail value $12,250 U.S.); vi) France (approximate retail value $7,300 U.S.).
4. Any winner may choose to receive any trip or a cash alternative prize of $5,000.00 U.S. in lieu of the trip.
5. Odds of winning depend on number of entries received.
6. A random draw will be made by Nielsen Promotion Services, an independent judging organization on January 29, 1991, in Buffalo, N.Y., at 11:30 a.m. from all eligible entries received on or before the Contest Closing Date. Any Canadian entrants who are selected must correctly answer a time-limited, mathematical skill-testing question in order to win. Quebec residents may submit any litigation respecting the conduct and awarding of a prize in this contest to the Régie des loteries et courses du Quebec.
7. Full contest rules may be obtained by sending a stamped, self-addressed envelope to: "Passport to Romance Rules Request", P.O. Box 9998, Saint John, New Brunswick, E2L 4N4.
8. Payment of taxes other than air and hotel taxes is the sole responsibility of the winner.
9. Void where prohibited by law.

PASSPORT TO ROMANCE
WIN 1 of 10 Vacations SEE INSIDE

VACATION SWEEPSTAKES

MONTH 1 ENTRY

Official Entry Form

Yes, enter me in the drawing for one of ten Vacations-for-Two! If I'm a winner, I'll get my choice of any of the six different destinations being offered — and I won't have to decide until after I'm notified!

Return entries with invoice in envelope provided along with Daily Travel Allowance Voucher. Each book in your shipment has two entry forms — and the more you enter, the better your chance of winning!

Name ______________________________

Address ______________________________ Apt. ______

City ______________ State/Prov. ______________ Zip/Postal Code ______________

Daytime phone number ______________________________
Area Code

☐ I am enclosing a Daily Travel Allowance Voucher in the amount of $__________ Write in amount revealed beneath scratch-off

- - - - - - - - - - - - - - - - - - - -

PASSPORT TO ROMANCE
WIN 1 of 10 Vacations SEE INSIDE

VACATION SWEEPSTAKES

MONTH 1 ENTRY

Official Entry Form

Yes, enter me in the drawing for one of ten Vacations-for-Two! If I'm a winner, I'll get my choice of any of the six different destinations being offered — and I won't have to decide until after I'm notified!

Return entries with invoice in envelope provided along with Daily Travel Allowance Voucher. Each book in your shipment has two entry forms — and the more you enter, the better your chance of winning!

Name ______________________________

Address ______________________________ Apt. ______

City ______________ State/Prov. ______________ Zip/Postal Code ______________

Daytime phone number ______________________________
Area Code

☐ I am enclosing a Daily Travel Allowance Voucher in the amount of $__________ Write in amount revealed beneath scratch-off

CPS-ONE